Here's What Critics Are Saying About Angie Fox

""With its sharp, witty writing and unique characters, Angie Fox's contemporary paranormal debut is fabulously fun."
—*Chicago Tribune*

"This rollicking paranormal comedy will appeal to fans of Dakota Cassidy, Mary Janice Davidson, and Tate Hallaway."
—*Booklist*

"A new talent just hit the urban fantasy genre, and she has a genuine gift for creating dangerously hilarious drama."
—*RT Book Reviews*

"Filled with humor, fans will enjoy Angie Fox's lighthearted frolic."
—*Midwest Book Review*

"This book is a pleasure to read. It is fun, humorous, and reminiscent of Charlaine Harris or Kim Harrison's books."
—*Sacramento Book Review*

This is a work of fiction. Names, characters, organizations, places, events, and incidents are either products of the author's imagination or are used fictitiously.

SOUTHERN SPIRITS
Copyright 2015 by Angie Fox

This edition published by arrangement with Moose Island Publishing.

First Edition

ISBN-13: 978-1939661210

Southern Spirits

The Southern Ghost Hunter Mysteries
Book 1

NEW YORK TIMES BESTSELLING AUTHOR

ANGIE FOX

ALSO BY ANGIE FOX

The Southern Ghost Hunter series
Southern Spirits
The Skeleton in the Closet
The Haunted Heist
Deader Homes & Gardens
Sweet Tea and Spirits – coming spring 2017

The Accidental Demon Slayer series
The Accidental Demon Slayer
The Dangerous Book for Demon Slayers
A Tale of Two Demon Slayers
The Last of the Demon Slayers
My Big Fat Demon Slayer Wedding
Beverly Hills Demon Slayer
Night of the Living Demon Slayer
I Dream of Demon Slayers - coming soon

The Monster MASH series
Immortally Yours
Immortally Embraced
Immortally Ever After

Short Story Collections
A Little Night Magic: A collection of Southern Ghost Hunter
and Accidental Demon Slayer short stories

To Sherrie Hill and Alexx Miller, for their great advice and for making this a whole lot more fun.

CHAPTER 1

I LIVED IN A GORGEOUS ANTEBELLUM house. Not too large. Certainly not too small. The white columns out front were tasteful, even though they had chipped in places. The porch was welcoming, if a little weathered. Over the years, my family had sold the estate around the house, piece by piece, so that the sprawling peach orchard and even the grand front drive had given way to tidy bungalows lining the long road to the main house.

Grandma had said it made gossip travel even faster, the way they built houses so close together these days. I always told her that the good citizens of Sugarland, Tennessee, needed no help.

Still, I loved the place.

And I absolutely despised letting it go.

"Anyone home?" my best friend, Lauralee, called from the front of the house. "Verity, are you in here?" She added a few knocks on the front door, out of politeness rather than practicality, since the door already stood open.

We'd endured a stifling hot afternoon, and I couldn't afford to run the air-conditioning. I needed any breeze I could get.

"In the back parlor," I called. "Mourning," I added, since there was nothing left in the once-stately room, save for a cooler filled with ice, my tea jug, and a lopsided futon I inherited from a roommate back at Ole Miss. The pink-papered walls and elegant wood accents appeared so strange without rugs and furniture, like a queen stripped of her jewels.

The estate sale was yesterday and the place had been picked clean. The vultures.

"I'm sorry." Lauralee's voice echoed in the empty room. She let her purse and a cloth grocery sack slip from her shoulder to the floor; then she wrapped an arm around me and squeezed, the curled end of her ponytail tickling my cheek.

I gazed up at the ugly black hole where the crystal chandelier had hung for more than one hundred years. "Thanks." I'd come to terms with this. I really had. I turned and looked her straight in the baby blues. "I'd live in a paper bag if it meant I didn't have to marry that bastard."

My friend drew back and tucked a lock of my hair behind my ear. "Seems like he's trying to make you good on your word."

"True. But I'm not done yet." I refused to even entertain the thought.

This past May, I'd scandalized the town when I jilted the most eligible bachelor in three counties—at the altar, no less. It was a disaster. Two old ladies fainted straight out of the pew reserved for the Southern Heritage Club. Then Beau's own mother collapsed, taking down a lovely hydrangea arrangement. I secretly wondered if Mrs. Leland Herworth Wydell III didn't want to be upstaged, even at her own son's ultimate humiliation.

Truth was, he'd brought it upon himself. But I suppose it was quite shocking if you didn't know the details.

I hadn't told a lot of people. I'd wanted to spare my sister.

Lauralee chewed on her lip as she surveyed what little remained in my home. "Tell me you at least made some decent money yesterday."

"I did." I'd sold everything I could lay my hands on and kept only the absolute necessities, namely my futon, my grandmother's pearl wedding ring, and the quilts she'd made for me. It had hurt like a physical pain. I'd had to remind myself that it was only furniture, clothes. *Stuff.* I still had my health. And my friends. Not to mention my family. I brought a hand to my throat, where I used to wear my grandmother's cross from when she was about my age. The delicate gold and silver filigree antique now belonged to my not-quite-mother-in-law. "I still owe more than twenty thousand dollars."

I gazed across the once-grand, now empty back parlor turned family room. I tried to ignore the hollow place in my stomach. Tomorrow, my ancestral home would go on the market. I let out a ragged sigh. "It's dumb, but I keep hoping for a miracle."

A hidden treasure in the attic. Gold under the stairs. Stranger things had happened, right? All I knew was that I couldn't lose this house. I just couldn't.

Lauralee wrapped an arm around my shoulder and gave me a squeeze. "You'll make it. You always do," she said, in a way that made me think she actually believed it. She took in the fourteen-foot ceilings, the crown moldings. "With the money you have left over from the sale, you can make a fresh go of things."

A new start. I certainly needed *something* to change. And yet...

"I can't believe it's all gone." What had taken more than a century to accumulate had become fractured history in the space of a day. "Except for that," I said, pointing to a god-awful vase on the mantel.

My friend made a face. "I never even noticed that before."

It would have been hard to ignore. "It was in the attic," I explained. "Where it belongs." The green stones that circled the top were sort of pretty, but a crude, hand-painted scene marred the copper exterior and a healthy dent gouged the lower half. The dotty old relic looked completely out of place on an ornate marble mantel with flowers and hummingbirds carved into the corners.

"Yeek." Lauralee crossed the room for a better look. She attempted to lift the monstrosity and then changed her mind. It was heavier than it looked, wider at the top and tapered down to a flared base at the bottom. In fact, it reminded me more of an antique Grecian urn. She turned to me. "Is it a spittoon?"

"I think it's a vase," I said, joining her. "Beau gave it to me. He called it an historic heirloom. Looking back, I think he just needed to get rid of it."

In the beginning of our relationship, Beau had given me heartfelt gifts—a pressed flower from the picnic we took on our first date, a little notebook with one of our private jokes written on the inside cover. Later, it was last-minute gas station flowers.

And objects like this.

"It's hideous," Lauralee said.

"A true monstrosity," I agreed. Or else he would have let me return it when I gave him back the ring. "You want it?" I asked, turning the dented side toward her.

My friend let out a snort. "Not unless I can thunk your ex over the head with it."

I shot her a conspiratorial grin. "You'd do that for me?"

She raised her delicate brows. "Nothing would give me more pleasure," she said in a sweet, Southern tone that would make you think I'd offered mint juleps on the verandah.

"I suppose I could toss it," I said. I still had one trash can left.

She waved me off. "Keep it out. It's a focal piece. The only one you have. Here." She scooted it over toward the pale shadow where my mother's crystal swan used to be. "It'll draw people's eyes to the fireplace instead of that hideous futon."

"Way to remind me that I'm sleeping in the parlor." No way was I going to try dragging a futon up a flight of stairs.

She crossed over to the opposite wall to retrieve her hemp grocery bag from the floor. "Maybe this will help you forget," she said, holding up a bottle of Malbec.

"Mine," I said, on her in an instant. Although I'd have to tell her Beau took the stemware.

She handed me the bottle and the opener, then pulled out a pair of plastic wineglass tops from her bag. "My kids used the bottoms to play flying-saucer frisbee, but I didn't think you'd mind."

I wound the opener into the cork. "Who won?"

"Who knows?" She held out both glasses and I poured.

It was well past cocktail hour in the Old South. In fact, the sun was beginning to set.

"Should we retire to the floor?" I asked, a bit punchy with the unreality of it all.

Lauralee handed me a glass. "We might end up there anyway,"

she said as we both took a seat.

I smelled lemon polish and old wood as I stretched my legs out over the floor I'd lovingly scrubbed. We leaned our backs against the plaster wall and sipped our wine as the shadows lengthened over the room.

It wasn't like I had any lamps.

"You ever think what might have happened if I hadn't come back home?" I asked her.

I could have gone to the big city after graduating art school. My father died when I was in fifth grade, my mother long since remarried. My sister had bounced around from college to college. I could have found a job at an advertising firm, or at a large company with an in-house graphics department. I wouldn't have been around when Beauregard Buford Wydell decided it was time to take a wife.

This place would have sat empty, but at least it would have stayed mine.

"You belong here, Verity," she said simply, as if it were the only truth.

She had me pegged. I cherished this town and my home. There'd been no other choice for me. Without my roots and my family's heritage, I'd be adrift.

Grandma knew. It was why she left the house to me when she died. The rest of the estate went to my mother, who bought an RV and embraced adventure with my stepfather; and to my sister, who used her portion to pay for her various semesters abroad and half-finished degrees.

But, truly, this place had been mine even before Grandma made it legal.

I took an extra-large sip of wine as Lauralee's phone chimed. She handed me her glass and pulled the smart phone from her back pocket. The glowing screen lit her pixie face and what she saw made her frown.

"Trouble in paradise?" I asked as she checked her text messages.

The faint lines around her eyes crinkled at the corners and she sighed. "It's Big Tom. Tommy Junior got his head stuck in the hallway banister again."

I should have faked some sympathy, but it happened at least once a month. The kid was forever getting stuck in something. "Do you have to leave?"

"No." She took her wine back from me. "Big Tom has it handled." She held her glass like a diva at a cocktail party. "Heck, if I was home, I'd be calling him. He's better at prying the railings off."

I tried to imagine it and failed. "I'm starting to think you need the wine more than I do." She had four children under the age of seven—all boys.

She gave me the old pishposh as she leaned against the wall. "It's the first two kids that get you. After that, you're broken in."

I'd take her word for it.

A beam of slanting sunlight caught the ugly vase and shone through the dust in the air around it in a way that reminded me of dozens of mini fireflies. The copper itself didn't gleam a bit.

"Oh my God..." Lauralee said, leaning forward, glass in hand. "It's dirty," she said with relish.

"I saw the dust," I told her. I'd give it a good scrubbing before the open house tomorrow.

But she was already halfway to her feet. "No. The painting on it is dirty. As in sexy time."

"No way," I said, practically leaping off the floor to get a look.

"It's so bad it's brilliant." She laughed as I pulled the vase from the mantel. "I don't know why I didn't notice it before. Now that I see it, I can't *not* see it."

"Where?" I asked. Yes, there were some highly styled, almost art-deco swirly bits. They were hard to make out. It looked like people dancing. Maybe.

My friend rolled her eyes. "Has it been that long since you got laid?"

"I plead the fifth," I said as I carried the vase over to a beam of fading sunlight by the window. I traced a finger over the crude painting. Then I saw it—a girl and a boy...and another boy.

Now how did that work?

"They're getting lucky," Lauralee said, crowding me to get another look. "It's a lucky vase."

I stifled a snicker. "Can you see Beau's mother displaying this in her parlor? Maybe she knows what the girl is doing with two boys."

"And I think there's a goat," Lauralee added.

"No," I said, yanking it closer to see.

"Made you look." She laughed.

Did she ever.

"Wait till the old biddies see this," I said. And they would. We'd have plenty of gawkers tomorrow.

Lauralee gave me a loving punch to the arm. "You might have to point it out to them. They'll gasp and moan, but they'll secretly love it."

My friend's phone chimed again. She looked, and this time her sigh was heavier. "Rats."

"Trouble?"

She held up her phone to show me a text photo of her five-year-old son sitting next to a pile of debris, grinning. "Hiram got hold of a screwdriver and took apart the hall clock while Tom was working on the banister. I'd better go."

Typical day in the Clementine household. I folded her into a hug. "Thanks for the support."

She squeezed hard. "Thanks for the laugh." She smiled as she pulled back. "I love you, girlie." She tilted her chin down. "And I, for one, am glad you came home."

She was a true friend, and for that I was grateful. "Me too."

🛈

After she left, I took that vase off the mantel and traced my finger over it. Boy, girl…and that really could be a goat. I smiled to myself. Lauralee was right. I would make it through this, despite Beau and his mother and every damned one of them.

I'd be strong. Free. Maybe not quite as free as those happy fun-time people painted on the vase, but I'd be a new woman all the same. My own woman.

I wet the pad of my thumb and used it to wipe the dust from the rim. As I did, something shifted inside of it. Strange. I lifted the small bronze lid and saw at least three inches of dirt.

Well, no wonder. Nobody had cleaned the thing or showed it any love in ages.

No problem. I'd take it outside and rinse it down with the hose. I could turn the dented spot toward the wall and this little piece of faded glory might pass for something worth buying.

Now would also be a good time to track down Lucy. That sneaky little skunk would spend all night outside terrorizing the neighbors if I'd let her.

I pushed past the screen door and saw she wasn't in her bed out on our sprawling back porch. A walk down the steps showed she wasn't under her favorite apple tree, either—or as she probably thought of it: the place where snacks dropped down from heaven. After a little bit of searching, I found Lucy catching the last bit of sun on the stone pavers lining the rose garden at the back of the house.

As soon as she saw me, she rolled right off the paver and landed on her back in the grass. She gave a chipper, skunky grunt and waddled over to greet me. I loved the way she walked, with her head down and her little body churning with every step. It was the cutest thing ever.

"Hiya, sweetie pie." I bent down on one knee to greet her. She thrust her entire snout into my palm and then turned her head for easy petting, making husky, purr-like squawks. She had the softest little cheeks. I stroked her there, then down along the neck and between the ears in the way that made her right back leg twitch. "You enjoying your last day at the house?"

An apartment just wasn't going to be the same for Lucy. I'd found a place that accepted exotic pets, but believe it or not, people around here held a certain bias against skunks. It wasn't enough that I'd had little Lucy's scent glands removed. They wanted her to stop being who she was.

Poor baby.

I'd have to make some adjustments as well after we moved. Our new home, The Regal Towers, was basically an old six-family flat down by the railroad tracks. So close, in fact, that the windows rattled every time a train went by. The doors were made of plywood. I wasn't even sure that was legal, not that management cared. Morton Davis, slumlord extraordinaire, had offered to save it for me on account of the fact we'd attended grades K through eight together at Stonewall Jackson Elementary. I knew it was available because no one else wanted it.

There had to be a way out of this.

Lucy snuggled up to me and tried to climb my leg to get closer.

"You want to help?" I asked, making sure I reached clear of Lucy as I dumped the contents of the vase over Grandma's rosebushes. She gave the little pile a sniff and sneezed.

"You said it." The dirt was loose and dry, which I was glad to see. I'd heard that sort of thing was good for the roots.

It certainly couldn't hurt.

When the last of the fine dust had settled out of the air, I hosed out the vase and poured the water on the roses. They needed it. I'd been neglecting them lately.

"How do you like that?" I asked my climbing vines.

A chilly breeze whipped straight up my spine and shot goose bumps down my arms. It startled me, and I dropped the vase. Lucy darted away.

"Nice work, butterfingers," I mumbled to myself, retrieving it. I spotted a stubborn patch of dirt down in the base and rinsed it out again, but the stuff wouldn't budge.

The rosebushes shuddered. It had to be the wind, but this time, I didn't feel it.

For the first time, I felt uncomfortable in my grandmother's garden.

It was a strange feeling, and an unwelcome one at that. "It's getting late," I told myself, as if that would explain it.

Quick as I could, I reached for the rose snippers I kept under the hose. I cut a full red bloom, with a stem as thick as my finger, and popped it into the vase with a dash of water. Then I hurried back toward the house, careful not to spill a drop.

"Lucy," I called, half-wondering if the skunk wasn't the source of the strange rustling in the rosebushes behind me. "Come on, girl."

She came running from her hiding place under the porch. Something had scared her, too.

The house had never been what you'd call ordinary. We had fish in the pond, each one big as a cat; more often than not, I found fireflies in the attic.

But this was unusual, even for my ancestral home. I didn't like it at all.

Especially when the windows rattled.

"What the hey, girl?" I asked Lucy. And myself.

She turned around and headed back under the porch. Darn it all. She tended to snuggle under my covers at night and I didn't want her all dirty.

You have no idea how hard it is to give a skunk a bath.

A low creaking came from inside the house. The hair on my arms stood on end. Perhaps Lucy was the smart one after all. Unfortunately, there wasn't room under the porch for me.

Instead, I took the steps slowly and crossed the threshold into the darkened kitchen.

My eyes strained against the shadows. Not for the first time, I wished I'd kept at least one light. With shaking fingers, I lit the big, orange, three-wicked candle I'd been using for the last few days.

The house stood still, quiet as a grave. Almost as if it were waiting.

"Is it you, Grandma?" I asked on a whisper. "Are you mad I'm selling?"

If she'd been watching down on me at all—and I knew she did—Grandma would understand I'd been given no choice in the matter.

"Oh no," said a ghostly male voice. "You're staying put, sweetheart." With shock and horror, I realized it was coming from the vase. I dropped it.

The door slammed closed behind me. The bolt clicked, locking on its own as the vase spun and rattled to a stop on the floor.

A chill swept the room. I retreated until my back hit solid wood. I'd never seen a ghost or heard a ghost although I watched *Ghost Adventures* on television and I certainly believed in them and sweet Jesus I was trapped.

I couldn't feel my fingers, or my limbs for that matter. My entire body had gone ice cold. "What do you want?" I asked, voice shaking. Seeing as I hadn't dropped dead on the spot from a heart attack, this had better well be my salvation. "Why are you here?"

The voice laughed, as if it were honest-to-God amused. "I'm here because you chiseled me, princess."

CHAPTER 2

I HAD NO IDEA WHAT THAT meant, but by his tone, I knew he wasn't about to thank me. I had to escape. *Run.*

But I couldn't go anywhere. A frigid chill radiated from the vase in front of me. I pressed against the locked door at my back, my skin slick with sweat and fear.

I tried to stay calm, be rational. But there was no way I could reason my way out of this. Okay, then, *think.* Grandma always said she talked to spirits, that it was a Southern thing. But I'd certainly never seen her do it. Or *heard* them answer.

I blurted the first thing that came to mind. "I'll return your vase to the Wydells. Tonight. You'll be there before you know it." Back to the grave, or at least back home. Isn't that what ghosts usually wanted?

A blanket of fog descended over me. My skin erupted with icy pinpricks. A disembodied voice spoke directly over my right ear. "We've got a bigger problem than that, babe."

"No, *you've* got a bigger problem." I screwed up my courage and forced my voice to steady. "Leave," I commanded. "I order you from this home. Now."

He chuckled low, right next to my ear. "Don't you think that's a little dramatic?"

Flames shot up from the candle next to me, from the fat candles by the stove, from my little tea lights on the windowsills. "You think *I'm* dramatic?" I choked.

A specter shimmered into view directly in front of me. He

appeared in black and white, but I could see through him. Almost. He wore a 1920s-style pin-striped suit coat with matching cuffed trousers and a fat tie. His chest was level with my line of sight, which made him unnaturally tall.

The blood froze in my veins as I forced myself to look up. He had a long face with a sharp nose, which made him appear utterly ruthless.

He softened a bit when he let out a long sigh.

I mashed my back flat against the locked door. He casually removed his white Panama hat and I gasped at the neat, round bullet hole in his forehead. He motioned toward it with one edge of the brim. "Hard to miss, right?"

I didn't know what to say to that as he fingered the broad black band of his hat. Perhaps I'd take the polite approach and pretend I didn't notice the large hole placed squarely an inch above his eyes. I really had to stop staring. "I'm sorry," I whispered.

"For what?" he asked, shooting me a scowl. "For dumping my ashes out onto your rosebushes?"

A new horror bubbled up inside me. "Those were…" Oh my God. "I had no idea."

He cocked his head to the side. "Are you sorry for trapping my spirit on your property?"

My throat went dry. "Is that what I did?"

He thrust his hat on. "This is worse than getting shot in the head," he grumbled.

He began to pace.

I stayed exactly where I was. "I suppose you would know," I ventured.

He reared back as if I'd slapped him. "Is that supposed to be funny?"

"No. Never." Just…terribly inconvenient. I didn't know what else to say. How does one have a polite conversation with someone so tragically deceased?

He adjusted his shoulders and shoved them back. "Nobody brunos with me. You hear? You know who I am? I'm Frankie the German. Men fear me. Women want me."

I hated to get picky with the ghost who'd cornered me in my kitchen, but, "Shouldn't you be in Chicago or something?" Isn't that where the gangsters lived?

He scoffed. "Let the Italians have Chicago. The South belongs to the Germans. And the flipping Harps," he reluctantly added.

"Who?" I asked.

"The Irish," he groused.

"That sounds reasonable," I managed. I didn't know what to do. I was used to fainting widows and shrieking Southern belles. Not real live—make that dead—gangsters. He was a criminal. Someone had seen fit to shoot him between the eyes, for heaven's sake.

I didn't know what this man, this ghost, was capable of. Obviously, he was used to violence. I shoved back my fear enough to ask, "Are you going to hurt me?"

He jerked his shoulders at the thought. "I don't do damage to skirts," he snapped, as if the mere idea offended him.

I wasn't sure I believed him.

"Listen, doll," Frankie said, his tone softening a hair. "When your great-uncle so-and-so dies, there's a reason you scatter his ashes. You *scatter*," he said, making a motion like he was feeding birds or something. "You let them catch the wind. You give the spirit freedom if he wants it." His voice grew tight. "You don't dump them all in one spot and then stomp on 'em," he added, fingers clenching.

"I didn't stomp," I pointed out.

He shot me a dirty look. "You've got to move your rear and get those ashes out of the dirt."

"I can't," I said, wincing. "I hosed them into the ground."

He huffed, as if physics were a mere technicality. "Well, un-hose 'em. I'm on you like a tick until you fix this."

That was impossible. "You don't understand. I'm sorry this happened, but there's nothing I can do about it now." I couldn't bend the laws of science and nature. Not even for an angry ghost.

He retreated to my grandmother's oak center island. It was bolted down or it would have been gone with the rest of the furniture. "I got time." He said it like a threat, running a hand over the countertop, as if he could actually feel it. Heck, maybe he could.

"Yes, well, I don't. This house goes on sale tomorrow." A familiar knot tightened in my stomach. No doubt it would sell fast.

He slammed a fist down onto the butcher block. "You're *not* going to ground me here and then sell."

"I will unless I can find twenty thousand dollars by the end of the week," I snapped back.

I'd asked my family. I'd asked my friends. Nobody could spare that much. We had a lot of pride down here in these parts, but it didn't always come with a lot of money. I'd even applied for a bank loan. They took one look at my student debt and turned me down. It was hopeless.

The ghost crossed his arms over his chest. "Twenty grand, huh?"

Maybe now he'd see how impossible it was and scram. "My ex-fiancé, who gave me your urn by the way, sued me for that and a lot more after the Incident." I crossed my arms over my chest. "Although how Beau Wydell came across your urn"—and gave it to me as a gift, the rat—"I'll never know."

The gangster sat on my grandma's nice countertop, which would have earned him a whooping if either Grandma or Frankie were alive. "I'm his great-great-uncle," he said, nonchalant.

"That explains a lot," I muttered.

The gangster shot me a look. "Damn. He must have done a number on you."

"He cornered my sister in the hallway outside the bridal suite after our rehearsal dinner." I'd invited her to stay with me in the bridal suite on the eve of my wedding. She'd left to grab a bottle of wine and come back in tears. "He groped her, and he would have done a whole lot more if she hadn't kicked him in the balls."

"I like your sister," Frankie concluded.

I snorted. "I can't believe he managed to hide that side of himself until it was almost too late." When I'd confronted Beau, he tried to deny it. Then he said it was a mistake. That I'd have to deal. It wasn't as if I could call off the wedding.

Little did he know.

Frankie scooted to the edge of the counter. "Now listen up. 'Cause here's what we do," he said, clasping his hands in front of him, his elbows resting on his knees.

"What we do?" I asked. I didn't recall teaming up with a dead gangster.

"Oh?" He opened his hands. "So you have ideas?"

"No," I said grudgingly.

He scratched at his long, thin nose. "Okay, here's the deal. Old lady Hatcher's not-so-dearly departed husband came across some cash in 1965." He gave me a long look. "It's more than you need."

My spine stiffened. He was talking about saving my house. Whatever he was about to suggest couldn't be good. Did I dare?

"How did the money come about?" I absolutely refused to get involved in anything illegal.

Frankie shrugged. "He bet his entire mortgage payment on a long-shot horse. The damn thing won. He hid the money on his property. Only he was an idiot and died right after he stashed it."

I'd heard that last part of the story. Maisie Hatcher had dug up every tree, shrub, and flower patch in her backyard, looking for the fortune her husband hid. "She swore there was money under one of the trees on her property. We always thought she was crazy."

The corner of his mouth turned up. "It's not under a tree. It's hidden in a box with a tree carved on the top."

Well, didn't that beat all? I strolled toward the ghost, feeling brave. Or maybe I needed to show him that I wasn't *as* scared anymore. "You'd think her husband could have left better directions."

He shrugged. "Oskar Hatcher was an asshole. Still is."

I cocked my head. "How do you know?"

"He's behind you."

The air left my body. I screeched and spun around fast, my heart jackhammering against my chest. I couldn't see anything in the dark. "Where is he?"

Frankie's chuckle behind me sounded like gravel over rocks. "Your friend's right. You really are gullible."

"You're such a jerk." A chill washed over me as the sweat on my body cooled. I turned back to him. "How long were you watching me?"

He didn't buckle under my stare. "Don't flatter yourself. I spend most of my time picking up dames at the cemetery. Or I tool around, see who's manifesting." He grinned. "Those Johnny Rebs from the 12th Infantry throw a wicked poker game. And half of 'em don't know how to bluff." He stood taller. "I did stick around for the sale. I can't believe that crappy lawn furniture went before I did."

He'd succeeded in wigging me out on about ten different levels. But now wasn't the time to think about it. I needed to channel my inner Scarlet O'Hara. I'd asked for a miracle and I'd gotten one...sort of. At least I'd been given one more chance, with money that was more or less clean. Abandoned, at least. "Okay, so we go to Maisie Hatcher's house," I began. "Wait. You can't leave here."

He cocked his head. "I can if I'm with you."

I stood surprised for a moment, and not in a good way. "Okay. We'll leave. We'll talk to Maisie," I said, thinking it through. "We certainly can't tell her you talked to Oskar."

He popped down off the counter. "Of course not. We sneak onto the property. We take the money. Simple."

I flinched as if he'd struck me. "I'm not going to rob her."

"Technically, it's not her money," the ghost pointed out.

I disagreed. It was her husband's win. Her property. "The poor woman's been searching for that treasure going on fifty years." I'd met Maisie several times through Grandma's church group, and I liked her. "She's an eccentric, and she doesn't have a lot in the bank."

Frankie rolled his eyes. "Fine. We'll tell her you can dig up the cash if she gives you eighty percent."

"No," I said quickly.

He crossed his arms over his chest. "Sixty."

"Forget it." My eye caught the shadows of candles dancing on the walls. "She might not even let us on her land. She's a recluse now."

Frankie tossed up his arms. "Then what the heck are you going to do?"

He stopped right in front of me. I stiffened my back and held my ground. "I'm not going to take advantage of an old woman." I had my integrity. And my pride. I thought for a moment. "I'll sneak onto the property, but only because we don't have a choice." It was for Maisie's own good. "Then if we find the money, we'll ask for a reward. Maybe Maisie will feel generous."

"Oh, brother." He rolled his eyes. "You need to be more ruthless if you want to keep this place."

I was tempted to point out exactly what being ruthless had gotten him, but I resisted. "I do just fine."

He shook his head, as if my mere presence amused him. "It's amazing the world don't eat you alive."

Sometimes it did, although I wasn't about to admit that to him. Not now.

Despite it all, I had to believe that honesty would be rewarded. That if I lived my life doing the right thing, good fortune would come back to me. The alternative was unthinkable.

"So are we really going to do this?" I asked, antsy down to my toes, trying to psych myself up. I'd never broken the law before, unless you counted a speeding ticket or two. At least I was dressed for adventure. I still had on my Keds sneakers and a casual, purple sundress from a steamy day of cleaning and loading boxes. "I think it could actually work." I needed it to, desperately.

An old woman would get her long-lost money, which would hopefully put her in a generous mood. And Frankie? Well, he'd still be trapped in my rosebushes, but we couldn't fix everything.

"My plans always work," Frankie said, with the annoying

self-assurance that had probably gotten him killed. Without meaning to, I glanced at his forehead hidden by the brim of his Panama hat. He caught my gaze. "Well," he corrected, "most of the time."

I'd have to take his word for it. My nerves pulsed with excitement and something else...anticipation? I'd never done anything like this before, and I was surprised to find I wasn't exactly opposed to it. "If this is going to happen, it has to be tonight."

Before the house showings tomorrow morning. Before I had time to think about how crazy this sounded.

I jumped as the back door clicked open. With a loud creak, it swung wide.

Frankie adjusted his hat and gestured toward the door. "After you, sweetheart." He lingered in the kitchen as I crossed out onto the porch. "Aren't you forgetting something?"

I stopped and realized I'd breezed right by the vase I'd dropped on the floor.

Urn. I corrected in my mind.

I still couldn't believe I'd dumped out his urn.

Slowly, I turned to face him. "So you can't leave with me unless I have your urn?" I was a little surprised at that. It wasn't like his ashes were in there anymore. Not that I was going to remind him.

He frowned, clearly uncomfortable with the topic. "You didn't rinse all of me out."

"Ah." I didn't know whether to be glad or sorry. "So if I don't have any of your ashes, you can't follow me."

He shoved his hands into his pockets, not eager to admit anything. "I can drive you nuts while you're on your property, but otherwise... What part of 'grounding' don't you get?"

"So you had the run of the whole world until I..." No wonder he'd been ticked.

The look on his face warned me it would be a good idea to let it drop. "Okay," I said, scooting past him and into the kitchen, shivering at the cold spot he created in my doorway. I opened the pullout drawer next to my sink. "I think I have a few grocery bags still left in here." Hopefully that wouldn't insult him. Darned if I knew the etiquette on this.

The air chilled ten degrees as he moved in behind me. "Get a backpack," he said, "I don't want you getting scared and dropping it."

Like I had in my kitchen.

"Listen here, I'm no simpering Southern belle." I straightened, shocking us both when I stood up right in the middle of his chest. It was like stepping out into a freezing cold rain. Or standing in a cloud. It felt cold, wet, and terribly uncomfortable, like I'd invaded his personal space in the worst possible way.

Each of us froze for a moment. Then he shot backward and I shuddered.

"Sorry," I said, patting myself down to get rid of the watery, chilled feeling of him, even as I tried hard not to make it look like I was wiping him away. I needn't have bothered. He wasn't looking at me. He huddled in the corner of my kitchen against the ceiling, clear on the other side of the room.

"Are you *trying* to make this worse?" he demanded, as if it were my sole purpose in this life to torture him in the next.

"It was an honest mistake," I said quickly, searching for something, anything else to say that wouldn't make us both feel like ten miles of bad road. The rough, tough gangster looked almost frightened up there above my empty mug rack.

So I did what my mother and my mother's mother before her most likely would have done. I changed the subject.

"I realize a bag that zips closed would be a better choice for your...urn," I said, trying to act as casual as possible, "but I don't have one. My backpack was a gift from my ex and he took it when he left." Because Beau really needed a pink leopard-print JanSport with double-zip pockets.

Frankie's long face set into a scowl. "I used to shoot people for less," he muttered to himself.

Yes, well, we all had our crosses to bear.

I grabbed a hemp grocery sack and shook out a few lingering onion skins into the sink. Then I retrieved Frankie's urn. I tipped it inside and dared him to say another word about it.

He didn't.

I grabbed a dish towel and swiped up the spilled water before placing the rosebud on the counter. It's not like I had another vase.

"All right, then," I said, holding the door open for him. "We might as well get to finding that hidden cash." I prided myself on being practical. We didn't have all night.

Frankie slid down, his shoulders hunched. Then he deliberately snubbed me by walking through the wall to get out to the porch. I sighed. It didn't matter. I used the door and closed it behind me, not bothering with the lock.

"I can't believe you thought my urn had sexy pictures," he grouched as we started down the steps.

The polite thing would be to let it go, but if I didn't stand up to the man, he was going to think he could walk all over me.

"How can you blame me?" I asked, catching him out of the corner of my eye. I mean truly, "There was a girl and a boy—"

"Dancing the tango," he snapped.

"I suppose that's one way to look at it."

He let out a regretful sigh. "I used to love to dance."

"What about the extra boy?" I asked.

He gave me the kind of slant look that suggested I was crazy. "He's playing a custom-made, highly decorative bandoneon, with ivory inlaid handles and feather accents. From Argentina," he added, as if that made a difference.

I pulled the car keys out of my pocket. "We thought it was a goat."

"My wingman, Suds, carved that," he barked. "It took him a week."

"Maybe Suds should have spent less time stealing, more time practicing art." I barely said it. Frankie heard me anyway.

"Can you think of any other way to insult me? I thought you outdid yourself when you dumped my ashes on your rosebushes, but you keep surprising me."

We reached my car on the side drive, a 1978 avocado-green

Cadillac handed down from my grandmother. Good thing it was worthless or I would have had to sell it. "You really aren't going to let that drop, are you?" I asked, opening my door.

"No," he said. He shimmered out of view and then reappeared in my passenger seat. Neat trick. "I'm more of the avenger type," he said, leaning back against the worn upholstery.

"Great." I slid in next to him and started the engine. "A vengeful ghost."

He shook his head as I started up the engine. "You don't know the half of it, sweetheart."

CHAPTER 3

MY CAR SET TO RATTLING before we even started hitting the bumps at the end of my street. Frankie was polite enough not to mention it. Or maybe my car performed about even with a 1920s jalopy.

We took a left and then followed Rural Route 7 until we came up on the main road that led into town. I steered that way without even thinking, until Frankie piped up.

"Whoa," he said, as if everybody didn't drive a little fast off Route 7. "Hang right." He pointed to a narrow asphalt road that disappeared into the underbrush.

"You've got to be kidding." I hit the brakes, forcing the Cadillac to lurch to a stop. The dim dashboard lights made the ghost look watery in the moonless night.

He had his directions straight. Maisie lived out east, past the civilized part of town, but there were nicer ways to get there, ones that didn't include a barely there road through the woods.

Besides, I'd been down there years ago, before I had more sense. "There's nothing that way but Johnson's Cave." We didn't need to be wandering along dark, deserted back roads, even if he did think he knew where we were headed.

"Trust me," he said, settling in, spreading his arms over the back of the seat.

Had the man forgotten I'd only met him tonight? Still, this whole mission had been his idea. I supposed it wouldn't hurt to do as he asked, even if it annoyed the spit out of me.

I clicked on my brights and made a right onto the uneven asphalt. My tank of a car lurched and every bolt shook as we tested the limits of my decades-old suspension system. Frankie cursed under his breath.

"Don't start," I shot back, daring him to make this more difficult as branches from the bushes on either side of the road scraped against the sides of my car.

"You drive like a woman," he said, flinching as a longer branch caught my windshield wiper and dragged the arm of it up before the stubborn old thing snapped back.

"You led me this way," I said, cringing as we bottomed out and something hard and crunchy scraped the undercarriage of my car. "So stop being sexist."

He let out a choked sound, but I wasn't about to take my eyes off the road, what little of there was of it. "I'm not the one who keeps bringing up sex."

"I have no idea what you're talking about," I began, and then it hit me. He didn't know he was being sexist. He didn't even know what that meant. How to explain... "Oh Lordy. I didn't mean *sex* sex, I meant—"

"Stop it. I'm not listening to another word," he said, like he was my father or something. "First you think there's a girl and a boy and a...goat on my urn, and now this. You might like to skate around, but I can't do that no more."

Sweet heaven. "I'm not coming onto you." I didn't even know how to explain. "Forget it."

"Gladly," he muttered.

I kept driving. "If it makes you feel any better, this is the first time I've ever had a conversation like this," I told him. I certainly hoped it would be the last.

"You're making it worse," Frankie said, his voice rising.

"Fine. You have my apology." I'd never met anyone who necessitated more subject changes. Frankly, I was losing patience for it, especially when we were running around hell's half acre because of him.

The road split in two. The path to the right led down to John-son's Cave. A thick chain stretched over the entrance, blocking that wider, easier route. We took the other road, the one less traveled.

Lord help us.

I blew out a breath. "I should turn around right now." I would have if I could have found anywhere to do it. I had a feeling we'd missed our chance.

"You thinking of backing out?" Frankie demanded.

"Yes," I said, slowing as I spotted Bambi's mom in the woods. I furrowed my brow, hoping the doe didn't dart out in front of my tank on wheels. "I told you. I'm not one for trespassing."

"Me neither," he grumbled. "Stealing's way more fun."

"No wonder somebody shot you between the eyes."

"Like I haven't heard that one from every dead smart-ass in the last ninety years." He pointed to a shadow up on our left. "Turn there."

I slowed and took another hard left onto a road that was even narrower than the one we'd been on. I'd have to be careful not to get lost. Until tonight, I thought I knew every inch of Sugar-land. This forgotten part of town was quiet. Creepy. "This may be a shortcut, but it's a dumb way to go." In fact, I'd have been worried the ghost was luring me somewhere shady if he hadn't been so wigged out by touching me.

Or maybe that was an act.

I shot him a glance. He caught me at it and raised his brows.

It felt like we were entering another world as the road opened up and I caught sight of an abandoned gas station. The sign read Tennessee Oil. My headlights caught rusted pumps under an old tin awning. The narrow windows of the building at the back were dark and broken.

"I've heard of this place," I said. I'd just never seen it.

"It's the land that time forgot," Frankie said, a little melodramatic for my taste.

"Don't tease." I was already a little freaked out.

Farther down, I spotted an old diner, its white tile exterior

chipping and streaked with graffiti, its parking lot all but lost
to weeds. "The boys in high school used to dare each other to
come out here," I said. I'd been too scared.

Now I realized it was sad, too. I'd read stories about disappearing rural towns, but never thought mine would be included.

"Unincorporated," Frankie said, "with a spotty police presence. A perfect spot for me and my associates back in the day."

Frankie watched out the front window with a faraway look.
He turned as we passed a lump of a building completely over-
taken by bushes and trees.

"The turn past Dolly's place," he murmured before clearing
his throat. "Up here," he said as we reached a lonely crossroad.
"Right."

I did as he instructed, glad to realize we'd left the ghost town
behind. No doubt someone had loved that place a long time ago,
like I loved Sugarland now. But the relic of a town didn't feel
right.

Maybe I was merely unsettled about how easy it was to lose a
home, a road, an entire community.

We drove until the road went from asphalt to dirt.

"Kill your lights," he ordered.

"Dang it, Frankie," I muttered. But I did as he asked.

Now we were really asking to hit something.

"Drive straight," the ghost said quietly as we crunched over
dry ground.

Off in the distance, I saw a single porch light. "That's Maisie's
house, isn't it?" I murmured. We were in about the right place
for it, although I couldn't see the rest of her 1940s-style bungalow. The place was too dark.

Frankie straightened in his seat. "Follow my lead. Sneaking's
one of the things I do best." He shot me a dark look. "Stop the
car."

He sounded like we were about to rob a bank or something. I
didn't like it. "I never should have agreed to this," I muttered as
I ground the car to a halt. The engine clicked and protested as I
shut it down.

Frankie adjusted the Panama hat low over his eyes. "The widow's been looking in the ground. That's the wrong place." He shot me a grin. "Oskar hid the cash in the old family homestead."

"You mean the haunted house on the hill?" I shot back. We'd told stories about the old Hatcher place, an abandoned Civil War-era two-story where candles still glowed in the upstairs window and the ghost of Jilted Josephine threw rocks at people. Word had it she'd pitched her lover headfirst out of her window before she'd hung herself. The widow Maisie hadn't let anyone near the place in forty years and I didn't blame her. "I'm not going in there."

Frankie shot me a dry look. "You'd rather take your skunk and live in an apartment by the railroad tracks?"

"That's not fair."

He disappeared from the seat next to me and materialized about ten yards ahead.

Criminy.

I popped open the locks, grabbed the bag with the urn, and hurried after him. "Can't we discuss this like rational human beings?" I hissed. It was dark and freaky and he'd better not leave me alone. "I thought you said you couldn't go anywhere."

As if determined to prove me wrong, he disappeared completely, abandoning me in the darkness. It was colder than it should have been. Blacker. A bloodcurdling cry rose up from the woods to my right and a twisting, hollow fear settled into my chest.

"I didn't go far," Frankie said, right up against my ear.

If I'd had a heart condition, that whisper would have been the end of me. "Stop it."

"Relax," he said, shimmering into view. "I'm just messing with you."

I shot him my dirtiest look. "Have you heard the stories of Jilted Josephine?"

"No," he said. "Focus on the prize." He motioned me forward.

I took a few tentative steps. A dark mass loomed up ahead,

surrounded by an overgrowth of woods. Josephine's lair, no doubt.

This time, Frankie stuck close. "If this Josephine dame lives up there, and she's a little squirrely, that's good for us. Most folks don't like that, so they won't have come close to the loot. We, on the other hand, don't care. We need the cash."

I stopped. I'd thought I was up for this, but I had my limits. "I'm not going to sneak into a haunted house."

He turned back to me, surprised. "What? Are you afraid of ghosts?"

I planted my hands on my hips. "I don't like them very much."

He broke into a grin. "That's only because you met me."

Heavens to Betsy. This was different and he knew it. He also knew I didn't have a choice. "You have to admit this is creepy." It wasn't merely the pitch-black, middle-of-nowhere spooky forest. I pointed to the shadows of the towering oaks surrounding us. "Did you see these trees? They have no leaves. I know it's almost October, but still. Nothing. They're all gnarled and dead."

"You done?" Frankie asked, completely unaffected by my outburst.

"I need my flashlight," I gritted out, fumbling for the one on my keychain. "It would be great if you could go in by yourself," I added, with just a hint of desperation. He could find it as well as I could. Maybe.

"It takes a lot of energy to move anything on your plane," he said, "much less do a full-out search. Don't you know anything?"

"Not about this," I said, flipping on my light. The watery beam spilled down onto the path in front of me.

Frankie stared out into the darkness, lost in thought. "If I could, I would have taken the cash already." His brow furrowed. "Not that I could have spent it. It would have been more like a force of habit."

He turned his back and began gliding toward the cabin. "Wait up," I said, chasing after him.

I had a hard time following the path, and my Keds didn't offer great traction, but I didn't dare fall too far behind. I kept as close as I could to Frankie. He was the least creepy thing here.

How messed up was that?

The closer we got, the more I wanted to turn back. Seeing the house straight ahead didn't help.

The rough, wooden boards looked like they'd been pieced together with nails, spit, and not much else. Darkened windows gazed out from both stories and the front door leaned drunkenly on its hinges.

Weeds invaded the path, winding around my ankles. The entire property felt dark, wrong, like it lay in wait for me to enter and make a mistake.

"How far in do I have to go?" I whispered to Frankie.

Maybe Oskar hid the money by the front door or something.

He glanced up at the house. "Let's get inside before we worry about that."

As he spoke, a candle sputtered to life in the upstairs window. I would have screamed if I hadn't been too busy trying not to fall.

"Don't let that bother you," Frankie said.

The light flickered even as I stood there, scared out of my wits. "There is a ghost up there," I said, as loud as I dared.

"It's her house," Frankie said simply.

Right. A hysterical giggle threatened to burst from me. I could relate to that. If I lost my nerve now, I was going to lose my house tomorrow. Or if not tomorrow…soon. Josephine was nothing but a ghost. A spirit. A remnant from another age, like Frankie. He hadn't harmed me, and I'd actually done something to tick him off.

I forced myself to take one step forward, then another, until I made it to the front door and touched my fingers to the latch. "What do I do when I get inside?"

"Follow your gut," Frankie said.

My gut told me to run.

But I knew I could do this. I *had* to do this. And so, I slipped inside.

CHAPTER 4

THE CHILL AND THE DARK seeped over me. The wooden floorboards creaked under my feet. Oh my Lord, this place was creepy. It made no sense for it to be colder in here than on the outside. *That's right,* I told myself. *Focus on the logic.*

I should have run out of there screaming.

Instead, I took one more step, then another, until I was all the way inside.

The thin beam from my flashlight reached tentatively into the blackness. I could barely see two feet in any direction. I had no idea what surrounded me or which way I should go.

I shuddered to think what might lurk just beyond my reach.

The whisper of a breeze stole over me and I jerked in surprise. *It was coming from inside the house.*

I sucked in a breath. "Calm down," I told myself. I wasn't some stupid horror movie heroine going into a dangerous situation for no reason. I was merely taking a gander inside a haunted house in order to help an old widow and save what should have been rightfully mine in the first place. This wasn't the same thing at all.

Plus I could run like the dickens.

I fought to keep my breathing slow and even, to ignore the pounding of my heart.

There were no axe murderers here. Nothing alive.

My bangs tickled my forehead, stirred by an imperceptible

force.

"Frankie?" I asked, my voice catching in my throat. "Please tell me that's you."

I wouldn't even be mad.

"It's not," he said quietly. He hovered on my right, behind my line of vision. I could feel him next to me. At least I hoped that was him. For once, he kept his voice down. "There's something in here that you can't see."

Sweet mother. "What is it?" I froze in place, as if that would keep anything from coming at me. "Tell me where to go." I'd get the money and break a land speed record getting out of here.

A chill tickled up my spine.

"Frankie?" My voice quivered. "Tell me what's going on."

"Act casual." He disappeared.

Oh, no. He did not just do that. Something was wrong. If I couldn't see what threat might be lurking, and if Frankie wasn't going to tell me, then I was in a lot of trouble. "If you're not going to help me, I'm leaving. Now." Or at least as soon as I could find the door.

I took one step backward, then another, inching my way toward a full retreat.

"Wait." Frankie snapped. "Stop. Fine, I'll do it."

"What?" I braced myself.

His voice spoke from the dark void to my right. "I'll make it so you can see the ghostly side of this place. Just this once."

I couldn't spend another second in the dark, so I nodded and found my voice. "Please," I said.

"If I do it, you'll stay? You'll help me find the cash?"

"I'll try." My skin prickled as I felt the air around me shift. "Frankie?" I asked, not trusting my own voice as the ghost of the gangster shimmered into view next to me. A dull light settled over us, casting the house in an eerie silver glow.

I stood in a single room. Gossamer cobwebs hung down from the ceiling like Spanish moss dripping from an age-old oak. The ends brushed over my forehead and tangled in my hair. "Yikes." I ducked and my breath hitched as a wiry shadow scrambled down the far right wall and burrowed into the corner by the floor.

"Oh God. Oh God. Oh God," I repeated like a mantra, as if that could hold back the faint images that slowly came into focus all around me. They intensified and formed a ghostly portrait of a life once lived. A fire crackled in the stone hearth. I could actually hear the wood snap. A three-pronged pot stand floated above it, with something thick bubbling inside.

To my right, several inches off the ground, hovered a table surrounded by rough wood chairs. I took a quick step forward when a delicate spinning wheel appeared almost behind me on the left, close enough to touch.

Loud creaks echoed from above, underneath, all around, as if the house was adjusting itself on its foundation.

Frankie faded in and out with the rest of my otherworldly surroundings. "You doing okay?"

"No," I said truthfully. Ask a silly question… "Why is everything floating?"

Frankie set his jaw. "That's how the dominant ghost sees it."

"Josephine?" I asked, not really wanting to know.

"Yes." He lowered his chin. "Now for that problem I was telling you about? It's behind us."

I heard a snarl and whirled to see the shimmering outline of a hound dog with bared teeth. I took a quick step back.

Frankie hissed out a breath. "I never did too good with the guard dogs."

The dog's yellow eyes pierced the darkness as it solidified. It took a menacing step toward me, growling deep in its throat.

"And now that I can see it, it's going to come after me," I concluded.

"Sorry 'bout that," Frankie said, wide-eyed.

The beast stalked me toward the back stairs. Step by step I retreated. Away from my only means of escape.

I grabbed hold of the banister with a quick prayer that the old staircase could support my weight. The curved wooden handrail felt freezing cold to the touch. I yanked my hand back.

New plan. I wasn't going to touch anything in this place.

Except for the hidden money box.

A high-pitched wail echoed from the floor above.

I gasped. "Jilted Josephine." It had to be.

Frankie appeared on the staircase a few steps up from me. "Let's do this fast."

He'd better know what he was talking about. We took the steps two at a time. Each footfall elicited a creak that seemed to echo throughout the house.

"What do I do if she's up here?" I asked, breathless, glancing back over my shoulder. The hound dog had stopped at the bottom of the stairs, its yellow eyes glowing in the darkness. Maybe it couldn't go any farther.

A girl could hope.

Frankie lurched to a halt next to me. I stopped as well. Ghostly portraits lined the wall. The quivering beam of my flashlight caught the elaborately framed paintings of men with stiff collars and ladies with artfully styled hair.

I didn't like this. And I was real unhappy our only exit was blocked. I didn't take well to being trapped—by a ghost dog or by anybody. It felt colder up here. Sinister.

The gangster looked as agitated as I felt. "Focus on the money," he ordered, with the kind of single-minded determination that had probably gotten him killed.

Fine. Okay. I took one more step, then another. "Where is it?" I asked as we neared the top.

He stopped cold, refusing to look at me. "I don't know."

"What?" It came out louder than I'd planned. But holy moly. He'd led me here thinking all I had to do was sneak onto this poor woman's land, break into a haunted house, uncover the money, and run. And then share it, of course, but in no way did Frankie ever mention that he didn't know exactly where to look.

"Relax," he snapped. "The dog made our decision for us. We'll start by searching the second floor. If it's not there, we'll look on the bottom floor when he goes away."

"Since when do guard dogs go away?" I demanded. "You are

the worst criminal ever." He was making this up as he went, and taking me along for the ride.

"I think I've been doing this longer than you," he shot back over my whispered, desperate, admittedly repetitive chorus of *oh my Gods*. He stared me down. No doubt if he could have shaken me, he would have. "Get a grip, sweetheart. Remember, you can move things and touch things in the physical dimension. You've got a huge advantage."

Fat lot of good it would do me if we didn't know where the box was.

"Oh, sweet mother," I gasped as we heard the door downstairs swing open. "Is somebody coming? Someone alive?" I almost hoped we'd get caught at this point. Rescued.

The ghost dog barked happily and went to greet our visitor. Frankie cursed under his breath. "It's probably someone who haunts this place."

"Oh geez," I swayed, fighting hard not to grip the banister.

"Go," Frankie said. "You look around upstairs. I'll try to buy us some time. If I yell, you run."

Lovely. "Run where?" I muttered as the image of Frankie disappeared.

The dog's barks grew harsh and aggressive as I heard Frankie's voice downstairs. Whatever he was saying, it sounded charming. Or whatever passed for charming among the cocky gangster ghost set. I hoped he knew what he was doing.

I took the last few steps at a run.

At the top of the landing, the ghostly cobwebs tangled all the way down to the floor, blocking my path. There was no way around them. I'd have to go through them.

It seemed like an impossible task. Then again, everyone around these parts knew, if you wanted something done—come hell or high water—you leave it to a Southern girl.

I gripped my flashlight and summoned up my courage.

"I love my house," I reminded myself on a whisper before squeezing my eyes shut tight. I steeled my courage, made sure my mouth was closed firm, and stepped forward. *I love my house.*

I held my breath and reached out my hands. They tangled in the cold, filmy, sticky, otherworldly web.

I love my house. I pressed forward as it touched my face and wound through my hair.

I love my house. I screamed it in my head as the fibers caressed my arms and goose bumps rippled over my skin. That web felt like a living, breathing entity. It stretched out in front of me, surrounding me, blocking my way until...

With a soft whoosh, I broke through.

I ducked my head, sucking in a harsh breath. "Get it off," I said, furiously rubbing at my arms and face.

But there was nothing there.

The filmy tendrils had disappeared completely.

I couldn't even hear Frankie or the dog anymore. It was as if I'd entered another realm.

I stood in a narrow hallway, a long stretch of wall broken apart by three solid doors. Light glowed from the one on the far right end and I knew without asking that we would find our ghost there.

I hurried the opposite way, to the far left door. Maybe I'd find the money in here, and then I could sneak down and somehow get past the ghosts on the first floor and get away from this house.

The door handle felt like a block of ice as I gripped it and turned.

I pushed the door, but it didn't budge. It was locked, no doubt by something otherworldly and terrifying, but I wasn't going to dwell on that. I simply drew my hand back, wiped it on my dress, and kept my eyes peeled for any hidden compartments as I moved to the door in the middle of the hallway.

Glancing at the glow coming from the door not taken, I steeled myself and reached for the knob in front of me. The chill of it radiated up my arm.

It refused to even turn.

"Okay," I said to myself shakily, knowing I needed to keep quiet, but at the same time, needing to remind myself that I was real. I was here. And no doubt whatever haunted this place knew that already.

I was out of options except the glowing door at the end of the stairs. I didn't even want to think about what lay in wait near the exit if I chose to flee.

But really, where would that get me at this point?

I'd already gone through so much and I couldn't, just couldn't, give up now. Not when I was—could be—so close.

The flashlight beam shook along with my hand, sending stark, flickering shadows over the wall.

Now or never.

Sweat slicked my skin despite the chill in the air.

The house went eerily still as I approached the third door.

As I reached for the knob, it began to turn on its own. I fought the urge to yank my hand back. Instead, I pushed the door open, shivering at the dank room that greeted me. It glowed with a silver light. I saw no bed, no dresser. Only a ghostly chair in the very center, with a perfectly formed hangman's noose stretched out above it.

I folded my arms over my chest and shuddered when I saw that my skin shimmered with silver light, as if I'd somehow gotten caught up in the illusion.

I jumped in shock as the chair clattered across the floor.

The rope of the noose creaked and I gasped in horror at the sudden appearance of a young woman, her neck in the noose, hanging.

The door behind me slammed closed. I ran for it, yanked at it, but it wouldn't open. The knob wouldn't even turn. I fought with it until I wrenched my wrist and tears ran down my face and I sobbed and I begged and—

"You," the ghostly woman uttered, nearly scaring me out of what was left of my sanity.

I refused to look. "Frankie!" I called, I begged, fighting with the door. "Frankie, get up here!"

No response.

"Frankie!"

Nothing.

I turned to face the ghost of the woman. She wore her long hair in a thick braid down her back, baring her neck, which lay crooked in the hangman's noose. Her chin tilted down, her head lolling so I couldn't see her face, which was perfectly fine with me. She wore an old-fashioned nightgown in ghostly flowing white. Her skin shone translucent, but her neck was raw and torn where the rope cut into it.

She raised her head and stared at me. She had been in her late teens when she died, and she was beautiful, if you didn't count her quivering chin and haggard expression.

The shadows under her cheekbones deepened. Her eyes shrank back into their sockets. She snarled and her entire face drew back into a skeletal sneer. She let out a deep, guttural moan. "Get. Out."

CHAPTER 5

MY BODY REFUSED TO MOVE. If it could, I'd be running. Or cowering in the corner and crying like a baby. Instead, I stood dumbstruck.

The noose swayed almost imperceptibly from side to side, rocking the woman, squeezing off her air. I wasn't even sure ghosts needed air. Her mouth formed an "o" and she let out a hoarse, wet moan.

She had been strung up, tied to the ceiling, strangled for eternity.

The poor girl. When it came right down to it, Josephine's story wasn't all that different from my own: jerky guy, public embarrassment, the whole town looking down on her. But it didn't have to end so terribly.

Maybe she didn't have a friend like Lauralee. Or a sister who loved her.

Her mouth opened and closed like a caught fish. She was haunted and tortured and had been *left* that way. In a terrifying moment of total clarity, I had to ask. I had to know the truth, not just the legend that didn't tell her side of the story. "What happened to you?"

Her eyes locked onto mine. My pity fled as her stare bored into me hard. She took a deep, sucking breath, and screamed.

I took one step back, then another. I didn't know where to go or how to get out of there, but she'd told me to get out and I meant to do it. I was just going to need a little help since she'd locked the door behind me.

I let out a loud hiccup. "I'm not trying to hurt you or invade your house. Or keep you from throwing anything you want out your window." Damn. I probably shouldn't have mentioned that. "It's just that I'm in a bit of trouble and…"

The ghost's hair unwound from the braid. The shadows in her face drew deeper. I watched, stunned, while her hair freed itself and spread out behind her as if carried on an unseen gale of wind.

My voice left me with a final squeak as she drew the noose off of her neck.

She drifted straight for me, her eyes cold, her face menacing.

I was sorry this had happened to her. I was sorry I intruded. I cringed, holding up my hands to shield my head. I willed myself to open my mouth, to speak without screaming. Maybe if I explained what I was doing there, she'd understand. Maybe she'd let me go. The words came out in a rush of desperation. "I'm only here because my ex-fiancé screwed me over."

She stopped her approach and hissed out a sharp breath. It sounded scratchy, weak, as if she hadn't spoken in a long time.

"Men," she said, her voice crackling. The ghost tilted her head to the side.

I swallowed. Hard. She'd just given me an opening. Maybe. I couldn't believe I was explaining this to a ghost. "He cheated on me. And he assaulted my sister." It made me angry just to think about it. "Then he turned the whole town against me when I called off the wedding."

She stared at me. My heart pounded. I'd probably said too much. But it was the truth. All of it.

She drew her hair over her shoulders, watching me all the while. "My former love also had trouble with the truth."

I tried a conspiratorial laugh, but it came out as more of a whimper. "Um…" My power of speech, which was my only true gift on this earth, had completely abandoned me.

She began to braid her streaming black hair. "I know what

they call me. I hear them say it." She flinched as if struck. "Jilted Josephine."

I cleared my throat. She might have heard me say it when I first walked into this place. Guilt gnawed at me. "I've heard it bandied about," I said weakly.

"Jonathan said he wanted to marry me." She snorted, and her watery black-and-white image grew stronger. She glanced at the window overlooking the front yard. "But then *it* happened."

Her back stiffened, and I could see a red haze form around her.

I had a feeling we were headed into dangerous territory, and I didn't want to test my luck. It was freaky enough to be standing here, talking to her. But at least she wasn't attacking me. She wasn't threatening me.

She was simply another girl with a crappy ex.

I shook my head. "Men can really do a number on us, can't they?" And as long as we were telling stories: "When I told Beau I couldn't marry him after what he'd done, he refused to listen. He said the wedding was going forward whether I wanted it to or not." I still remembered his smug words.

Her eyes widened. "He forced you to the altar?"

"No. I didn't show up." I couldn't believe I was having this conversation. "Once he realized I was standing by my word, he painted me around town as a flaky gold digger who realized too late that his parents controlled the money." I crossed my arms over my chest.

Her image swirled in an unseen wind, her hair loosening and flying out behind her as she clenched her jaw. "My fiancé left town without telling me and married his cousin. He said it 'just happened.' How do you 'just happen' to get married?" She held out her hands and a silver locket shimmered into view. She gripped it hard, turning it over in her hands. "Of course, his cousin had a bigger dowry."

Her white gown streamed around her as she rushed to the window and hurled the silver necklace straight through the broken panes. I heard the glass shatter anyway and listened as broken shards clattered onto the ground below. "If I was a better shot, I'd have hit him in the head with it."

"I'd have helped you practice your aim," I told her.

Her expression softened and she appeared almost vulnerable. "I really loved him." Her gaze focused on the rough floorboards. "Enough to compromise my virtue. I couldn't marry anyone else." She raised her head to watch out the window and I saw a faint silver light gleam amid the weeds and the overgrowth. "Then he arrived at my home, thinking to apologize, when he had *her* in his carriage." She turned to me. "So I cast the contents of my hope chest out the window as well. Along with the chest itself."

"I hope it landed on him," I said.

She smiled. And when she did, she was truly lovely. "I would have liked that very much."

I smiled back and the ghost gave a small shrug. "Maybe we can start over," I suggested. "My name is Verity. I'm from Sugarland as well."

She tilted her head and watched me closely. "Most of the time, people can't see me," she said slowly.

Oh, how I missed those days. That time. An hour or two ago when I would have classified this as the stuff of nightmares.

But nooo. I'd explicitly requested to be open to this and to everything else that was happening in this godforsaken house.

"Let me see." Ha. I should have run from this place and never looked back.

"I don't like when people come into my house," she said grudgingly. "They come and they gawk, and I hear what they say about me. It's never kind."

She had a point. "I don't know why the gossips enjoy other people's pain. I don't think most people do it on purpose. If you haven't been on the receiving end, it's hard to understand." I certainly hadn't until it happened to me. "Why do you stay here if it bothers you so much?"

"My mother," she said simply. "She told me Jonathan was a bad choice. She wanted me to marry the man my father picked out for me. I refused. I thought I would prove them wrong.

Then *it* happened." She turned her haunted gaze toward me. "She sent me to my room to think about what I did."

"For a hundred years?"

She nodded. "It's very lonely."

"I should think so." I almost offered to come back and visit, but this ghost-seeing was a onetime thing. I didn't want to make a promise I couldn't keep.

Josephine shrugged. "I'd like to leave, but I'm afraid of what might happen. Ma has a temper. She went poltergeist once and tore off the chimney."

Wait. "Poltergeist?" I didn't understand what she meant. The only thing I knew about poltergeists was not to put your hands on a TV around one, especially if you were a little blonde girl.

She kept her eyes on the door behind me. In the silence I could hear a faint scuffle from the kitchen downstairs. "I hope it doesn't happen tonight. Your friend provokes her. She doesn't like intruders; they make her feel unsafe."

I drew in a breath. "What's going on down there?"

Josephine gave a small smile and tamped down a giggle. "She is scaring him with my dog. I almost feel sorry for that insufferable man."

If she did, she was a better woman than I was. Still, he was my one connection to the other side. I needed to give Frankie a break. "Would you mind calling your dog back?"

She pressed her lips together and whistled. "Here, Fritz." I heard the clicking of dog claws on hardwood as the hound trotted straight through the locked wood door, tail wagging. Josephine reached down and stroked his head. "Fritzie has made my confinement bearable. He loves me."

He ate up the attention and appeared like a totally different animal than the one I'd met downstairs.

"Do you wish to pet him?" she asked. "He is quite friendly once he has been introduced."

Fritz lolled his head and gave me a serious hit of adorable-dog syndrome.

"No. That's okay," I said, resisting his charm. His body would be cold and wet and, "I don't want to make my skunk jealous."

Josephine raised an eyebrow at the mention of my skunk, but she nodded as if she understood. "All animals want to do is love us," she said, stroking Fritz's knobby head. "He has been more protective lately, ever since the last time a living person came up here." She winced at the memory. "A strange man barged into my room. He ripped up my floor right there," she said, pointing to the spot right underneath where she'd hung. "He didn't even care that I was here."

I stiffened. "Did he leave anything?"

She shook her head, her thoughts far away. "I'm not sure what you mean."

My stomach tingled. "I came here because a man hid money on your property a long time ago. I need it to save my house."

Her mouth formed a hard line. "I don't know what I'd do if I lost my house."

"It's a terrible feeling," I told her.

She gave a short nod as Fritz nosed her, trying to get her attention back. "If the money is there, you can have it."

The Southern manners in me screamed to ask her if she was sure, but I knew better than that. "Thank you," I said quickly.

Before I lost my nerve, I stepped around the ghost and knelt down over the place where that poor girl had died. I held my flashlight between my teeth, aiming it at the floor, and ran my fingers over the rough wood planks. None of them were the same length. I traced the length of each of them, searching for a break that would indicate a hideaway of some sort underneath.

The beam of my flashlight shook, its light flickering over the old hardwood. There were four round marks where the legs of the chair had rested.

My skin prickled as I touched one of the marks. I glanced up at Josephine as my finger found purchase next to it, under a knothole that had long since rotted out. She was staring at the door, focused on whatever was going on downstairs. I thought I heard Frankie yelp.

One problem at a time.

The board groaned as I lifted it away from the others. Then I shone the flashlight inside.

A tangle of small white bones greeted me. "Oh my Lord." I reached in and knocked them away. A long wood box lay underneath, with an oak tree carved into the lid.

I let out a joyful, disbelieving snort. "This is it." I reached down, my fingers closing over the prize just as I felt a cold whoosh of air rush into the room.

Josephine let out a gasp. "Ma, no!"

A wall of energy slammed down onto me, stunning me. My ears tingled, my legs felt weak. I looked up and saw the disembodied face of a woman with stark red eyes and a vicious, angry sneer.

She swooped down on me. I grabbed the box and rolled to the side, looking for somewhere—anywhere—to run.

"Stop it, Ma!" Josephine stood between the specter and me.

The older woman's hair was pulled in a severe bun. Her nostrils flared and she vibrated with malice. "What did I tell you about letting people in?"

The door to the room flew open. Frankie stood on the other side, hat gone, suit rumpled. "You get it?" he asked, eyeing the box in my hand. "Let's go!"

I found my feet and dashed past all three ghosts, straight out into the hall.

Fritz barked like crazy, his nails scrabbling against the hardwood, but someone—most likely Josephine—held him back. "It was lovely to meet you," she called. "Please do come again sometime!"

"She's a crazy woman," Frankie hollered, hot on my heels.

"She's getting us out of here," I countered. I clutched the box to my chest and about fell over making the corner around the landing without touching the banister.

Frankie zipped ahead of me. "Not Josephine. The other one."

I thundered down the stairs like the wood under my feet could open up and swallow me at any second.

For all I knew, it could.

I jumped the last three stairs and hurtled past the ghostly table and chairs. The only thing I cared about was the exit straight ahead.

I swore if I made it, I'd never do this again. I was done with Frankie and his money schemes and ghosts and all of it.

My fingers closed around the knob. It was ice cold. I twisted it hard, threw the door open, and ran straight into the blessed freedom outside.

A shotgun blast ripped through the side of the house next to me, peppering my back with shards of wood.

Holy—

"Stop!" I screamed, holding out a hand as I gripped the box under my other arm. Darkness surrounded me. I'd suddenly gone from the glow of the ghostly visions to pitch black, and my eyes needed to adjust. I couldn't see.

"Run!" Frankie screamed, dissolving into thin air.

I crouched and started back for the house, even as I felt the anger and the energy of Josephine's crazy mother radiating down to my very core.

A second shotgun blast tore into the ground in front of me, sending up a spray of plants and dirt. Sweet heaven. I dropped the cash box and kept going.

Rumbles echoed from inside the house. The dog barked like mad. A cold wall of air rose up, whipping my hair into my eyes, stinging my cheeks, and driving me back.

"I mean you no harm!" I screamed at my attacker, at the ghosts, at anyone who would listen.

A sharp double-click echoed in my ears as my assailant cocked a gun.

"Then stay the hell off my property!"

CHAPTER 6

I FROZE. I KNEW THAT VOICE. It was cracklier than it had been. Sharpened with age. But I had no doubt who it was: Maisie Hatcher. Heart pounding half out of my chest, I stopped with my back to her and straightened.

Making sure to be slow, painfully restrained, I raised my arms up and away from my body. I didn't dare turn or speak.

Not yet.

In the moonlight, I could see the spray of small bullet holes torn into the wood next to the door. I gulped. That could have been me.

"Where are the rest?" she demanded. "I want to see every goddamned one of you hooligans."

My mouth and throat went as dry as the Sahara while the rest of me sweated buckets. I was reluctant to speak, afraid of what might set her off. But I knew I had to say *something*. It was my only chance to calm her down.

"It's just me, Mrs. Hatcher. Verity," I began, voice shaking despite my efforts to sound soothing. "I'd like to turn around now."

"Trespassing delinquents," she mumbled under her breath. "Let's see your face."

I turned.

Mrs. Maisie Hatcher stalked toward me, her legs bent and wide. She held fire in her eyes and a shotgun aimed straight at my chest. A shabby tan bathrobe covered her high-necked blue nightgown. She'd aged twenty years in the ten since I'd last seen her.

Her eyes briefly widened when she saw me and I took that as a victory.

"You," she snarled, taking fresh aim. "Aren't you a little old for this malarkey?"

Definitely not the greeting I'd been hoping for.

"I'm sorry, Mrs. Hatcher," I said, the words running together. Without conscious thought, I found myself reverting back to the tone I'd used when I spilled tea on her skirt during one of my grandmother's church group get-togethers. "I needed something. Badly. And I didn't want to bother you."

Her eyes narrowed. "What do I have that you want?"

Okay, yes. This was bound to be an uncomfortable situation.

I racked my brain for a way to tell her that I'd come onto her property in order to find the cash she'd desperately sought all these years. Sure, I'd been rather enthusiastic about dashing out of the house with it. But I really had planned to give it to her.

It sounded suspicious, even to me.

"Well?" she demanded, adjusting her aim.

Maybe she was just shocked, scared like I was. She'd been sleeping very hard, if the hair sticking straight out from her head in clumps was any indication. Last time I'd seen Maisie, her tresses were thin, teased straight up, and stained an unnaturally orangeish auburn that could only come from a bottle. It didn't quite work, but I had to give her credit for making an effort.

I knew I must look guilty. I felt guilty. And every moment I stood tongue-tied in front of Mrs. Hatcher no doubt made me look even worse. Only there was no plausible explanation for my presence on her property at this hour of the night.

So I set my goal lower. Maybe, just maybe, I could get her to stop aiming her shotgun at my chest.

It was a start. "Mrs. Hatcher, I…"

Right when I thought the entire sordid, unbelievable, damning story would come spilling out of me, I caught the glint of something out of the corner of my eye and found inspiration.

Josephine's locket.

It lay in the grass a few feet to my right, directly under the ghost's favorite window.

I took a deep breath. "I came here once on a dare," I said, the words spilling out of me as if they were true. "When I was a teenager, a young, dumb kid," I stressed that last part, ignoring the widow's huff of agreement. "I came here with some friends. While I was here, I lost my grandmother's locket."

She wasn't impressed. "I always got kids sniffing around my 'haunted' property." She frowned. "This is private property. It ain't for kids."

"I know," I said, raising my arms higher, even though they were starting to ache. It was time for the truth, at least the part that didn't involve a ghost named Frankie. I cleared my throat. "I'm not sure if you've heard, but I had some money troubles."

She snorted. "We all have."

Indeed. "I've had to sell most everything my grandmother gave to me." I swallowed hard. Maisie watched me carefully. At least I had her attention now. "That locket," I said, motioning with my eyes, "lying right over there… It's the last thing I have left of her." I shook my head. "I know coming here was dumb and wrong. And rude," I added, "but I was only trying to get it back."

She hesitated, relaxing her stance a fraction. "Then why were you inside?" she asked, tipping her gun toward the door of the house.

I slowly began bringing my hands down, relieved when she let me. "I left it in the upstairs bedroom." A sharp, chilling breeze whipped up her hair and chilled me to the bone. Goose bumps raced down my sweat-slicked skin.

"I never went up there," she said, her eyes darting to the side as she thought. "'Course, I've only been inside once." She eyed me carefully. "Once was enough."

She lowered her gun all the way. At least we were having a conversation now, and not a standoff. "I'm sorry," I said, quite honestly. "I shouldn't have come so late at night. But my house goes on sale tomorrow and I panicked."

"Had to find it, huh?" she asked, glancing at the upper bedroom window. She patted her hair down, or at least she tried. "I knew your grandmother pretty well, back in the day. We went to school together."

I hadn't realized, but it made sense. We only had one elementary. "I remember you from her ladies parties."

The corners of her mouth turned up and she coughed a little. "Now those were some pleasant afternoons. Your grandmother was a real nice lady."

"I know," I said simply. "Thank you."

I eased over toward the locket in the grass. And when Maisie didn't stop me, I reached down for it. Until that moment, I hadn't stopped to consider whether I could still touch a ghostly object. I hesitated for a split second before my fingers closed around the chilly metal. I'd take good care of it, I vowed, as I slipped it into my pocket.

When the widow's brows furrowed, I realized what I'd done.

"The chain is broken," I explained quickly. I didn't feel right about wearing Josephine's necklace.

I'd polish it up and return it to her later.

Maisie paused. "I didn't see it until you had it there in your hand." She rubbed a hand down the side of her face. "I must be more tired than I thought."

"It is late," I agreed. We were both a little stressed. I should have realized she wouldn't be able to see the ghostly object. But then I'd touched it and brought it into her reality. Amazing.

I glanced up to Josephine's window. The ghost stood over us, watching. She caught my eye and gave me a small wave.

The widow clucked. "I don't know why anyone in their right mind would set foot in that house."

"It's not all bad," I said, surreptitiously returning Josephine's wave. I shivered as the necklace in my pocket went cold. I slipped my fingers over it and felt it melt away into nothing. Okay, so maybe I wouldn't need to go back.

Maisie frowned. "That place is more haunted than the *Queen Mary*."

"If there's a spirit lingering here, she's probably a little lonely." I glanced back at the house. The ghost still stood in the window. I was no expert on the paranormal, but, "Have you tried saying hi?"

I mean, who wouldn't want to be acknowledged?

Josephine had lived a hard life, a tragic one. And her afterlife was no picnic, either. It must be the worst feeling in the world to be feared, maligned—alone.

Maisie had to think about that one. She gestured toward the house, with a rolling motion of her wrist. "You think I should say hi to Jilted Josephine? Like she's a person or something?"

"I'd call her by her Christian name only, for starters," I suggested. "But yes. When you walk your property—"

"Every day," she interjected proudly.

Why was I not surprised? "Every day," I repeated, "wave and greet her like you would any neighbor." I paused, thinking of the stark isolation of that girl inside. "I'll bet things in that house might even calm down a bit if you do."

She let out a small huff. Then to my surprise, Mrs. Hatcher raised her hand—the one that wasn't holding the gun at her side—and gave a small gesture of greeting. "Well, hello there, neighbor." She blew out a breath. "Not that I want her returning the favor and coming by my place with greetings, but I know what it's like to crave a visitor from time to time."

I didn't doubt it. Maisie didn't have a lot of people she could count on. There weren't many of her generation left.

And with that, I was reminded of my true reason for being there. "I have to tell you something," I said, retreating to search for the box I'd dropped. It lay on its side in a tangle of grass, half-bathed in moonlight. My hemp bag with Frankie's urn lay nearby. I shouldered the bag and then picked up the box. Hope flared in my chest. I'd done it. I'd solved both our money problems.

"I found this with my locket," I said, carrying it back to her, eager to see what it held. "I think it might be what you've been looking for."

She gasped when she saw the wooden box with the oak tree emblem.

She placed the gun on the ground. Shaking, she took the box from me with both hands. "It feels like I've been looking for this for half my life." She glanced up at me, wary, before her excitement got the better of her and she unlatched the metal clasp.

When she lifted the lid, we saw bundles and bundles of twenty-dollar bills, neatly paper-clipped together. My heart lifted.

She simply stared, her eyes welling with tears.

I grinned like mad.

"You—" she stammered, unable to find the words. She shook her head as she struggled to compose herself. "I—"

"Grandma told me stories of how your husband left money for you." He'd treated her poorly, but that was over now. She shouldn't have to struggle so hard, not at her age. And it seemed as if she had plenty extra. "This should be more than you need, right?"

A single tear fell, bypassing her cheek and falling into the box. "Thank you," she said, suddenly quite proper, and for a brief moment, I caught a glimpse of the woman she'd been twenty years ago.

"You deserve it." Here was a woman who lived on her own, walked her property, and stood up for herself. She might not welcome all that many visitors, but she'd more than earned a helping hand and I was glad to be the person to give it.

A cold spot materialized to my right. I didn't see Frankie, but I could certainly hear him. "Ask her for the money."

He was like the devil on my shoulder.

I opened my mouth. Closed it. Exactly what does one say to persuade an old woman to part with a chunk of her long-awaited inheritance?

"That's a lot to spend," I said, in the worst lead-in ever.

Frankie groaned.

"Be kind," I muttered.

Truly, I could speak plainly with the best of them, but not about money, in the middle of the night, with an old woman who stood crying in front of me.

She wiped her nose on the sleeve of her robe. "You don't know what this means," she said, blinking back grateful tears.

"Here," Frankie said, "you just take it. Like this." I watched the bills ripple under Maisie's fingers. "Well, not like that, but you get the picture."

I took Maisie by the shoulder and steered her away from the sticky-fingered ghost.

"Don't you be high-hatting me." Frankie chilled the air at my back. "She's holding at least forty g's in the box. She won't miss half of that."

"Maisie," I began, "I don't know if you have plans for that money, but—"

She clutched the box to her chest. "I can pay my medical bills now. I was going to lose the house, the farm. This still might not be enough. But it's a lot. It'll go far, don't you think?"

My heart grew heavy. "Yes."

She needed it just as much as I did. And it was hers.

"I'm glad I could help," I said, fighting back the lump in my throat.

"Did my hearing go out, or did you just let that dame off the hook?" Frankie's voice was incredulous. I waved him off.

I'd made her happier. And I think I'd also helped Josephine. It would have to be enough, I decided as I reached into my pocket for my car keys.

Maisie was a woman alone. She and I both were.

"I'll come by and visit you," I added, "this time in daylight." I'd bring cookies when I could afford all the ingredients. If I recalled, she favored oatmeal crunch.

The urn bumped against my hip. "You're just gonna give up? On our house?"

My house.

It meant more to me than he could ever imagine, but there were some lines I couldn't cross. "This isn't right," I said under my breath.

"What's not right, dear?" Maisie asked.

I didn't realize she could hear so well. I turned back to her. "I'm losing Grandma's house." It hurt to even say it. "I wanted to ask you for a loan, but you need the money as much as I do."

Maisie sighed. "I love that old house. It used to be the heart of Sugarland when your grandmother was alive."

I nodded. "Our family has so much history there, but after what happened with Beau and me, nobody in town will lend me the money to save it, and I don't have a fortune buried in the backyard."

She thought for a moment. "How much do you need?"

"Twenty thousand," I told her solemnly.

She let out a surprised cluck of sympathy. "I can't give you that much."

I understood, more than she realized. "Three thousand would cover lawyer fees to put off the judgment for another month. If you could spare that much of a loan." Of course I'd still have to figure out another way to earn twenty thousand dollars.

I doubted Frankie had another box of money up his sleeve.

Maisie Hatcher fingered the lid, not saying a word.

Then she nodded hard, a tear spilling down her cheek. "Oh, sweetie. I can lend you that. I'd be happy to."

I couldn't believe it. "Thank you," I squealed, hugging her before either one of us could think about it too much. "I'll pay you back as soon as I can."

She pulled back, flustered. "I'm sure you will."

I'd get a job, one that paid a lot better than having an art degree in a small town afforded. I'd work day and night if I had to. I'd even move away to Chicago if it meant I had a chance to make this all right.

She opened the box a crack and carefully removed three thousand dollars.

"Thank you," I whispered as she gave it to me.

I was about to breathe the biggest sigh of relief ever when police lights flashed. I about jumped out of my skin when the siren blipped.

Headlights turned on us, bright as day, and I realized Maisie was as frozen as I was, pressing a wad of cash into my hands.

Surely that wasn't illegal.

Although there was the issue of me breaking and entering.

And I hoped she'd registered that firearm she'd been discharging.

"Stay where you are," the officer ordered, exiting his car.

I knew that voice. And I ignored it long enough to stuff the three thousand dollars into the pocket of my sundress.

Right now, the officer was a tall, looming shadow surrounded by lights. But as he drew closer, I grew a bit dizzy.

Ellis Graham Wydell strode up wearing the badge of the Sugarland Sheriff's Office. He was the bold one, the black sheep, not to mention my ex-fiancé's brother. And he was the very last person I wanted to see.

CHAPTER 7

HE SLOWED AS HE APPROACHED. "Verity Long," he drawled, as if he expected me to be caught red-handed in the woods after midnight.

Damn the man and his assumptions.

Ellis Wydell was as handsome as the rest of the men in his family, which was to say drop-dead gorgeous. He stood tall and lean, with broad shoulders, bulk in all the right places, and a dimple in his chin that deepened when he smiled the same as when he frowned.

I planted a hand on my hip and waited as he drew the flashlight over me. "You get a good look?" I asked. I wasn't armed and I wasn't doing anything wrong. Not at the moment, anyhow.

His piercing hazel eyes raked over me. "We had report of a trespass."

"Maisie and I were just visiting," I said. That might have been the lamest excuse ever, but it's not like I'd ever planned to get caught.

His eyes narrowed. "I was addressing the property owner."

Right. Well, then he should stop looking at me.

"It's good to see you again, Ellis," Maisie said, hurrying to latch the box of money and stuff it under her arm. "He likes to check up on me."

"I heard gunshots," he said before saddling her with a long pause, one that would encourage her to spill her guts, no doubt.

She looked like Lucy when that darned skunk stole the potatoes out from under my sink—guilty as sin. I wanted to assure Maisie it was quite legal how she'd come about her fortune, and how she'd loaned me some, but the less we said to Wydell, the better.

She patted at an errant tuft of hair that was sticking straight out. "You're absolutely right, young man. I did fire my gun." She cleared her throat. "I thought I saw a bear. Only it was Verity."

"And she stopped shooting as soon as she knew," I added, as if that meant I belonged here.

Ellis stood for a moment, his forehead crinkling as if he couldn't quite believe that was our official story. People must try to sell him on bull all the time, but I had a feeling our explanation went beyond the pale. For a split second, I actually pitied the man.

He moved closer to Maisie and placed a comforting arm on her shoulder. "Why are you giving this woman money?" he asked her.

Oh, so now I was *this woman*.

Maisie chewed at her lip, and for a second I thought she was going to spill the whole story. "It was a loan," she said quickly. It didn't sound good, even if it was the truth.

His radio buzzed and he answered it. "Officer Wydell." He might have turned his back, but his manner suggested this was far from over.

The radio crackled with static. *"Requesting update on shots fired off Saw Mill Road."*

He lifted the speaker to his mouth and acted like it was our fault when he had to say, "Subject believed she saw a...bear."

"A black one," Maisie added.

He ignored her. "No injuries."

I crossed my arms over my chest. "You know, you'd think in all his years on the force, he wouldn't be so put out by a wildlife sighting."

Maisie's mouth fluttered into a brief smile, but I could tell from the way Ellis's eyes narrowed that he was fast losing patience.

"I'm going to stay and ask the witnesses a few more questions," he reported to the dispatcher before signing off.

Lovely. Maisie looked like she'd just drunk about ten cups of coffee. As long as she didn't break, we'd make this work. We'd get rid of Ellis and say our good-byes. I'd thank her profusely. Again.

And then I'd get right home and call my real estate agent.

The sale would be off—at least for tomorrow.

Ellis tucked his radio into his belt and strolled straight for me. The man was bound and determined to make this hard. Well, I'd been through plenty tonight already, and I think I'd proven that I didn't scare easy.

Still, that didn't mean I wasn't affected. Ellis towered over me. He was taller than his brother, lean and tan. It was as if he'd been born to be more intimidating, more rugged.

He regarded me as if the intensity of his gaze would let him see straight into me. For a brief moment, I wondered what it would be like to have a man look at me like that when he wasn't trying to figure out if I was up to something nefarious. "Want to tell me what really happened?"

I tilted my chin up. "I was out walking."

"Ten miles from your home. In the dark," he added, not being helpful at all.

"I needed to clear my mind," I said. "As you and your brother must realize, I'm having some difficulties as of late."

He clenched his jaw. "I know. I was there when you threw the engagement ring at him. You hit me in the forehead."

"I was aiming for *him*," I said, keeping my tone lofty. Besides, Officer Wydell had surely been hit by worse than a flying two-carat princess-cut diamond.

"Bad move for a gold digger," he mused.

For the love of Pete. "Ever stop to think I might have had a good reason for leaving your baby brother?"

He was back on me in a second. "Then tell me," he demanded.

"Ask him," I said, knowing Beau would never tell the truth.

He'd threatened me with my sister's job if I ever said anything, and I knew he wasn't bluffing. She was a part-time employee at the library and he was on the board.

Ellis sighed, put out. "Can you at least tell me what happened tonight?"

Not quite. "It was a misunderstanding," I offered.

A muscle in his cheek twitched and he didn't even notice the unearthly breeze ruffling his dark hair. "She shot at you," he said, with no trace of irony, as if he'd been there.

"Not really," I said. She'd hit the house.

We were both fine. In fact, we'd gotten a lot done tonight. We solved some of our problems, made a few bucks, and everyone was going home happy.

If Officer Ellis Wydell would let us.

But he was like a duck on a June bug.

"Come with me," he said, walking me back to his patrol car.

I went along willingly. Sort of. "I'm not under arrest, am I?"

He gave me a slanted look. There was that dimple again. "Now why would you think that?"

"Because that's the only way you'd get me in the backseat of your car."

I said it to shock him and it worked, although I didn't count on the mild blush creeping up my cheeks.

Ellis was two years older than my ex. Beau was the young-est, then Ellis, then Harrison as you went up. Harrison was a fancy-pants judge who loved having his name in the papers. Beau was a big-shot lawyer, just like his dad. Ellis had stunned them all by opting out of the family business and going into law enforcement.

Truth be told, I hadn't seen much of Ellis over the years. The middle brother had always been somewhat of a mystery—elu-sive, taciturn. He hadn't gotten wrapped up in family politics. He loved the law for its own sake, which was quite unfortunate for me at the moment.

The police cruiser's flashing lights made me wince. I knew he was only doing his job, and a tough one at that, but I hated being the cause of his late-night investigation. I had to tell him, "This is all rather innocent."

"I'll bet." He leaned in close enough for me to catch the scent of him, a pure male earthiness that had nothing to do with perfume counters or aftershave. What you saw was what you got, it seemed. He cocked his head and leaned in closer. "My brother said you were sly."

Of all the—"That's not fair."

Ellis Wydell had known me all my life and ignored me for a good portion of it. I didn't even see him much when I dated Beau. The brothers didn't run in the same social circles.

Then Ellis had been off in Virginia at some FBI institute for police, and now he was back, poking his nose in where he wasn't wanted, ready to judge me on a word and a glance and a pile of bills I'd stuffed into my pocket.

"I didn't mean any harm," I told him. "Truly." I wasn't exactly sure why, but it was important for him to understand that.

He simply opened the back door. "Get in the car."

Right. Of course. I had to wait here while he got the facts from someone he trusted.

My heart sank as I eased inside. It didn't matter what Ellis thought, I tried to convince myself. He was one person, a biased one at that.

"Now you stay here," he warned before he closed the door.

I watched him walk back, squirming a little in my seat. Maisie was a loose cannon, and it seemed like those two had a pretty good relationship.

Still, he had nothing on us as long as we stuck to the truth. And that was good because I had to get out of here and use the three thousand dollars that was burning a hole in my pocket.

In the meantime, I felt rather small sitting in the backseat of the police cruiser.

I'd never been in one before. The smooth vinyl seat felt hard against my backside, very different from my well-worn velvet cushions in the Cadillac. Steel mesh separated me from the front seat, where the radio buzzed with reports of police activity in progress.

Reckless driver on Alvin York Boulevard.

Stumbling drunk at the Circle K on Fifth and Main.

Surely either of those was more urgent than a girl escaping a haunted house with a pile of money.

Ellis returned to Mrs. Hatcher. I couldn't read the widow's expression. She stood several yards away, out of the light cast by the headlights of the patrol car. Yet I saw her hands flutter near her neck. She'd better not be telling him about the locket. Not when I couldn't show it to him.

It was all facts with him, nothing else. I tried to tell myself that his good opinion of me didn't matter a whit.

That his words hadn't hurt.

I tucked my long hair back behind my ears and straightened my sundress around me. I'd never had anyone think the worst of me until the Incident. Now it happened far more than I liked. But no one had ever been as blunt or as bold as Ellis. That man was in a league of his own.

At this point, nothing should have startled me, but still, I jumped when Frankie shimmered into view in the seat next to me.

He glanced from the dash-mounted GPS system to the lit-up police computer crowding the front seat. "The fuzz has gotten fancier over the years." He ran a hand over the seat between us and gave me a pointed look, like he was instructing a six-year-old to stay out of the street. "You realize now is the time to run."

"I'm not a criminal." Not really. "You of all people should know that." I shifted to face him. "And speaking of running, why'd you leave me alone in a haunted house with a poltergeist inside?"

He let out a huff. "You gotta be kidding me. I held off the crazy mamma so you could get the loot."

"Fine job you did. The spirit ambushed me."

He pursed his lips. "Well, maybe if you hadn't spent so much time yakking about your love life, you could've gotten out of there before she got tired of me. And before the cops showed up."

"Oh, so this is my fault?" I began.

A harsh chill whipped through the police cruiser. "Zip it," barked a voice from the front.

A ghostly figure glowered at us from the front passenger seat. He wore a tan Sugarland Sheriff's Department uniform with black trim and a gold badge. He had to be at least sixty, but he was built as solid as a drill sergeant. He wore his gray hair in a crew cut and his name tag read Hale.

He wasn't black and white, and he wasn't as translucent as Frankie, but he was definitely a ghost.

I turned to Frankie. "How come I can see him in color?"

The gangster shrugged. "He probably hasn't been dead that long."

My heart lodged in my throat. So this Officer Hale was as real as Frankie or Josephine. I flopped against the seat. "Oh my God, I can't believe I'm seeing random ghosts now."

"You asked," Frankie shot back.

Hale raised his brows and I was almost perversely glad to see I'd surprised him. "She knows I'm here?"

"Verity Long," I said, reaching out a hand and then thinking better of it. I gave him a short wave instead. "Pleased to meet you."

The officer answered my wave with a stern frown. "I'd say you're in a lot of trouble, young lady." He gave Frankie a stony look. "And you've always been bad news."

Frankie sneered. "How do you know? It looks like you just got here."

"Word gets around," Hale shot back.

Lordy. "Okay, stop." Maybe he could help us out. "We're suffering from a misunderstanding," I said. "Your police buddy seems to think there's a problem here and there isn't."

Hale braced an arm on the seat between us as he twisted around. "Wydell's a damn fine officer. As for you…" He assessed me coolly. "What I don't get is why you had to leave that poor boy at the altar. Little Beau didn't deserve that."

Heavens to Betsy. Now I was taking flack from the dead.

Besides, 'Little Beau' was twenty-eight. "I didn't leave him," I said automatically. "I mean, yes, I refused to marry him, but—"

Hale grunted his disapproval. "You found out he didn't have as much cash as you thought and so you called it off. Guess my nephew was lucky to be rid of you."

I drew in a sharp breath. "Hardly." Now I remembered who this guy was. One of Beau's uncles was a police officer who'd been killed in the line of duty. I barely knew him.

"Now we've got you red-handed, taking money from an old lady," he said.

"Is that what you think?" Of all the… "Does Ellis know you're here?"

The ghost didn't answer. Instead, he pulled a pack of Marlboro cigarettes out of the front pocket of his patrol uniform. He knocked the pack twice against the seat and pulled out a smoke.

I crossed my arms over my chest and hunkered down in my seat. "Those things can kill you, you know."

He didn't even look at me as he felt his pockets for a lighter. "So can a bullet."

Frankie pulled out a box of Tiger Head matches from his front suit pocket and struck one against the seat of the cruiser. He held it out to Hale and the officer leaned forward for a light. He breathed in a long drag of his cigarette and nodded to Frankie. "I keep forgetting I left my lighter under the steps."

"Now remember that was me doing you the favor, right?" Frankie said. Even in death, it seemed he wasn't above getting in good with the fuzz.

Smoke curled from Hale's nostrils. "I ain't that hard up for a cigarette."

The door opened and Ellis stood outside. He didn't acknowledge the ghost cop or Frankie. Of course, why would he? I was the only one living this crazy nightmare. "Come on out." He didn't look happy. I hoped it meant good news for me.

I shimmied out of the car and saw Maisie behind him. "I'm very proud of you," she said, giving him an affectionate squeeze on the arm, even as he grimaced at her words. "Now I'm going home. It's late and I need my rest."

"Stay here for a minute," he said as she began her way down the road. "I'd be glad to drive you."

She kept going toward her house, her shotgun hitched over her shoulder. "I'm fine," she said, waving him off. "I walk my property all the time." She was a strong woman defending what was hers. It was our way here in Sugarland.

"I'll stop by soon," I called after her. "We have to set up a repayment plan for my loan."

Ellis turned his anger on me. "Don't pretend."

"Has it ever occurred to you that I might be a nice person?" I snapped.

"No," he shot back. "Poor Mrs. Hatcher might have bought your act, but I know better." He clenched his jaw, the lights from the police cruiser playing over his rugged features. "I'm telling you now: You need to do the right thing."

I dug for my keys. "And you need to learn to have a little faith in people."

He snorted.

My mamma taught me to be kind, but in that moment, he deserved the truth. "I always thought your brother was the delusional one, but you're just as bad."

His eyes hardened. "If it were up to me, I'd have you in cuffs."

"Well, I didn't do anything wrong, so I guess you're out of luck. Now may I please leave?"

He gave a sharp nod. But he didn't let up. He stuck with me all the way down the path. "It's good to hear you're done with your walk. A girl shouldn't be strolling alone after midnight." We neared my Cadillac. "Oh, look," he added, "you brought your car. Most pedestrians don't think of that."

I shot him a withering glare. "Are you done being sarcastic now?"

"Hardly." He glanced back at the darkened house. "You took advantage of poor Mrs. Hatcher. She's old. She doesn't have any family left. She's the perfect target." He held up a finger between us. "I'm going to see she gets her money back."

"She wouldn't have anything at all if I hadn't gone into a haunted house," I shot back.

"You want me to believe some bullshit story about how that place is haunted?" He made it sound so absurd, so stupid. Like I was some kind of liar.

"Go on in and see what happens," I dared. Let's see how he did with Josephine's crazy mother.

He gave a huff. "If it's so dangerous, how did you make it out?"

"I have skills," I said primly.

I didn't like the way he'd treated me this evening. In fact, I didn't like anything about tonight. But I was sick of being called a liar, by him and everybody else in this town who found it easier to believe a cheating jerk than to give me the benefit of the doubt.

"I can talk to ghosts, okay?" I said, almost dropping my keys. There. I admitted it. "I walked in there and hung out with Josephine." Let him put that in his pipe and smoke it.

"Jilted Josephine?" he scoffed.

"Don't call her that."

"I've heard some crazy stories come out of people, but that takes the cake."

"Has it ever occurred to you, Ellis Wydell, mighty arbitrator of what is right and wrong, that someone could be telling you the truth, even if you don't believe it?" I held my hands out. "No, of course not. You and Hale have all the answers."

Ellis blanched. "What do you know about Hale?"

"Only that he's dead, and his ghost is hanging out in your cruiser." I pointed my keys at him. "Old Hale says he can't get his lighter out from under the steps, and I'll bet you think that's my fault, too." I started walking to my car.

He stood, his mouth slightly open, working furiously to recover. "How'd you know Hale smoked?"

"That's what you want to focus on? Fine," I said as I passed him. I turned around, walking backwards. "I saw him light up a few minutes ago. Right there in your squad car. Bet that's a violation, right? You'd better check the manual on that one. He said you were a damn fine officer, so I'm sure you'll want to make sure everybody's following the rules."

Let that wind up his little brain and make smoke come out his ears.

I was done.

I opened the door to my car and slid inside, tossing my sack with Frankie's urn on the floor. The gangster could deal with that, too. It's not like he hadn't been dropped before.

My skin flushed pink. My whole body felt like I'd been running the fifty-yard dash. I wiped my eyes before I started up my old tank of a Cadillac.

Oh, Lordy.

As the adrenaline seeped away, I felt exposed, invaded.

I never should have told that man about my newfound ability to communicate with ghosts, but it slipped out before I'd had a chance to think it through. I'd never had a secret this big before.

"Calm down. It's not like he believed you," I chided myself. Still, ever since that incident with his brother, I was enough of a strange duck around town. No need to be giving people ammunition. "Just get yourself home. Plenty of time later to worry about what people will think."

As I left the property, I felt a tingling surge whip down my body. I slammed on the brakes, flinging out a hand on instinct to steady the purse that would ordinarily be in the passenger seat.

"Yow!" Frankie shouted, making me jump.

I hadn't realized he was next to me. But of course he was. He didn't know how to leave me alone.

I braced a hand on my chest and pressed the gas again. Quickly, I glanced into my rearview mirror. Ellis had better not be behind me. He'd probably love to give me a ticket for careless driving. "You scared me," I said to Frankie.

"Yeah," he said, looking a little green, "because I'm the scary part in all this."

I cringed as the car lurched over a particularly deep rut in the road. "You shouldn't just pop up on a person."

Frankie shook his head. "What? Do you want me to knock?"

I ignored his sarcasm. "What was the shock I felt back there?"

"When you left the property, your connection to the spirit world snapped," he said. He tried to make himself more comfortable on his seat. "Good thing, too. I can't keep feeding you that kind of energy forever."

"You okay?" I asked him. He was missing his left knee.

"It'll come back," he said, stretching out his foot. "We just mucked with my energy is all, and it's affecting my manifestation." He shot me a sideways glance. "I ain't never done that before."

"Join the club." I didn't want to see what was on the other side anymore. I just wanted to go home.

The roads were dark and, until tonight, unfamiliar. Still, I managed to find my way back well enough. I was good with things like that.

"Hey, cheer up, Verity," the gangster said, leaning back against the headrest. He looked tired. "The good news is you didn't give away every cent we needed for the house, only most of it."

"Don't start. It'll buy us some time." I hazarded a glance at him. He sat there fiddling with his matchbox. "Do you have any idea what we can do after this month?"

He had his eyes closed. With practiced ease, he spun the matchbox with two fingers. "Not a clue."

"Glad you thought about it for more than a half a second."

"A thousand apologies, princess," he said, shoving the matchbox back into his pocket. "You think gangsters buried their money like pirate gold? We laundered it like sensible crooks and put it in banks." He cocked his head. "Or we spent it."

"Fine." I didn't want to talk about it anymore. At least I'd bought a little time. I didn't have to sell my house tomorrow.

Next month was another matter.

CHAPTER 8

THE NEXT MORNING I WAS up bright and early. Mostly because I'd sold the curtains.

I poured Lucy a bowl of kitty chow (yet another way society discriminated against skunks—no skunk chow) and left my girl crunching and swishing her tail while I went to answer the avocado-green wall phone in the kitchen. It tring-a-linged the same as it did when I was a child. I smiled at that, and because I knew who it had to be.

I'd called my sister first thing, even though I knew she was probably in the shower. It never took her long to call back.

"I heard your message," Melody said as soon as I lifted the receiver. "You're not selling? What did you do? Did you get a loan?"

"Stop talking and I'll tell you," I said. She was five years younger. In times like these, it showed. "One of Grandma's friends came into some money. She loaned me a little. Anonymously," I stressed. "I still have to come up with the rest."

Luckily my sister was too focused on the problem to grill me on the particulars. "But we have time." She whooshed out a breath. "I'll have another hundred by the end of the week."

"You don't need to give me your money," I told her. She needed it. Melody worked part-time at the Sugarland Public Library. She'd also taken a part-time waitressing job at the diner Lauralee managed, but she barely made enough to cover student loans and rent. I'd offered to let her move back here, but she was locked into a lease. Melody was naturally curious, and smart. But none of her almost-degrees had quite panned out and she'd need to go back to school eventually.

"I'm so sorry I caused this," she said, her voice racked with guilt.

"It's not your fault," I said. It was the truth. "You saved me from a lot worse."

"I'm coming by with a chicken after work," she said, in the ultimate Southern subject change. As if food really could fix things.

"That sounds good," I told her.

She had to get to the library, so we signed off. Meanwhile, I'd get busy with my breakfast and my day.

Frankie shimmered into view next to me while I stood at the stove cooking zesty pork-flavored ramen noodles in my old Girl Scout camp pot.

I'd hoped he'd be the type to sleep in. Or at least leave me to my thoughts.

"I called my lawyer," I told him, taking the pot of noodles off the burner. Tim Caruthers didn't come cheap, but he was good. "He's going to use the money from last night to file another appeal." It wouldn't help in the long run, but it would buy us time.

"This is how you celebrate?" The ghost gave a delicate sniff, as if he were some type of French chef. He retreated through the kitchen island and to the other side of the room. "It stinks."

It wasn't the raspberry smoothie I preferred, or the roast chicken I'd get tonight, but I had to get used to a new standard now. "Leave me alone, I'm hungry," I said. "And I didn't feel like picante beef noodles," which had been my other choice.

The dollar store tended to stock the less popular flavors.

I poured the noodles and the water into a plastic bowl and mixed in the flavor packet. Frankie watched with barely contained revulsion. "Okay, so you got them off your back for now, but we're still in trouble."

How sad is it that I liked the word *we*?

My family meant well, but I still felt ashamed I'd dragged them into this. And Lauralee had responsibilities of her own. It was nice to have someone in my corner who didn't have to be there.

I placed my breakfast on the kitchen island and gave myself a mental shake. It wouldn't do any good to feel sorry for myself.

Meanwhile the mobster couldn't take his eyes off the noodles swirling in my bowl. "You're seriously going to eat that?"

"Frankie!" It was one thing to have someone care and quite another to endure his pestering. Was it too much to ask that one thing in my life be peaceful? Even if it was only breakfast?

I turned and located the bag with his urn. It was on the counter, exactly where I'd left it last night.

"What are you doing?" he demanded as I hefted it over my shoulder and made for the door

"Fish and houseguests stink after a few days. This is my home, not yours," I reminded him as I placed his urn on the back porch swing. "You can stay outside."

"Now if that don't beat all. Southern hospitality sure has changed in the last ninety years," he said, laying it on thick as if he thought I'd feel guilty and change my mind. "Because you grounded me, babe. That's as good as making me family." I gave him the hairy eyeball and he threw up his hands. "Fine. You know what? I'll humor you." He vaporized into a fine mist, although I noticed the volume of his voice didn't go down a bit. "I could use some shut-eye anyway."

With a small sigh, I headed back inside, the screened door flapping closed behind me. On second thought, I bolted the oak door as well.

As if it would keep out a ghost.

Less than a year ago, my life had been so simple. I had a nice little freelance design business going. I was marrying a man I thought I loved. And then—poof. Ghosts in my kitchen and ramen for breakfast.

The smell of broth filled the kitchen. It was quite homey,

actually. Soothing. I rinsed out my pot and placed it in the dishwasher. Then I made my way back to the kitchen island.

I'd figure a way out of this mess. I'd never been the type to give up before. I scooped up a bite of noodles, blew on my spoon, and was about to taste it when a knock sounded at my back door.

I was seriously going to lock Frankie's urn in the car this time.

And hope he didn't go for a joyride.

I set aside my spoon, wiped my hands on my pink flowered sundress, and stalked for the door, ready to give that ghost a piece of my mind.

But it wasn't Frankie. It was worse.

Ellis Wydell stood on my porch.

My pulse sped up and my palms grew damp. He'd better not be here to arrest me.

On second look I was relieved to see he hadn't worn his police uniform. Instead, he had on a gray T-shirt with the police department baseball team logo on it. It revealed what his uniform hid last night—a nice set of arms and shoulders wide as a barn.

I placed a hand on my hip. "Just so you know, I didn't break any new laws since last night. A girl's got to sleep sometime."

"Can I come in?" he asked, glancing at my neighbors' house down the way. "I'd rather not be seen at your place."

"Charming." No wonder he'd used the back door. "I'd offer you a seat, but there isn't one."

It would be nice to hear him apologize for our rude start. Instead, he strolled right into my kitchen like he owned the place. He turned to face me. "How did you know where to find Vernon Hale's lighter?"

He looked at me like he expected an answer.

Fine. Nobody would believe him anyway.

"Your uncle told me himself," I admitted. "We had a conversation last night when I was sitting in the backseat of your car, like he was a real person." It would be nice if his nephew started treating me like one.

He shook his head, as if there had to be some other explanation. "That's impossible."

"Yes," I agreed. "Only lately I've expanded my view of what's possible."

He reached into the pocket of his jeans and pulled out a lighter shaped like a whiskey flask. "This is it. It was under the porch at his old house."

"Well, would you look at that?" Hale said it would be there and it was. I held my hand out and Ellis gave it to me. The silver shone and it had the letters VRH etched on one side. Ellis had obviously given it a polish after he found it. "This is real nice," I told him. "I wish we could get it back to your uncle." That way, he wouldn't always be counting on people like Frankie for a light. Nobody wanted to deal with that for eternity.

Ellis regarded me for a long moment. "Can you? Get it back to him, I mean?" he asked, as if he couldn't quite believe he was saying the words.

I sighed, not wanting to get his hopes up. "I don't know." I was surprised when I'd been able to pull Josephine's locket out of the ghostly realm, and I had no idea how I did it, much less how to send things the other way.

He began pacing and part of me started to wonder why he'd even come. It was clear he wasn't ready to believe me, not really. And I had no doubt my presence made him uncomfortable.

He stopped, refusing to meet my eyes. "How does he look?" Ellis asked quietly.

Damn. Right when I was getting used to him being a judgmental jerk, he had to go and say something to make me feel sorry for him.

"Your uncle is…strong," I said, searching for the right words. "You'd never even know he was hurt." I couldn't help but grin. "With that buzz cut and that attitude, he could be a drill sergeant."

The corners of Ellis's mouth turned up and at the moment when I thought he might share my smile, he winced. He straightened, his expression devastatingly calm and his tone firm. "I know you don't like me."

It was true and it wasn't. "As long as we're being honest, I think it's more that you don't like me."

A muscle in his jaw jumped as he clenched it. "I can agree to that."

Dandy. "So are we finished here?" Last night was enough. I didn't need round two with this man.

He shoved his hands into his pockets and stared at me hard. "I need your help."

Of all the... He could have knocked me over with a feather. "You need *my* help?" Unbelievable. I crossed my arms over my chest. I didn't know if he was nervy or just plain nuts. I mean, he didn't even want to be seen in my house.

He took one step toward me, then another, like a man on a mission. "I need you to do a job."

A sinking feeling invaded my insides. "You're not talking about graphic design, are you?"

He stopped a few feet in front of me, serious as sin. "I need you to clear out a ghost."

"But you don't believe in ghosts."

"It doesn't matter what I believe." He held up his hands in a form of surrender. "Look, I don't know what you do. Or how you see...*them*." He clenched his fingers and brought them down to his sides. "I don't even want to know."

"Okay." He had this all wrong. "The first thing is that I don't *clear out* ghosts. I'm not Bill Murray with a proton pack and a ghost trap." I ran a hand through my hair, thinking about how much I wanted to explain. People in this town thought I was crazy enough. I didn't need to go telling Officer Wydell about my recent spiritual troubles. "I accidentally washed some-one's ashes into my rosebushes, well, into the soil around my rosebushes," I corrected. "Anyway, that allowed me to see him, and then he did something that made me be able to see other ghosts." I could tell by the expression on Ellis's face I'd said too much. "I'd appreciate it if this didn't get around town."

He shook his head slowly. "Nobody would believe me."

"I'd sure deny it." I was enough of a pariah as it was. I didn't want to be the whacked-out nut job with my own personal ghost. Sure, people in the South called those individuals 'colorful,' but everyone knew it was just a nice word for *bat-shit crazy.*

"Look," he said, in an obvious attempt to sugarcoat something I probably didn't want to hear. But then he couldn't quite figure out how to spin it, so he said it plain, "I don't even want it getting around that I'm talking to you."

"You sure know how to ask for a favor," I said tartly.

"Can you blame me?" he shot back.

"Maybe." Maybe not, since he'd been so corrupted by that brother of his. I knew how convincing Beau could be. I leaned up against my kitchen island and tried not to think about my breakfast getting cold. "Tell me your problem. I'll see what I can do."

He gave a sharp nod. "I'm in the middle of renovating a piece of property I bought a few years ago, the one up on Wilson's Creek Road."

I'd heard of the place. It used to be an old distillery. He'd bought it with someone, an uncle. My heart gave a little squeeze. "You and your Uncle Hale bought it together, didn't you?" It made more sense now.

He stood stock-still. "We were renovating the carriage house into a restaurant. Then we planned to start in on the other buildings. It was going to be our project. Something for him to do when he retired."

Instead, he'd been killed in the line of duty.

Ellis cleared his throat. "I didn't feel much like going out there in the year or so after."

I remembered. "You left town there for a while, didn't you?"

He nodded. "Now I'm back. I'm investing in the place again. I'm taking it building by building. Eventually, it'll have festivals and events and a whole line of beers aged in reclaimed whiskey barrels."

"Well, that sounds really nice," I said. We didn't have many modern hangouts like that around town, and it would be a great place for people to gather.

"Only I've run into a problem," he said, apparently not in the mood for pleasantries. "Vandals destroyed the walk-in freezer. After that, I put in video surveillance." He gave me a hard look. "Two nights ago, the serving line was destroyed. Literally taken apart and smashed."

"That's terrible," I whispered, disturbed for him and also by the hard way he looked at me. He made it so that I almost felt like confessing, even though I was quite sure I wasn't guilty.

He braced his hands on the kitchen counter next to me. "Nobody did it. Surveillance shows it coming apart, but no human caused the damage."

It took me a moment to grasp his meaning. I gasped when I did. "You have a vandal ghost."

His hands whitened where he pressed them against the counter. "I'll pay you to get rid of it or them or whatever it is doing this. And I want you to keep it between us."

No problem on the second request. As far as the first one...

I didn't know how far my abilities went, especially since I'd borrowed them from Frankie. Besides, I wasn't a ghost hunter. I'd lucked out with Josephine. My limbs felt light and my mind raced. "How much are you willing to spend?"

He huffed out a laugh. "How much is the going rate for ghost extermination?"

"More like relocation," I said, as if I knew what I was talking about. Actually, I did in a way. I wasn't going to hurt a spirit merely because it caused a few problems. I was sure we could come to a reasonable agreement that suited Ellis's needs. I mean, look at poor Jilted Josephine. We'd had a lovely conversation once she'd come down out of her noose.

"What are you thinking?" Ellis asked. "Will you do it?"

I blew out a breath. "I don't know."

"Look," he said, "I don't know who else to call. I mean if it's not you, it may have to be the Psychic Friends Network or something."

"That's not funny," I told him. I wasn't a freak or a swindler.

But I was a girl in a bind. I didn't know how I could turn this down, not with my house on the line. "If I do this, it'll cost you."

"Name your price," he said flatly.

I was going to ask him for what I needed. What did I have to lose? "I want twenty thousand dollars," I said in a rush.

He didn't even think about it. "Done," he said.

I about fell over.

"Don't even think about asking for more," he warned. "I know what you owe my brother. I figured you'd ask as much."

"I'm not a gold-digging manipulator, no matter what the rumormongers say," I gritted out. "And by rights I shouldn't owe your brother anything. He's not the victim here."

"I was at the reception, honey." Ellis smirked.

After he'd forced me to stand him up at the altar, Beau called and invited me to our reception. The whole town was there, he said, enjoying our five-course sit-down dinner. Dancing to the ten-piece band his mother had insisted we hire. Consoling him. Assuring him he was better off.

He sent me photos of the cake.

I snapped.

That he would play the victim, that he would humiliate me like that after what he'd done...well, maybe I should claim temporary insanity—or maybe it was the most sane thing I'd done in my life—but I drove straight to the Hamilton Hotel, marched right into my almost-reception, and plastered Beau's face straight into our almost-wedding cake. In front of his family, God, and about two hundred of Sugarland's most admired citizens.

Ellis's mouth twisted into a wry grin. "The best part was when you tried to run away and knocked over the gift table instead."

"I did *not* run," I said hotly. "There was frosting on the floor, and I slipped."

"Do you want to review the tape? It's all recorded," Ellis reminded me slyly. "My mom tried to upload it onto YouTube. You're lucky she can barely turn the computer on."

I wouldn't put it past her to take lessons. She would love to humiliate me. Again.

"Your mother hired four videographers. Flew them in from Atlanta. How insane is that?"

He rested his hands on the counter behind him. "I didn't hear you complaining."

"That's because she wouldn't let me get a word in edgewise. She assured me she'd pay for the whole crazy show if I let her have her way. And I'm about to lose my house because I believed her."

His brows shot up. "So now you're blaming my mother?"

Yes. I was. "She's the one who stuck me with the bill."

"Because you ran out on the groom."

"Because he cheated on me. With three different women. He even admitted it." I left out the part about him attacking Melody. No reason to bring her into this.

The thunder drained from him. "What? Jesus."

I crossed my arms over my chest, clutching my elbows. "So now you know."

He still didn't look one hundred percent convinced. "If this is true, you need to defend yourself."

"Against your mother?" I asked. Mrs. Leland Herworth Wydell III would relish any excuse to go after me, and she had the money and the power to do it.

He knew how she was. I could tell by the way his jaw tightened and released. "I don't know what to say."

I didn't either. I hadn't exactly planned this. "Let's not say anything," I told him. I didn't want his pity or his sympathy. It surprised me enough to see a crack in the Wydell family armor. "I'll try to help you with your problem, and then we can go back to hating each other."

"You *will* help me," he corrected, both of us glad to be on more familiar terms. "There's no trying. It has to be done."

"Let's leave off the pep talk, officer perfect."

He took a slow breath as he steered us onto more solid ground. "That kitchen equipment cost me more than you're asking. You clear out my vandal ghosts, every damned one of them, and you've earned the twenty grand."

"All right, then." This was a business arrangement, pure and simple.

He pulled a set of folded papers out of his back pocket. "I took the liberty of drawing up an agreement."

Before he'd asked.

"Confident much?" I murmured as he spread it out on my counter. But I signed it. So did he.

I just hoped I could pull it off. I hadn't asked for Frankie's help yet. Even if I got it, I didn't know what we were up against.

If I failed, which I very well might, Ellis would most likely go back to thinking I was some sort of con artist. And his family would love exploiting the tale of Verity Long, failed ghost buster.

Either way, I'd have to take another harrowing trip into a haunted building.

Don't think about that part.

"Meet me at the Wilson's Creek property tonight at eight," Ellis said, folding the agreement and sliding it back into his pocket.

"I'll be there," I said, all business.

I felt a part of him give a little as I escorted him out. Or perhaps that was wishful thinking. "Don't tell a soul," he warned.

"Of course not," I said.

Well, just the one.

CHAPTER 9

A S SOON AS I SAW Ellis's black Jeep bounce down the road
away from my house, I sprang into action.

"Frankie!" I called, banging out to the back porch. The white-
painted swing rocked the gangster's urn lightly in the breeze.
"Frankie, come out here."

He didn't respond. The jerk. Now was not the time for him
to sulk.

I waited one second. Two. The morning air was deceptively
balmy for fall. Honeybees buzzed over the hydrangeas near the
back rail.

I picked up the urn. "You're going to want to hear this," I
told him, rubbing it, as if that would get his attention. Maybe
I should give it a little flick. That seemed rude, but darn it, we
needed to plan, to strategize. To see if we could pull off what I'd
promised to do.

"I'm not the genie in the lamp," his voice echoed behind me.

I spun around, but saw no one.

"Over here." His voice floated from across the yard, and then
I saw him sprawled out under the apple tree, waving.

I left his urn on the swing and hurried down the back steps
and out into the yard. "Nice trick." I could have sworn he was
behind me. "I suppose you can do all kinds of things now that
you're dead."

He leaned his head back against the thick tree and scratched at the bark with his fingernail. "You have no idea." He straightened as I neared and wrapped his arms around his knees. "By the way, while we're having a heart-to-heart, I don't like that word. *Dead*," he said, as if there were something rotten in the air. "It's a terrible reminder of my accident. Call it something else."

Hmm…what would that be? The gangster formerly known as 'alive'?

I hesitated only a moment before I went ahead and sat right next to him. He scooted down a bit for me, but I stayed where I was. "Did you see who came by? The police officer from last night."

Frankie tensed. "Deny everything."

"He's going to pay me what I need to keep the house," I said.

Frankie grew still. It was as if he knew there was a catch. In this case, he was right.

"In exchange, he wants me—us," I corrected, "he wants us to neutralize some 'formerly living' souls who are vandalizing an old distillery he bought."

Frankie drew his shoulders back. "Let me guess. You said yes without even asking me."

Okay, maybe I'd overstepped a little. "I couldn't exactly ask you in front of Ellis."

Frankie rubbed the back of his neck. "I was in the ether anyway."

I wrapped my arms around my knees. "I don't know what that means."

"Kind of like being asleep," he said, leaning back against the tree. "Lending you that power really did a number on me."

"Sorry. You look a lot better now than you did last night, though." He even had his knee back.

Frankie stared up at the sky. "Bridging the planes is probably against some natural laws, too."

"That's why we'll only do it once more," I told him.

He slanted a look my way. "I ain't no do-gooder, honey. Don't ask me to drain out my essential life force so that you can run around solving other people's problems."

Fair enough. "You got a better way for me to keep my house?"

He rubbed at his chin. "Did your cop friend say what was inside the place?"

"Some stainless steel kitchen equipment was broken," I said, watching him wince.

"Not that," he interrupted. "I mean the spooks."

"No. But I'm sure it's nothing we can't handle."

He grew as serious as I'd ever seen him. "It takes a whole lot of energy to move an object. Dark, negative force is easier to use—and better for smashing things. This ain't some weepy broad tossing jewelry out the window."

I didn't like the sound of that.

But it didn't change things. "We can't go back on the deal, not until we at least try to make it work." I ignored the stark unease trickling down my spine. "You need to show me what's going on tonight at the Wilson's Creek property." I couldn't do it without him.

He frowned at that. "You ever stop to think maybe I got my own life on the other side?"

"You know some of the ghosts there," I said, surprised. I could see it in his face.

Frankie shifted uncomfortably. "I might." He picked a piece of imaginary lint off his pants leg. "Damn sure he don't wanna see me."

"Just this once," I said. "Please," I added. "You know it's our best shot."

He stared me down. "You think everything's jake in this."

I had no idea what he meant. "No," I said, feeling it was the safest answer. "This is the last time I'll ask." I hoped.

"Fine," he said, taking off his hat, crumpling it in his hands. "We'll go. I'll let you see again, but just this once."

"Thanks," I said, fighting down a smile.

"Eh, go chase yourself," he muttered as he shimmered away. "You ain't gonna be smiling come tonight."

❦

The sun hung low, throwing out a burst of reds and yellows across the evening sky. We'd left more than an hour early so we could get the lay of the land before dark. And so I had time to talk Frankie into following through on his promise in case he gave me trouble.

I'd cancelled on my sister. I told her I had taken on a new freelance job and asked her to stop in and see Lucy if she got the chance. Melody had been all too happy to oblige and said she hoped it would pay off.

That made two of us.

The Wilson's Creek property stood in a wooded area toward the west side of town. Gorgeous sugar maple trees, bursting with fall color, joined oaks and sassafras. They stretched over the road to form a canopy prettier than any postcard.

I wondered what kind of ghost Frankie knew on the property, and why he seemed to think he wouldn't be welcome there.

"This would be a funky cool location for a restaurant," I said, making conversation.

Frankie slouched in his seat, less than impressed. "Turn off the radio. Please. I don't know how you listen to this rap stuff."

I snarfed. "It's Michael Jackson. I thought 'Thriller' might lighten the mood."

The gangster looked at me as if I'd sprouted wings. "We do good tonight, I'll show you some real music. Introduce you to Benny Goodman."

I wondered if he meant for real or just his records.

We had the windows down and the wind tousled my long blond hair. Frankie's didn't move an inch. Naturally.

Another twist on the country road led to a smattering of orchards, roadside fruit stands, and antique shops.

Whitewashed fencing gave way to a battered limestone wall. Moss clung to the uneven top. Clumps of grass and weeds sprouted from gaps in the mortar and the GPS system on my phone told me we were getting close.

Frankie cringed every time the overly pleasant woman's voice chimed in with directions.

I shot him a glance. "You've been hanging around for how many years and you never heard this before?"

He shifted in his seat. "I know what's going on," he said, focusing on a gathering of black crows on the fence up ahead. "Only I usually tune you people out."

Poor ghost. After we solved the issue with the house, we'd have to figure out how to send him on his way.

I'd packed some light snacks in the bag with Frankie's urn, along with a brand-new flashlight in case the mini-flashlight on my keychain ran low. The light cost more than a week's worth of ramen, but tonight had me more worried than I was letting on, and I refused to go in unprepared. I'd also managed to scrounge up a few half-burned Christmas candles, along with some matches. Backups for my backup.

The rock wall rose higher on both sides of an open iron gate. A large stone marker read Wilson's Creek.

Frankie straightened and peered out the front window, as if he was searching for something in particular.

"Tell me about this place," I said. "It sounds like you have some history here."

"It was a long time ago," he said, his attention diverted.

"I'll drive slow," I told him. "The more I know, the easier this will be."

He huffed. "Not now."

We turned into the drive, a narrow dirt road. A large brick building stood at the end, with wide wooden carriage doors at the front. Tall green-painted windows lined the first and second floors, sheltered under red brick arches. I spied what appeared to be an aged, wood turret off the back. Faded letters, hand-painted in white on the brick, read Southern Spirits since 1908.

To the left, on a small rise, I spotted a large Victorian that had probably been quite grand at one time. A wide sitting porch gave way to three stories, complete with a slate roof. The tiles had cracked in places and the bronze embellishments bled green.

"It's nice," I said as we bumped over the unfinished road. "Once you spruce it up and mow the lawn and—"

"Get rid of the ghosts," Frankie finished.

"Only the troublemakers," I said. Then I realized that was exactly who he would be friends with. "We're not going to hurt anybody," I told him. Not unless we were forced to defend ourselves. And even then, I didn't know what I could do to hurt a ghost.

It bothered me all the same, although I had no idea what to do about it. And as we drew closer to the carriage house, I realized Ellis had beaten us here.

He walked around the side of the building and held up a hand in greeting. A peace offering, perhaps. Although I couldn't imagine how I'd get that lucky.

I didn't see Ellis's car, so I went ahead and made a spot for myself out front on a patch of crumbling pavement that could very well have been a parking lot at one time.

The sun had begun to sink lower onto the horizon, casting blinding rays of light between the shadows of the century-old buildings.

"It's gorgeous," I called out to him. And I meant it.

He shoved his hands in his pockets and appeared almost pleased. "There's a lot of work to do," he said as I walked up to him.

True. It wasn't only landscaping. The brickwork crumbled at the edges and spiderwebs clung to the window corners. Overgrown bushes flanked the entry doors and even the matching iron carriage lights had seen better days.

Ellis glanced out over the property. "There are nine buildings total, including the carriage house." He reached down for the door handle. "This one is the most convenient to the road and needs the least amount of work, so we're starting here." He caught himself and corrected. "I'm starting here."

That's right. He'd lost his business partner. I could see his uncle attacking this place head–on. Ellis, too. Although it had to be harder to do it alone. I hesitated. "I don't want to insult you, but it looks a little…forlorn."

He gave a small smile. "The inside is almost done. Speaking of work, you're an hour early."

"I wanted to see the property before dark," I told him. "Have you been here long?" He didn't look like he'd run into any angry spirits.

"I had to unload some pavers out back," he said. "The rear porch is starting to sink." Ellis stood by the entrance doors, looking remarkably casual about hanging out in front of a haunted building. "Hey, Harry, come on over and meet someone," Ellis called as a bearded man emerged from the side of the carriage house. He wore blue jeans and a sleeveless work shirt, and he scowled when he saw us.

Ellis didn't appear to notice. "This is Harry," he said to me. "He's been helping me out." Then, quietly, he added, "Don't tell him your last name or what you're doing for me."

What a sweetheart.

But I didn't have to worry about spilling the beans to the handyman, because Harry hunched his shoulders, kept his head down, and pretended he didn't even notice us.

"He's not great with people," Ellis said, not at all bothered. "Maybe you can meet him later when he's feeling more sociable."

And maybe I'd get the job done tonight and never come back.

Ellis opened the carriage house door for me. "Come on in."

I made my way past the skeleton of a rusted-out brewery wagon and climbed the stairs, glancing back for Frankie as I did. He'd disappeared somewhere between the car and the carriage house. I knew he had to be close. Still, I jumped when I heard his voice in my ear. "Don't go inside."

He had to be kidding. That was why we were here. I stiffened. "What do you see?" I murmured. "Show me."

Ellis eyed me. "I don't see anything."

"Great," I said, pasting on a smile.

Frankie, on the other hand, remained mum. The jerk.

I looked from the darkened windows to the man in front of the age-old doors.

Was it me, or did the air seem chillier as I drew closer?

Inside was pitch black. A slight breeze ruffled the hair at my shoulders, stirring up the dry leaves on the trees in the woods beyond. My stomach twisted.

Good sense screamed at me to heed Frankie's warning, but I couldn't stand out on the front porch forever. The ghost hadn't said another word. I didn't even know where he'd gone. And I was just as blind as Ellis without him.

"What's the matter?" Ellis at least had the grace to look concerned. "Are you picking up on something already?"

I put on a brave act. "No. Let's go in." I couldn't find out what haunted this place if I didn't venture inside. Still, I half expected a lecture from Frankie as I passed the flickering carriage lights and entered the musty-smelling relic.

Modern lantern-style light fixtures flickered to life overhead. They hung from the newly constructed, exposed rafters above. The smell of fresh lumber mixed with century-old brick and woodwork.

I blew out a breath. It all appeared so...normal. For now, at least. I wondered what exactly I didn't see. It could be anything. Ghostly furniture, scraggly black creatures slinking in the corners...or worse. I wanted to stay within a quick dash of the exit, so I waved Ellis over to the carved wooden bar near the doors. It had to be at least a hundred years old, definitely worth a closer look.

"Is this original?" I asked.

Ellis ran a hand over its polished surface. "The South Town gang installed it in the days they used to run liquor from this place."

"That's bold," I said.

Ellis shrugged. "So were they."

I wondered how many of them were still around. And just where Frankie had gone.

Far above, gray light filtered in from the tall second-story windows.

"We took out the second floor. The boards rotted too much to be safe." His voice sounded hollow as we moved farther back into the dim space. The windows back here, boarded from the outside, glowed with light around the edges. "After automobiles took over, the family opened a distillery in the carriage house building. There's a water wheel out back, from when they mashed grain for whiskey, so I'm going to call this place The Rumor Mill. The bar here is more of a waiting area. It'll have a restaurant in the main part."

Racks upon racks of old whiskey barrels lined the wall to my right with numbers painted on the sides and a thick cork pounded into the top of each one. It felt like we'd entered another era. "Come on," Ellis said, venturing deeper into the building. "I'll show you the rest."

I didn't want to follow him into the dark beyond, but I wasn't about to stand around by myself. I rushed through the shadows to catch up.

"You know where you're going?" I asked. We'd left the lights behind, and he hadn't turned on any more.

"No worries," he said, as if he didn't hear every echo of his boots on the stark concrete floor. I stepped on something soft and I winced.

And where the heck was Frankie? I had his urn. He couldn't leave me. Unless he'd gone back into the ether somewhere.

Apparently gangsters didn't understand teamwork.

I searched for him, but all I could see was pale dusk fading from dirty windows. It would be dark soon.

Ellis plugged in a set of construction lights. They illuminated a large space at the back. Arched doorways opened up on the left. Horse stables no doubt. To the right of the open area, I saw a set of black double doors. He cleared his throat. "The...ghost got the lights right here. They were heavy iron. It tore them apart."

I shuddered despite myself. I was in over my head here.

Ellis shoved his hands into his pockets. "Harry, the guy you almost met, is working with me on replacing the fixtures and repairing the ripped-out wiring."

Something about that man bothered me, but I couldn't put my finger on it. "Is he from around here?" I thought I knew most everyone in town.

"He is now," Ellis said, directing me toward the double doors on our right. "He's been a big help since my uncle died."

"Who are his parents?" I pressed, thinking I had to know them.

Ellis shrugged. "I don't think he's on the Sugarland social radar. Harry lives at the Good Samaritan House."

"That's the one near First Presbyterian." I'd been there with my mom's church group. Her friend Georgia helped run it. They gave people a place to stay while they found work and tried to get on their feet.

"The guy's good with a hammer and saw," Ellis said. "Getting better every day." He opened the doors and reached for a plug. "Here's the kitchen."

The lights were broken in here as well. Of course. Ellis had replaced them with temporaries. The glow of industrial construction lights revealed a modern kitchen with stainless steel everything. A refrigerator, two stoves, and a grill lined the back wall. The remains of a stainless steel serving station stood in front of it. The top had been ripped off, the metal torn from the bolts. I looked closer and saw a series of large dents in the countertop, as if a giant had skipped a boulder straight down the serving line.

I sucked in a breath. "I can't imagine what did that." I pushed against a piece of the metal heating unit on the top, torn almost completely in half. "You saw this happen on the video?"

Ellis watched me, grim. "Ripped apart by an unseen force," he said, as if he couldn't quite believe it. I almost didn't believe it myself. Something like that could easily kill a person. He ran a hand through his hair, frustrated. "It's completely ruined. I can sell it for scrap or pay to have it hauled off. But if I replace it with a new one, is it going to happen again?"

Most likely, yes.

There was something really wrong about this. Whatever did this wasn't just destructive. It was angry.

"Do you want to see the deep freeze?" Ellis asked.

I wanted to leave and never come back. "Yes, of course," I

said. I'd agreed to this. It was my job. We walked to a small hallway near the back. The door of the freezer hung from one hinge, crushed like a tin can.

Shadows bathed the end of the hall. Behind them, the back windows gave up feeble light, glowing gray with dusk. "Whatever it was also smashed the shelves," Ellis said, shining a flashlight over the inside. I saw the hooks where the racks had been bolted in. Otherwise, it was empty as a tomb.

Frankie was right. It would take a lot of energy to do that kind of damage.

I moved back out into the kitchen. Ellis adjusted one of the construction bulbs and shone it down like a spotlight onto the ruined serving station.

"Feel free to explore, get used to the place," Ellis said, moving to clean up a few more things.

"Right," I said, ducking back out into the hall. If I could find my spirit buddy.

The windows reflected the approach of night and I fought off a shiver. This place creeped me out on its own. And Frankie had yet to show me what truly lurked in the darkness.

The gangster shimmered into view next to me. At last.

"Where in heck have you been?" I demanded.

"I told you to stay outside," he shot back.

"How can I do that when I need to find the ghost that caused damage inside?"

His forehead shone with sweat. I didn't even know ghosts could perspire. My gaze traveled to the bloody circle between his eyes.

He drew his Panama hat out of thin air and yanked it down over his wound. "I was trying to smooth the way," he gritted out. "This is South Town turf and folks can get territorial. As you saw last night," he added. "I figured maybe I could warn them that I was about to show you some stuff. Maybe we could be polite."

I liked that. "And?"

He shifted uncomfortably, digging his hands into his pockets.

"They don't want you here."

That didn't help. But we were still figuring out the rules. No doubt they appreciated his attempt. These were Southern spirits after all. "Did you happen to meet the vandal ghosts?" I looked around. "Are they here now?"

"Yeah, because they're wearing name tags that say 'I bust things.' Think before you talk."

"You think this is easy for me?" I didn't like to ask for help with anything, and he was making it so difficult to work together on this. I understood he had issues beyond what we were facing right now, but that didn't give him the right to be a pill. "You left me, so I made an executive decision to walk in the door. You're not the only one having a hard day." My life hadn't exactly been a patch of roses since I'd dumped out his urn. "And anyway, I don't like your tone."

"I don't like you ignoring me."

Ellis's voice broke through the darkness. "Who are you talking to?"

My heart seized up. "Nobody."

"See?" Frankie said, next to me. "You just called me a nobody."

I ignored him.

I stepped back out into the kitchen and found Ellis watching me as if I were about to reveal a ghost to him, or at least continue the conversation.

His gaze flicked to the darkness behind me. "I was hoping to stay longer, but I got a call when you were out in the hall," he said, guilt coloring his tone. "We're short two officers tonight. I have to go in to work."

For heaven's sake. "You're going to leave me in a haunted building by myself?" That wasn't part of the deal. Or maybe it was. We hadn't specifically agreed he'd be staying with me. I didn't like the idea of being in this place alone.

"It's not how I would have planned it, either," he said, cringing, but at the same time standing his ground. "But you did it last night, right?"

"I admit nothing," I reminded him. Besides, this place felt

much darker. And I hadn't even seen anything yet.

He glanced up to the rafters above. "I've installed security cameras there and there," he said, pointing to a pair of lenses sticking out like large bug eyes. As if that would keep me safe. "We don't even know if anything will happen tonight."

"Ha." According to Frankie, these spirits already knew I was here, and they didn't like it. "So what if they have three guys out tonight instead of two? Can't you take off work until we figure this out?"

He huffed out a breath. "Sure. I'll explain to the chief that my carriage house is haunted and I have to babysit my little brother's ex-fiancé while she attempts an exorcism." He dug around in his pocket for a business card, then turned it over and wrote a number on the back. "Call me if you need me and I'll be right over."

After a ghost removed my intestines with a fork. "This doesn't feel right."

He drew the contract out of his pocket and turned it over in his hands. "We can call it off. I understand." He let out a sigh. "Some things just aren't worth the money."

Yes, but we were talking about the funds I needed to save my house. "Put that contract away, Ellis Wydell. I said I'd do it," I told him.

"Thank you, Verity," he said simply.

I didn't want to talk about it. "Just…go."

He gave me a long look. "I get off at six a.m. I'll be back then."

I watched him fade into the shadows until I could only hear the sound of his boots on the hard floors. The door opened with a creak and closed behind him with a bang that echoed throughout the cavernous space.

Then I heard his car start up. Rocks crunched under his tires as he drove away.

Oh my God. "I'm alone," I whispered to myself.

"You wish," Frankie replied.

I turned to him, my palms sweaty and my knees weak. "Don't joke." This was bad enough. I knew what had to happen next, even though the last thing I wanted to do was open my eyes to what was really going on around here. What we lived with now, in this reality, gave me enough of the creeps.

Frankie watched me, as if he expected me to freak out.

"Stop it," I muttered.

He rolled his eyes.

"I know, I know." I'd made the deal with Ellis. I'd asked Frankie to do this. I screwed up my courage and willed everything to be okay, or at least not too terrifyingly awful. "Show me what I need to see."

"Remember," he said, "you asked for it."

A low rumble sounded throughout the room. Silver mist, like steam, settled over us until I could see rusted iron trusses supporting the remains of large wooden brew kettles along the side wall. Barrels littered the floor, some broken open. Where I'd expected to see the old building in its glory days, instead I saw ruins.

"Holy moly. It looks even worse than before." I turned in a circle. My foot caught a discarded bottle and sent it into a wobbly spin. "Why does it appear this way?"

"This is how the strongest spirit sees it," he said quietly.

A hollow wail echoed from below the floor. I shivered, not missing the irony and frankly not caring as I drew closer to Frankie.

I felt the anger in the room, the desperation, as if it were a living thing.

"Is it the South Town gang?" I asked.

Frankie pursed his lips. "No. They're being held down, same as a lot of other ghosts. You get this thing, the South Town boys are back."

"Great." As soon as I got rid of this vandal ghost, I'd be long gone. The South Town boys were Ellis's problem.

My arms glowed with the ethereal gray light, as if I were part of the vision.

"The good news is there's only one sick bastard creating this," Frankie said. "Concentrate hard and you might be able to tell."

I realized he was trying to instruct me, to help me understand.

And I did feel it, low in my gut—a single shot of welling despair and pain.

"Can it hurt me?" I whispered.

"Yes," he said, his voice low in my ear.

Right. It took apart a serving station. It could take apart me.

I didn't know how I was going to reason with it, to convince it to leave, not when every cell in my body vibrated with the spirit's anger. I had to get a grip. I rubbed my hands on my dress, drying my palms, screwing up my courage.

There was something bad in here. We both knew it. And we couldn't solve anything until I confronted it face-to-face.

"Please come out," I said, my voice a little uneven. "I need to speak with you."

A high-pitched sob broke the silence. This time it came from above and I fought the urge to wince. My heart thundered in my chest.

Dang me. I didn't know anything about luring a ghost.

But I wouldn't run now. I stood firm, ready. I parted my feet, locking my knees. "Come on. This isn't helping anybody. Come on out. Now."

The lights fell, smashing to the ground. Darkness descended over me and I screamed.

CHAPTER 10

"HERE IT COMES!" FRANKIE HOLLERED.
A wall of energy smashed down as the ghost launched itself at me. The blast raced along my skin, pricking every hair on my body to razor points. It coursed through me, sizzling with electricity as it shook me from the inside.

I lost my breath. My voice.

My mind swam and my blood turned ice cold.

Frankie let out a battle cry like he was the one attacking. His image stretched and flickered. Either he broke in half or two ghosts raged against our attacker.

Steel groaned and bent, bolts shook. My teeth rattled as frigid wind shot up from under me. I gripped the metal cooktop, shrieking when it came off in my hands. I tossed it aside and grabbed for the cold burners. I held on until my fingers ached, clinging for dear life.

The force intensified and I felt myself go light for a brief second before it tore away, up into the ceiling.

It left me trembling in the darkness, sweating and trying to make sense of the tears running down my face and the hitch in my throat when I tried to breathe. The air tasted like saltwater.

I wasn't so sure this was worth twenty thousand bucks anymore. I tore my shaking hand away from the grill in order to pull the tangled hair from my face.

Frankie stood directly in front of me, hunched with his hands on his knees. He wheezed like he'd just battled a monster, which he kind of did. One of his feet had sunk into the floor. His Panama hat lay near my left foot. It glowed against the red industrial floor tiles. Frankie cocked his head and struggled to find the place on the ceiling where the energy had disappeared.

A knot in the wood glowed softly.

With shaking fingers, I reached in my bag for a candle and placed it on the service station. I hastily struck a match and lit the wick, needing the light. Any light.

I let out a small squeak as a second ghostly gray image appeared near the ceiling.

He wore an old-fashioned military uniform, complete with leggings and a wide-brimmed hat that I assumed had been dark brown at one point. It was hard to tell. His wide moustache joined a set of crazy sideburns. The translucent, gray-skinned man pointed his rifle directly at me.

"Don't shoot," I said, fighting for my voice, holding up my hands. No telling if a ghostly bullet could hurt me, but I preferred not to take the chance.

In an instant, the ghost appeared directly in front of me, the muzzle of his gun inches from my chest. I could see the crinkles at the edge of his eyes, the way his prominent nose dipped before it curved back up to a sunburned tip.

I tried to lean away, but I had nowhere to go, not with the stove at my back. He had piercing gray eyes and was younger than I first imagined. He couldn't have been more than thirty. He wore a pair of matching oak leafs on his collar. Next to them, in blocky embroidered text, I read the letters UVC.

Holy heck. I was a good Dixie girl. I knew my history. And I was looking at a lieutenant colonel in the First United States Volunteer Cavalry.

"You're a Rough Rider," I gasped, the words tumbling out. Amazing. I'd never considered this particular turn of events, that I'd meet dead people that had actually done things, seen things. "You guys are legends."

He blinked twice. "Well, I…" he drawled, lowering his gun.

"Did you know this man fought under Teddy Roosevelt?" I asked Frankie. "I'll bet you even met him, didn't you?" I geek gushed. He must have. Teddy Roosevelt recruited the Rough Riders personally. This was too much.

The ghost blew out a breath that made his moustache ripple. His eyes darted over to Frankie. "She can see me."

The gangster nodded. "You get used to it."

The Rough Rider kept his back straight, his shoulders rigid. "Colonel Clinton Maker, at your service," he added, almost as if by habit. He eyed the mark my attacker left on the ceiling. "This is a strange, strange night."

He didn't have to convince me. "Did you see the entity that attacked us?"

"Couldn't miss it." He hitched his gun over his shoulder. "I'm afraid one of our own has gone poltergeist."

"Poltergeist?" Josephine mentioned that about her mother. That she'd gone poltergeist once and tore the chimney off the house. Sweet Lord in heaven. He couldn't mean—

Frankie drew his foot out of the floor and shook it off like it had gotten dirty. "A poltergeist is a manifestation of negative emotions," he said, as if that explained it.

I stood for a moment in shock. Her mother had been very, very angry, but she didn't strike me as demonic. At least I hoped not. "I thought poltergeists were evil spirits that came from hell."

Frankie barked out a laugh. "If it was only that simple."

The colonel appeared less than amused. "Any spirit can manifest into a poltergeist, given enough anger. It's the negative energy that turns you."

Yikes. I'd have to think a little more carefully about how I interacted with the spirits in this realm. I crossed my arms over my chest and glanced up at the glowing knothole on the ceiling. "It's not permanent, though," I said.

"A spirit can be soothed back to sanity," the colonel agreed.

Frankie shot him a look. "If you want to call it that."

"I've seen it," the colonel insisted.

I wasn't sure I wanted to try. "Whatever or *whom*ever we just met…that was the scariest thing that's ever happened to me."

After Josephine's mother, that was saying something.

The colonel regarded me carefully. "I wish I could say the same." He followed my gaze. "Leave, and I doubt it will bother you again."

"We can't go yet," Frankie said. He shifted uncomfortably. "Verity's here to deal with it." Naturally, he left off the part about how Ellis would prefer we got rid of all the ghosts, not just the poltergeist. I noticed he also omitted the part about him helping me.

The colonel drew back. "You leave that to me," he said, irritated. "This is my property. My problem."

"You used to own this place?" I asked.

A faint, grayish blush crept up his neck and cheeks as he cleared his throat. "Not exactly. But after so many years of lingering here, I look at it as mine."

I could see where that would be an issue with spooks. You haunt a spot long enough, you feel like you own it.

"We'll stick around, learn what we can," I said.

"And try not to piss it off next time," Frankie added.

The colonel sputtered. "You will not."

Frankie ignored him. "I suppose it didn't work out half bad." The gangster leaned against the counter. "It used up most of its energy on angry wind and less on beating the hell out of you."

"Thanks for the support," I said, keeping an eye on the colonel. "But why is the spirit so angry?"

The colonel scoffed. "My dear, we're all angry," he drawled. "Workmen are tearing apart our home." He headed for the doorway and paused. "But now somebody's out of control. It takes a lot more than anger to manifest like that."

"Wait," I said, my sandals crunching over broken glass, "what do you mean more than anger? What else does this apparition have?"

He turned to me. "Rage. A burning desire for revenge. And I can't say as I blame it."

He walked away.

Oh my. Okay. "Wait," I said, following him out, not at all sure I was doing the right thing. The colonel was the best lead I had so far. I couldn't let him leave without asking more questions, even if he didn't want to answer them. I glanced back at Frankie. He'd stayed in the kitchen, and he was missing his entire right leg from foot to thigh. Dang it. He was losing energy faster tonight than he had last night. I needed more time.

The colonel passed through the arched main hall of the carriage house and over to the nooks that had once held horse stalls. I dodged a glowing, broken-down case of Southern Spirits Finest Whiskey as I rushed to catch up with him. There, in an alcove that would soon hold a table for eight, stood a gorgeous gray mare with a snip of white on her muzzle and a swirling cowlick between her eyes.

The colonel stopped in front of her. "Don't scare her," he said, refusing to acknowledge my presence in any other way.

"She's beautiful," I said as he stroked her head and neck.

"Her name is Annabelle." She nuzzled his palm.

"I can see why you stay," I said, itching to touch the horse, knowing I couldn't. I remembered what happened when I'd accidentally stood up in the middle of Frankie. Still, she looked so sweet and soft. I could almost smell her horsey hair.

"It's not only Annabelle," he said, scratching her between the ears. The horse dipped her head toward him. "My Sally is buried out back in the family cemetery near the woods. Her daddy built this place." He gave a wistful sigh. "She wanted me here, but the town insisted on burying me under a monument in the big cemetery. An honor, you see." He dismissed it with a chuff. "Some honor. To take me from my wife."

"That's so sad." Maybe we could get him moved. I didn't want to promise anything, but I'd look into it. "At least you get to see her."

His face fell. "Maybe someday. I'm starting to think she's already gone."

Annabelle nudged me, her nose slipping into my skin. Where I should have felt a velvety horsey muzzle, it felt like someone had pressed a large chunk of ice into the soft center of my palm. I trembled, yanking back. My skin pebbled with goose bumps that I couldn't rub away.

"She makes friends easier than most," the colonel said.

I wouldn't be riding her anytime soon. "She just wants a carrot," I told him, trying to keep the mood light.

He produced an apple out of his pocket and fed it to her. She took the entire thing in one bite, crunching it happily. The colonel smiled, watching her for a moment. He turned to me, his manner anything but friendly. "I've enjoyed meeting you, Verity. But you must never come here after tonight."

I took a sharp breath. "I don't have a choice. Whoever's mad has caused too much trouble."

He fixed me with an intent stare. "There are certain things that are not meant to be disturbed. Dangers you can't imagine. Places like this are abandoned by the living for a reason. Do you understand?"

I must not have looked like I got it because he drew back a hair and swore under his breath.

This could be a neat restaurant—would be if Ellis had his way. I just had to find the ghost who was causing the trouble and somehow…help.

If only I knew where to start. There were so many places to hide around here. The stable as well as all twenty acres of the property had to be full of nooks and crannies. I hadn't even begun to explore it all.

My eyes fell on an old wooden trapdoor built into the floor right outside Annabelle's stall.

Some things wouldn't be fun to explore at all. "What's down there?" I asked, moving toward it.

The colonel stood in my way. "If you know what's good for you, you'll tell your friend Ellis to leave this property alone."

So he knew about Ellis. He'd been watching.

I dodged around him. "Are you stronger than those gangster ghosts? Do you have more power than the others?" This world seemed to revolve around strength and energy. "Is that how you can be here and they can't?"

He refused to answer, so I tried another tack. "Tell me how to fix our problem in the kitchen." If I could calm the troublemaker, or at least find the spirit, it would be a start. "Who around here is angry enough to get destructive?"

He blocked me from the wooden trapdoor in the floor in a disconcertingly simple way: he hovered above it. "It could be my mother-in-law," he said in a righteous tone that left me wondering if he was serious or not. "Although she prefers to storm around the main house and terrorize the servants' quarters. It could be a half-dozen others as well. It's hard to say."

I didn't buy it for a second. "Hard to say or you won't say?" I could have gone through him. I considered it. But I needed his help and I'd upset him enough already. "You know who it is, don't you?" Maybe he was friends with it. Maybe he worked for it. Maybe that's why he could move freely while the rest of the ghosts had been tamped down.

He stood his ground, directly on top of the trapdoor. His voice grew deeper, louder. "None of this started happening until you living people came around and started digging. Now the negativity is spreading and there's no peace."

"Whoever it is, we can help," I began.

His voice boomed over mine. "We like things the way they are. I don't wish to sound rude, but I don't know any other way to say this. You shouldn't be here. This isn't a place for the living anymore." I felt the agitation rolling off him. "Tonight, I felt the poltergeist manifesting and I did what I could, but I can't always protect you."

"If you don't want me here, why didn't you let the poltergeist have its way with me? Why did you protect me?"

He seemed surprised at that. He drew back and his voice calmed, his manners returned. "How could I not?"

He truly was a gentleman to the end. Then a startling thought occurred to me. "Are you trying to protect it as well?"

He ignored the question. "I implore you to listen to me," he pressed. "Talk to your male companion. Stress the urgency."

"I'll pass along the message, but you and I both know that won't work." I didn't want it to.

"You've disturbed enough today," he said, almost to himself. His mouth formed a thin line as he placed his rifle down on the floor. "This rooting around has to stop."

He crouched down over the cellar door and placed his hand on it. I didn't understand what he was doing. I sure as heck didn't want to go underground. Not unless I could drag Ellis with me. Ghosts were one thing, spiders and snakes were another.

His hand glowed stronger and I watched the energy ripple from it. His eyes glowed hot, his face set in determination. It appeared as if he were willing the door closed. I watched as the rest of his body flickered and faded, even as his hand remained steady. His brow furrowed, his jaw clenched. He drove every bit of heart and soul into blocking that door until he was spent with the effort and blew away like smoke on a breeze.

I drew in a sharp breath. It sounded loud in the absolute silence that followed.

"That was weird," I said aloud.

"He seemed decent enough," Frankie said, scaring the daylights out of me.

I whipped around. He'd chosen to stand directly behind me. Not next to me so I could have seen him coming. I brought a hand against the heart threatening to thump right out of my skin. "You've got to stop doing that."

If he cared, he didn't show it.

"How are you?" I asked.

He shrugged. "It would be nice if I could feel my toes." He winked. "That was a joke. I don't technically have toes anymore."

I shook my head, still unsettled by what I'd learned tonight. "Anything else I need to know about angry spirits that you haven't told me?"

"Hey," Frankie said, as if I were out of line, "I didn't know it would be a poltergeist in here. I was hoping for a pissed-off group of winos. Maybe a hard-partying jazz band."

I turned away from him. "Be serious." I didn't like the idea of a ghost who could attack like that. "Could *you* actually become a poltergeist like the colonel said?"

Frankie stood next to me, rubbing at his chin. "Nah. It's easier to get tanked." He sighed at my reaction. "You gotta understand. Spirits don't always consciously decide to become like that. It just happens. They lose whatever it is that makes them *them*. They morph into pure negative emotion."

"What kind of emotion did this?" I asked, looking down at the sealed trapdoor.

The room glowed with ghostly gray light.

"He's protecting somebody." Frankie shrugged, watching the trapdoor like it might haul off and bite him. "It can wait for daytime. You're not getting paid enough to mess with that."

Yes, but that would mean borrowing Frankie's power for longer. I didn't want to impose, but since he didn't bring it up, I decided I wouldn't either. "So is it locked?" I asked, not quite willing to try to touch it.

He shivered, despite himself. "Might as well be. I wouldn't want to touch the field he put around that thing. It's going to give you that hair-standing-up-on-the-back-of-your-neck feeling if and when you try to go down. You're going to swear someone is behind you, ready to pounce."

Shadows flickered over the ominous-looking trapdoor. "Will it be true?"

Frankie clenched his jaw. "It just might be."

CHAPTER 11

THE REAL COURAGE WOULD BE telling Ellis I'd failed to protect his kitchen. I pulled the flashlight out of my back pocket as we made our way back to the scene of the crime. Hopefully, the beam would help me illuminate what truly existed in the kitchen versus the illusion. I hadn't even checked the damage before. Perhaps I didn't want to know.

I paused beneath the bug-eyed security cameras Ellis had set up in the rafters. At least he'd know I did my best. The service station was well and truly ruined. It lay on its side, even more beat up. Still, it had already been ready for the scrap heap when we started the night. Maybe Ellis wouldn't count that.

I made my way around the scattered contents of an overturned trash can while Frankie retreated to a small space behind the mess of a serving station. I sincerely hoped more parts of him weren't about to go missing.

Slowly, I made my way back to the stove where I'd taken refuge. It was intact. Hallelujah.

Except for a large, fist-sized dent between the burners.

"That's not pretty."

"Smashed?" Frankie asked, still holed up.

"Only the top." If you wanted to look at the bright side. I'd done my job. It wasn't in pieces on the floor.

Who was I kidding? Ellis would still be ticked.

I inspected the rest of the remaining kitchen appliances and breathed a somewhat agitated sigh of relief. Everything else remained unscathed. For the most part. I'd have to use this encounter, this failure, to learn more about what was going on. I righted the overturned trashcan and began reloading it with scattered construction scraps, amused that for once I wasn't annoyed at the man in my life for not helping during cleanup.

Frankie had the best excuse ever.

Glass snapped under my feet. I didn't see a broom.

An hour into our first night protecting Ellis's investment and we already had a dented stove, crushed lighting, and smashed-up cookware. I couldn't afford to be fired from this job.

There are more dangers in here than you can possibly imagine, the ghost had warned.

I didn't doubt it for a second.

I moved toward the candle I'd left on the serving station. Deep shadows lingered beyond the dancing light. I screwed up my courage and doused the fire hazard. It would be okay.

Maybe.

I pulled up Ellis's number on my phone and hit *connect*.

The phone didn't even ring and I realized I couldn't catch a signal. Hopefully, it was the lay of the land outside or the thick walls of the carriage house and not something else utterly and frighteningly paranormal.

"I'm heading outside," I told Frankie. "That won't disconnect me from you, will it?"

"Don't leave the property," he warned.

"Of course not." I wouldn't go far. "If the poltergeist comes back, you holler and I'm right back here with you."

He gave me a dry look. "I'm sure I'll feel much safer because you did such a bang-up job earlier."

"Can it," I said, grabbing my flashlight and moving past him. I'd done the best I could. We all had.

"No, really," Frankie called after me. "The screaming did help."

A long sigh escaped me. I wasn't crazy proud of how I'd handled myself with the poltergeist, but I certainly wasn't ashamed.

Two nights ago, if you had asked me to tell a ghost story, I'd have spun a tale about the faceless guy in the woods with the hook-hand who liked to run it along the sides of cars and scare teenagers.

That was spooky. This was real.

I kept an eye out for the colonel as I made my way past the main part of the carriage house and into the stables. The shadows seemed thicker here, more ominous. I tried to shake off the feeling.

Up ahead, I spotted the trapdoor in the floor. I could walk straight over it if I wanted. Instead, I detoured around. No sense tempting fate.

Maybe Ellis had already explored the cellar. Maybe we had nothing to worry about down there.

And maybe the colonel had filled it with stuffed puppy dogs and candy.

My body felt heavy. The skin on the back of my legs pricked as a chill wound up my spine and settled on the back of my neck. I could almost feel someone behind me, ready to touch me.

"Probably just Frankie," I whispered to myself.

"What?" he called from the kitchen.

Dammit.

I turned to look behind me, hoping to see the colonel.

But I saw nothing. Only the ghostly ruins of the old building, glowing in an ethereal gray light.

I let out a shuddering breath. Walking quickly, I headed straight for the heavy wood carriage house doors. I yanked the right one open with both hands and slipped outside, into the night. It closed behind me with a deafening boom. I don't think I'd ever felt so isolated, alone in this place save for an annoying "friendly" ghost and a host of other spirits who may or may not want me hurt…or worse.

At least the air felt warmer outside. Lighter. There were no glowing whiskey barrels, no rusted iron trusses, no broken crates. I walked to the right, holding my phone out in front of me until it caught a signal. I dialed up Ellis and he answered on the second ring.

"Verity," he said, as if he wasn't quite sure what to expect from me.

He'd have to put his doubts to rest real quickly. "I met your ghost."

I stared out at the pitch-black night and could feel him stiffen on the line. "What happened?" he demanded, the phone gathering static as he moved. A police radio droned in the background. "Are you okay?"

That depended on his definition of okay. "A poltergeist attacked me. It dented up your stove and delivered the final death blow to your serving station." I stepped up onto a small stack of patio bricks, the weight of my discovery spilling out into nervous energy. "I'm sorry. It also got the construction lights." I tried not to picture what would have happened if they'd come crashing down on me.

He cursed under his breath. "But you, you're all right?"

"Yes." His concern was a surprise. I'd expected him to be mad at me over his stuff. His brother Beau sure would have been.

I heard movement over the line. "I'm coming right now. I'm not that far."

"I'm glad for that." Now for the even harder part. "Ellis?" I asked, moving to another stack, my jittery legs getting the best of me. "They don't like us here."

"Tough shit."

I let out a small cry as I slipped, the patio bricks clattering out from under my feet. I leapt sideways and jogged a few feet to regain my balance.

"What's happening?" Ellis asked, as if he were ready to leap through the phone. "Where are you?"

"Outside. I'm fine." I shook out my legs, glad I didn't turn an ankle. "I'm not ordinarily this clumsy." A chill pricked the small of my back.

In all fairness, it had been an unusual night.

He let out a breath. "I know you can handle it," he said. "I just wish I hadn't had to leave you tonight."

"You and me both," I said, staring out into the darkness, the sheer isolation of the place starting to get to me.

This was the longest night of my life and it was barely past ten o'clock.

Headlights turned onto the property and my heart lifted a little. "Is that you coming down the drive?" He'd said he was close, but this was great.

"No. It's not me," he said, his voice like ice. "What do you see?"

"Lights. A car. Maybe Harry the handyman?" I hoped, fear skittering up my spine.

"I'm not expecting anyone," Ellis said, his tone clipped. "Go inside. Lock the door. I'm coming for you right now."

Oh God. I hurried for the stables, the rock-strewn ground slowing me down. Gravel crunched as the car continued down the drive, right for me. I shoved my phone in my bag and held it tight as I took the crumbling steps two at a time and opened the oversized carriage house door.

Headlights swept my face, blinding me for a moment. I ducked inside, slamming the door closed with a boom that echoed throughout the stables.

I shoved the bolt closed and leaned my forehead against the aged wood, the hard panting of my breath sounding loud in my ears. Hot orange circles of light danced in front of my eyes as my pupils adjusted to the darkness once more.

No telling who could be outside.

He said it couldn't be Harry, and with a sinking feeling, I realized he was right. Harry wouldn't come back this late. The shelter had a curfew. He wouldn't risk his bed to drop by unannounced.

I moved silently to the narrow window on my right. Construction dust and age clouded the glass. I rubbed it with my hand, trying to see if the intruder had come any closer. I felt like a sitting duck here all alone.

There could be entrances to this place I didn't even know about. I hoped they were locked.

The car idled about twenty feet from the door. From the height of the headlights, it had to be some type of sedan. I couldn't see the plates, the color, the make, or even how many people were inside. Two headlights, reaching for me as if to say, *I know you're in there.*

"Frankie, I need you," I hissed.

"We got trouble?" the gangster asked, appearing with his back to the wall on the other side of the window. He peered out, reaching under his suit coat and drawing a revolver from a side holster. He made a quick check of the chamber and I could see it was fully loaded. "Stay low."

"You think a shoot-out is the answer?" I asked, realizing I was well and truly alone in this. Frankie could fire all the ghost bullets he wanted. I didn't believe for a second it would stop the living.

My lack of faith must have been apparent. Frankie glared daggers at me. "Excuse me. I was under the impression you called for help."

The gangster pointed his gun through the window, which was a pretty neat trick all things considered. "They're driving around the side."

There was a narrow wooden door to our right. I tested it. Locked. I hoped they didn't have the key. "What should I do?" I whispered.

"You hide. I'll torpedo these mugs," he said.

I stumbled back into the darkness. First the poltergeist, now this. There was no way I was heading back to that haunted kitchen. That left me with precious few places to go. I didn't know this space or where I could go that they wouldn't follow. Unless...

I spotted the cellar straight ahead. No one in his or her right mind would go down there. The colonel had seen to that.

"Colonel," I whispered, my voice wavering, "I need some protecting. Please?" He seemed to be the strongest ghost here, except for the poltergeist.

He didn't respond, but at least he'd left me with an option, a terrible, horrible option.

I rushed for the trapdoor. The hair on the back of my neck stood up. Terror pounded through me. I grabbed the handle, yanking hard. The door felt heavy, sealed tight.

"The driver's side door just opened," Frankie said, watching out the window.

Ohmygosh. I battled the instinct to run as I gripped the ring harder. I pulled with all my strength and felt the door give an inch. Cold air rushed from the hole, seeping over my ankles and filling me with an inescapable dread.

Ignore it.

It had to be better than what was behind me.

"Just one fella. A mean-looking sucker, head down, making tracks for the side door," Frankie called.

I crouched above the horror seeping from the hole and redoubled my efforts. My abs twinged and my arm muscles stretched as I forced the creaking door open. It fell back onto the floor with a crash loud enough to wake the dead.

Okay, that was a bad choice of words.

Keep it together. I shook out my arms and tried to ignore the pure malice leaching out of the hole.

"The colonel made it feel nasty," I reminded myself. He'd laced the door with fear and dread. "That doesn't mean it's real."

Only that it *could* be real.

A rough, homemade ladder descended into the abyss. With my satchel over my shoulder and the mini-flashlight bouncing in my dress pocket, I said a quick prayer and began my descent.

It was awkward climbing backwards, but I kept at it, moving as quickly as I could. Barely a few rungs down, my legs chilled. It made me go faster. Lord in heaven. I half-expected something or someone to grab one of them. But I was more afraid of what awaited me if I didn't move than if I did.

I reached for the trapdoor and closed it behind me.

The tang of rust and mildew assaulted my senses. *Keep going.*

Something slithery wrapped around my ankle.

I gasped, jumped the last four feet, and spun to face my attacker.

A dull light penetrated the room, bathing it in an eerie silver glow. Stacks of horse feed piled up against the walls on either side of me. An unearthly gossamer cobweb wrapped around my ankle.

"Ick, ick, ick!" I shook it off and it disappeared.

More of them floated in the air, as if suspended on an invisible breeze. I drew my arms close to my body as another silky web threatened to wind itself along my forearm.

My flashlight lay on the floor at my feet, but I didn't need it. The silver light down here was weaker, like looking through smoke, but I could still see.

I shoved the flashlight back into my pocket. *Get a grip.* I'd done this before.

I heard a scrabbling behind me and gasped as I saw a wiry shadow clamber toward the trapdoor. I forgot to breathe as I watched it scurry like a spider and escape through a crack in the wood.

Holy Moses. Had I broken some kind of seal?

Yes.

But what kind, I had no idea.

Images flickered into focus all around me. I saw baskets of corn and carrots near the base of the wooden ladder. A nearby shelf held several cloudy glass jars of Tuttle's Elixir: Special Veterinary Horse Liniment. Hay littered the stone floor. Ghostly lanterns cast shadows along the century-old brick walls.

I adjusted my bag over my shoulder. The clanking of its contents sounded as loud as a brass band in this otherworldly place.

I had to find a way out of there. Every instinct I had screamed for me to claw my way out of this haunted hole, back the way I came.

But I couldn't go back. The only choice was forward.

Hollow, ghostly gunshots echoed from above.

Frankie swore. "Die, you bastard!"

The door creaked closed.

The intruder was inside.

I breathed in the stark bitterness of decay as I pressed deeper

into the cellar, past the horse feed and toward an arched doorway on the far left wall.

Maybe I could find some kind of weapon down here and pull it
into my dimension, just like I had done with Josephine's locket.
Of course that necklace had also disappeared rather quickly.

The air felt heavier in here, the room still as a tomb.

Rough-hewn wooden shelves clung near the walls, stocked
with jars put up for the winter. Only instead of peas and carrots,
tomatoes and pickled onions, I saw rot. It muddied the glass in
shades of muted gray and black.

A pitiful cry rose up behind me, stiffening the hairs on the
back of my neck. I spun to face human attackers, a ghost, I didn't
know what.

The corridor stood empty.

The shelves to my right flickered as I heard another hollow
cry. "Help me." It echoed. A woman wept.

Oh geez. "It's okay," I said, low under my breath. "Everything's fine."

I wasn't sure if I was talking to the ghost or to myself.

It didn't matter. We both needed to get a grip. I was one freaky
encounter away from melting into a shivering puddle on the
floor.

Footsteps echoed directly above my head.

"Help me," the watery voice called.

I forced my voice, at least, to remain calm. "Where are you?"

No response.

I saw no other exits to this room, no weapons, no new places
to hide. If I didn't find something soon, I could be in a lot of
trouble. The colonel had certainly been hiding something down
here. Perhaps the cellar held a secret door. I touched the brick
wall at the back of the room. It felt smooth with age, cold. Solid.

I turned to the shelves lining both walls. Perhaps I'd missed
something in the first room.

Then I spied a large piece of weathered plywood flush with the
left wall. I hadn't noticed it before, not with the putrid jars in the
way. But now that I gave it a second look, I could see it was real.

Black dirt lay in clumps around the bottom. Fresh dirt, if I wasn't mistaken.

The colonel had been especially angry about *digging*.

Oh my God. Was this where the intruder was headed? My neck flushed and I broke out into a cold sweat.

Maybe not. Maybe this was the way out. I searched for a space between the jars, one big enough for my hand. If I could knock the wood away and see...

The ring on the cellar door clanked.

Please let it be a ghost.

I rubbed my palms on my jeans and reached out, to the left of a jar of brackish sludge, between that and the one with the round globules. I closed my eyes and stretched up to the shoulder, my fingers barely touching the edge of the rough lumber. Tiny splinters pierced my fingertips as I squeezed a little farther around the back of the panel. I held my breath and tipped it just so...

The board fell forward and I jumped back. It whooshed straight through the unearthly illusion, tearing it apart in a rush of prickling energy and dust. The grit made my eyes water.

The board hit the stone floor with a resounding thud. I slammed my eyes shut and prayed that the intruder hadn't heard.

The footsteps stopped directly above my hiding place.

CHAPTER 12

IN FRONT OF ME STOOD a narrow passageway, brick lined and as tall as I was. The silver light didn't penetrate more than a foot or two inside. This could be my escape.

Or the trap that would corner me.

Either way, it was the only place left to hide. Heart pounding, I reached for my flashlight.

It occurred to me that no one knew I was down here. Not my mom, nor my sister. Certainly not Ellis, although he might eventually figure it out. My only link to the outside world was Frankie, and he couldn't talk to anyone I knew, nobody alive at least. If I became trapped, there would be no one to rescue me.

My light flickered against the walls, casting its beam a few feet ahead. Beyond that, pitch darkness.

I counted each stride I made. Five steps in. Ten.

A pile of crumbling dirt and rock brought me up short.

This was the end of the line for me. The trapdoor to the cellar creaked open. I'd run out of time.

Panic seized me. They were coming. And here I stood in the very place where the intruder was likely to go. I hurried out of the tunnel, each step feeling like ten. I needed to move faster, step lighter. I slipped on a fallen rock and my shoulder hit the side of the tunnel hard.

A ghostly wail echoed behind me and I doubled my efforts.

I ran faster than a hot knife through butter and burst out into the empty underground room.

The fallen board had dislodged the ghostly illusions. I had no shelves to hide behind, no jars. Not that anyone would even see them, except for me. I passed through the arched doorway and found falling-apart wooden whiskey crates, some red and white rusted-out signs advertising Southern Spirits, and a whole lot of dirt. None of it had been there before. It seemed a new ghost now held sway over the cellar. My breath caught in my throat. It could be the poltergeist.

The hard beam of a flashlight pierced the darkness directly in front of me, scattering light around the room. I cringed and sank back against the wall and prayed that Ellis wasn't too far, that I could hold out long enough. With every cell in my body I tried to be invisible.

"Verity," Ellis called from above. His voice sounded clipped, worried. I'd never been so glad to hear from him in all my life.

"Ellis!" I burst from my hiding place into the bright beam of his light from above.

He let out a huff. "What are you doing?" he asked, not half as relieved to see me as I was to find him.

I climbed the ladder fast as a whip. He placed the light on the floor and helped me out of the cellar. He never looked so good, so right and strong as he wrapped an arm around my back and steadied me.

Maybe I had a damsel-in-distress complex or maybe the sheer adrenaline of the night had gotten to me, but in that moment, I could have kissed him.

I surprised him with a monster hug instead. "Thank you. Thank you. Thank you." I clung to him. He felt so good. Smelled good. So warm. So *real*.

"I—" he began, trailing off. I was hugging him too long.

I didn't care.

But I was a little surprised when I pulled a few inches away and realized he was still hugging me back.

I gave him a squeeze. "I'm really glad it was you."

He dropped his hands like I was on fire.

I hadn't meant anything by it, but just that fast, we'd lost our moment. He rubbed at the back of his neck, as if he wasn't quite sure what to do with his hands. For a split second, I wondered what would have happened if I had kissed him. Scandal, no doubt.

I almost wished I had kissed him. It's not like this night could get any stranger. Besides, the man looked amazing in uniform.

"Stay here," he said, bringing a hand down to the Glock on his gun belt, as if to remind him who he was. "I'm going to check out the property."

Oh, no. "Not without me."

I could tell he wanted to argue, but he stopped himself. Yes, I was a liability and I'd probably slow him down, but we both understood that I didn't want to be alone.

"He came through the side door," Ellis said, straightening. "Kicked it right in." We made our way over there and Ellis frowned as he inspected the broken metal. "I should have gone for new locks and not kept the antique hardware."

"You wanted to do right by the building," I said. He couldn't know the old locks would break so easily.

"Should have done right by you," he said under his breath.

I followed Ellis outside as he shone a light down onto the brick patio.

"He stopped the car out front," I said, following Ellis along the side of the carriage house, careful to step only where he stepped. "Then moved around here to the side." We shone our lights on the cracked and broken asphalt, looking for tire tracks.

We found nothing.

"I think it was a lone intruder," I told him as we headed up the steps, trusting that Frankie had gotten it right.

Ellis nodded. "I saw him slide in the driver's side and take off down the road as I pulled up. I called it in, but so far none of our other units have spotted the car. He had the license plate covered with cardboard and left fast."

He'd come to check on me instead of chasing the person who trespassed on his land? "You didn't try to follow," I said, surprised. Ellis wasn't the type to let go easily.

He let out a huff, his expression impossible to read. "I needed to make sure you were okay."

"Thanks." That I hadn't expected. I wasn't sure what else to say. "So inside here is safe?" I asked, pausing outside the door.

He opened it for me. "Stay alert, but I think so." He glanced down the road, as if that would trace them. "Did he see you?"

"Yes. He got a look at my face and everything." The headlights had shone directly on me.

He swore under his breath. "I've got to be more careful with you."

"Okay," I said, not exactly sure how he planned to accomplish that. In fact, now that the adrenaline had begun to wear off, I found I didn't have the energy to say much more. I was tired of being alone in this place and more than a little relieved to have him here. He'd surprised me tonight by being supportive and brave and on my side. It felt good, even if it set me off course a bit. I realized I was shaking. My bag slipped off my shoulder. "Damn it," I said, reaching down to grab it.

"Let go." He eased my bag out of my grip, placing it down on the steps. "It's all right. I'm here."

I gazed down toward the main road, afraid of the vulnerability he'd see if I faced him.

"Look at me." The beam from his Maglite illuminated the porch. His expression was earnest, his tone sincere. "Tell me what happened."

"He drove straight up the drive, as if he didn't expect anyone to be here." Of course, my presence hadn't stopped him. "I didn't get a good description. I'm sorry." I let Ellis hold me by the shoulders as I explained, the warmth of him seeping into me, giving me strength. I told him how I'd decided to head down into the cellar and how scared I'd been.

He not only listened, but I could tell he really thought about everything I told him. It seemed Ellis wasn't the type to do things halfway. I don't know why I expected less, except that his brother had been very, very different.

"We'll check the inside, but it sounds like our intruder is long gone," he said, tucking a stray lock of hair behind my ear. "I'm sorry to put you through this," he said, his hand warming my cheek as it lingered there. "I shouldn't have left you here by yourself."

"You didn't know," I told him. None of us could have anticipated this.

But he held firm, refusing to abdicate responsibility. "This property, it's strange. You hear things. You sometimes see them out of the corner of your eye. Or at least you swear you do." He stopped for a moment, his expression softening. "I was anxious to get you started tonight. Our talk at your place didn't do anything to calm me down, either." At my snort, he added, "What I'm trying to say is I'm sorry. I should have been more cautious."

"Apology accepted," I said lightly. The truth was, I'd needed to hear that. Badly. Ellis and I might never be friends, but we didn't need to be at odds all the time. "Believe it or not, some good has come of this." I tilted my chin down. "When I was hiding in the cellar, I found a hidden passageway."

He hesitated. "I don't know what you mean."

"It's a tunnel," I clarified. "Or at least the beginning of one. There's a bunch of loose dirt, as if someone's been digging down there. I think it's what has the ghosts worked up. I'd hoped it was you."

A muscle in his cheek jumped. "Son of a bitch." He pulled away from me. "I haven't been down there since we bought the property." He glanced in the direction of the trapdoor. "It's not the most practical space, so it wasn't a high priority." He thought for a moment. "Maybe we should take another look."

"Oh, joy," I said as he headed inside and motioned for me to follow.

He either missed my sarcasm...or ignored it. "When we're done with renovations, the cellar opening will be behind the wine bar. I'd thought about using it to store a few bottles."

He placed his flashlight on the floor and forced the door open. I found myself cringing as he shone his light into the hole. He noticed. Not a lot got past Ellis Wydell. He braced a hand on his knee. "Are you up for another trip underground? If you can manage, I'd like for you to show me what you saw."

"Only for you," I said, surprised that I meant it.

His gaze lingered on me. "Before we go down, I'll secure the building. Just in case our visitor decides to come back."

"Great," I said, as if that would make it better.

Cold air seeped from the open trapdoor as he locked the carriage house doors, and double-checked a lock on a door in the back. Then he dragged a heavy construction saw to block the side door. "Best I can do," he said, breathing heavy as he stepped away from it.

A chill swept over me and I had the distinct feeling we weren't alone. "Colonel?" I called softly.

No response.

When Ellis drew near, I cleared my throat. "Maybe we should wait until daytime," I told him. "I already saw most of what there is to see and, well…" I had to be honest. "I'm not getting a good feeling."

"I'm not either," he said, in a way that made me wish he were the type to sugarcoat things. "Which is why we should head down there. We'll figure this out together, okay?"

Right. Together. I nodded.

I let him go first down the ladder into the darkness. As he descended, I saw Frankie standing in the doorway to the kitchen, motioning me back. Or at least that was what I thought he was doing. He'd lost the other leg from the knee down.

"What?" I hissed. He needed to come over here and tell me if we were walking into an ambush. If he was just trying to warn me we were running out of time, I knew that.

When the gangster started arguing with someone I couldn't see, I made my decision and followed Ellis down.

❦

Ellis shone his beam onto the stone floor of the cellar as I stepped down off the ladder.

This time, I witnessed no silver light, no ethereal objects. The space felt cold and dark, as if the ghosts had abandoned it. I reached for my flashlight and flicked it on.

"This way," I whispered, screwing up my courage and pressing forward, leading us deeper through the subterranean rooms.

"Did you see anything else down here?" he asked, studying the brick walls as the light bounced off them.

"One secret passage isn't enough for you?" I asked, half-joking.

"I like to be thorough," he said, moving slower than I'd have liked.

The less time we spent down here, the better.

We passed under the archway into the space where I'd found the tunnel. My beam caught the plywood board on the floor. "It was behind that."

Ellis crouched over the board and turned it over. I watched it rattle against the cold stone. "This doesn't look like it's been down here long," Ellis mused.

He was right. I didn't see any signs of wear, no cobwebs or water damage.

I stood and ventured as far as the light allowed, rubbing my tennis shoe along the floor. The dirt was moist, fresh.

"Is this where you tried to hide?" Ellis asked, closing in on the passageway cut out of the wall.

"I was hoping to escape," I clarified. Too bad that hadn't worked out. It appeared smaller, more cramped than I remembered next to his overlarge frame. "I'm not sure we should go in." For all I knew, the poltergeist could cause a cave-in and bury us.

He gave a slight grin at that. "I just want to take a quick look."

I chewed my lip.

"We can't get a good idea of what we're facing if we don't know all the facts," he pointed out. He sounded so reasonable. Too bad what we were dealing with went beyond normal logic.

"Let's do it quick, then," I said, ducking inside. "Follow me."

Now that I wasn't scrambling for my life, I found myself noticing more. Where the cellar had been painstakingly constructed, this tunnel felt rushed. The bricks didn't line up as precisely, the space felt claustrophobically tight.

Dirt covered the stone floor, or perhaps that was the floor. The ceiling dipped a few feet in and he had to duck in order to move farther.

A cold chill slithered down my spine. Instinctively, I stepped back. Straight into Ellis.

"Walk much?" he asked, catching me.

"Hush," I said, forcing myself forward.

I took one step, two. I made myself keep going.

Ellis followed close behind. I could hear his deep breaths.

When I didn't believe I could make myself move another inch, we came upon the wall of debris. I fought the urge to bite my lip. "It didn't occur to me before, but this could very well be a cave in," I said, tone hushed as if my voice alone could trigger disaster.

The tangle of bricks and stone blocked the passageway and ate at my light. I lowered my focus to where the debris scattered over the ground, directing the beam so that I could see the immense pile in front of me. It reached as high as my chin and seemed to stretch back pretty far.

Ellis stood close. "One sec," he said, touching my shoulder, reaching his other arm past me, in order to raise his light up over the blockage. He held it as far back as possible. The passage continued into the abyss, but to where, well, that was a mystery. "The ceiling's missing up ahead, but that's not what caused this pile ahead of us." He let out a small sigh, his warm breath tickling hair near my cheek. "One thing's clear," he continued, "a real, live person is in the process of excavating this tunnel. The next question is why."

I slid my light off. I missed it immediately, but I had an idea. I began digging through my bag. "I have GPS on my cell phone. We can map the tunnel."

I glanced up at Ellis and found him grinning at me. "I like how you think."

It embarrassed me, to have him look at me that way. It also made me proud.

"Think you can catch a signal down here?" he asked.

"Can't hurt to try." My fingers felt clumsy as I called up the app. It took a few extra seconds. The signal wasn't especially great down here, but at least we were far enough outside the carriage house walls that I got one.

Within moments, the app gave me a happy spin of a cartoon compass and followed up with a readout. "Do you have a pen?"

Ellis pulled one out of his shirt pocket.

I wrote the coordinates on my arm: 35.48944, –82.53370.

He seemed amused at that. "What?" I double-checked. I'd copied them right.

"You surprise me," he said as I handed his pen back.

As long as we were being honest, "You're not what I expected, either," I told him. "Now can we please get out of here? I want to see what's above this tunnel." And I wanted out. I'd never been crazy about closed-in spaces on a good day and this one had shot my last nerve.

"Lead the way," he said as I ducked out around him.

It's not easy rushing out of a secret passage. Each step felt like an eternity. And while I was glad to have Ellis down here with me, it didn't mean both of us wouldn't feel a ton better above ground.

When we hit the underground room, Ellis lifted the board and covered the passage again. He even kicked the dirt back around the other side. "I'm going to install a camera down here."

"Good," I said. In the meantime, I booked it straight for the ladder and launched myself right up in to the dark carriage house. I still felt the prickles on my neck, the sense that we weren't alone. "Hurry up," I called down into the hole. "You don't have to make it pretty."

The hole remained dark and silent. Oh my word. Something had gotten him.

"Ellis?" I asked.

Nothing.

I screwed up my courage. Lord almighty, I was going to have to go back down. I gave it one last shot. "Ellis?" I hissed before I caught sight of a milky white light directly below. For a second, I thought it was a ghost. Then I realized it was simply the beam of Ellis's flashlight.

He grinned as he made his way up the ladder. "I went back and got a few pictures."

"You could have told me," I said, relieved. He placed the flashlight on the floor and slammed the trapdoor down. The *boom* echoed throughout the stables.

But it was hard to stay too mad. We were out. Alive and together. A situation I most certainly did not take for granted as we both started for the front door.

He quickly drew ahead—longer legs and all—so I picked up speed.

Ellis pulled ahead again. "I don't know where you think you're going," I told him. "I have the coordinates."

"And I have the door," he said, unlocking the front of the carriage house and swinging the large wooden door open for me.

"Always a gentleman," I said, treading out onto the crumbling front steps.

"That's open for debate," he muttered, joining me.

I forced myself to slow down, if only to call up the GPS display on my phone. I plugged in the coordinates from my arm and it directed me to the right, toward the side yard and the old house.

"This way," I said, following the compass, careful of the rocks and the discarded bricks. The security sensors popped on and cast the yard in light. "Nice," I murmured.

"I installed them after someone or some*thing* tore up a section of my new brick patio."

Earlier this evening, I'd have wondered if it was a ghost. Now, I suspected someone very much alive wanted to access whatever was housed in the tunnel.

"Here," I said, leading him to the exact spot of the tunnel blockage, wishing the bricks under our feet could give any clue as to what lay underneath.

"Son of a bitch." I turned back toward where Ellis stood and saw the bricks had been ripped up in a neat circle, about five feet farther out into the yard.

Oh, wow. "If the tunnel continues straight, and if we could follow it…"

"Then somebody's trying to find something right there," he finished. The bed of gravel underneath remained in place. "I'm still installing it and they're ripping it up." He took a stone from a mound that reached as high as his knees, turning the rock over in his hand. "This doesn't make sense if they're digging for something below. They'd get to it much faster underground."

"Yeah, that's weird," I said. "And I really don't get what this has to do with the ghost in the kitchen."

He shook his head and tossed a rock out into the yard behind us. "And here I thought owning this place would help me relax."

I let out a small laugh. "Maybe after you figure this out."

"Maybe," he mused. He absently wiped the dirt from his hands onto his shirt. "Thanks for staying. I know it wasn't easy. I think most people would have been out of here."

"Not you," I pointed out.

"Yeah." The corner of his mouth tipped up. "But I'm crazy."

"Then that makes two of us." His praise, and that dose of respect, meant a lot after tonight. I had worked hard and it felt good that he noticed. "Didn't your brother ever tell you?" I asked. "Set me to a task and I'm like a tick on a hound dog."

"No," he said, growing more somber at the mention of Beau and me. "No, he didn't."

Of course, everything hadn't exactly gone according to plan. My enthusiasm faded. "I have to show you what happened in the kitchen."

"All right." We walked together in the dark, our footsteps loud in the utter silence surrounding us.

"It's not as bad as before," I said quickly, leading him to the scene of the destruction.

"Why do I get the feeling I'm still not going to like it?"

"Because you won't. An angry ghost came straight at me. It

smashed your lights and pummeled your stove."

He shone his light upon the mess in the kitchen and I caught my first full view of it as well. Shattered glass littered the floor, the half-dozen lamps smashed amid the chaos. Heavy cookware had been tossed around like confetti. I was lucky I hadn't been hit.

Frankie lingered next to the fist-sized dent in the stove. He flickered in and out and he was still arguing with someone I couldn't see.

"I'm sorry," I said to Ellis. "I tried to stop it."

He scanned the room, taking in every detail. "I should have been here."

"You couldn't have stopped it either."

His light searched the corners of the room, the floors and the ceiling, as if exposing the gloomy corners of this place could also reveal the darkness that dwelled here. "I never would have believed it if it hadn't been for that video. And now, you."

"I know exactly what you mean." Only for me, it was the terror of actually experiencing it.

He turned to me, wary. "Do you think you can get rid of it?"

"Yes." I wouldn't allow myself to think otherwise. Frankie and I would just have to rally our strength. This was our job. We had to learn enough about the ghost and the situation in order to make it safe for me and for everyone involved. "Meanwhile, you handle the living."

He drew closer. "I'll help in whatever way I can. Just tell me what you need."

It was disconcerting to have him this near. I shook it off, trying to focus. "I'd like a new lock on that side door."

"That goes without saying." He glanced around the room. "In fact, I'm sleeping here tonight. I can't leave the place unlocked."

"I'll stay too," I said, before I could change my mind. "I don't think the poltergeist will come back. It's used up a lot of energy already. But if there is a problem of the ghostly sort, I'd like to help."

He nodded. "Thanks."

So that was that. Ellis would handle the living and I'd handle the dead. I hoped I was up for it.

He drew close to me. "I have some blankets in my cruiser that we can use to bed down. Tomorrow, I'm going to start removing the rock from the tunnel. Maybe we can figure out what someone's been digging for."

I leaned back against one of the metal countertops. "I want to know what made them look at this property to begin with. Have you heard of anything being buried here?"

"No." He dug his hands into his pockets. "When this place came up for sale, my uncle mentioned something about a shoot-out back during Prohibition." He glanced at the old brick walls, as if they could tell us something. "It was more of a passing interest than an actual concern."

I glanced at Frankie.

"What?" he asked, defensive.

I waited for Ellis to head out and grab the blankets from his police cruiser before I started interrogating my ghost buddy.

"Quick," I hissed. "Tell me what you know about this place."

The ghost frowned. His face appeared sweaty and his hair was a mess, like he'd been running his fingers through it. "How about, 'hey, Frankie. How you doing, Frankie? I see you're missing both your legs, Frankie.'"

"Right." Although we didn't have time for pleasantries. "I'm sorry." Oh my. His waist had begun to disappear as well.

He notched a finger under his collar. "I don't know nothing about your poltergeist."

"Not even from the ghosts who live here? Who are you arguing with?"

He drew back, angry, and his image flickered. "My brother."

"Oh." I hadn't expected that.

"He's the one who got me in with the South Town gang," Frankie grumbled, shoving his fingers through his hair. "Haven't seen him since I died."

It didn't look like a happy reunion. "You weren't surprised to find him here."

The gangster glared at me. "Yeah, but he's not the one causing trouble."

"Okay." I hoped he was right. "We'll figure out who is. Maybe we can help your brother."

Frankie didn't respond and I decided not to push him.

Ellis returned with sleeping bags.

"Thanks," I murmured as he passed me one. I found a quiet corner in the kitchen.

A weary Frankie stood next to me, as if on guard. "I doubt you'll see much more tonight." He scrubbed a hand over his eyes. "The poltergeist has got to be tired."

"Manifesting is hard work," I agreed quietly. "You should get some rest, too."

The ghost nodded as his physical form faded away.

Ellis set up near me, and I didn't protest.

I didn't sleep well, but we did rest in peace until morning. Ellis helped me stow the sleeping bag and we agreed to meet back at five o'clock that night.

"I'll bring dinner," he said as he tucked my bag under his arm.

"Great," I told him. I hoped Frankie would be well enough to help us out. Maybe if I gathered enough information today, he wouldn't have to work as hard. It was worth a try.

Every old property had a history. I wondered if this one would reveal more about our intruders' motives.

I knew one way to find out.

CHAPTER 13

"SPILL," I TOLD FRANKIE AS I steered my car away from the haunted carriage house. "What did your brother have to say?"

Frankie shook his head. "Not much. He and the guys are being held down by the poltergeist. It's getting scary in there."

"Yikes," I said, considering the source. "We'll help him."

"Yeah, I didn't think I wanted to." The gangster shrugged. "Now I don't know."

As I drove through the gate, his energy left me with a mild zap that felt noticeably softer than the last time Frankie's energy left me. "You okay?" I asked, worried.

"Yeah." Frankie sighed. "That actually felt good."

"Speak for yourself." Muted or not, the zing still made my hair feel like it was standing on end. I ran a hand through it while I waited to pull the car out onto the main road. "Cripes," I muttered as Mayor Thad Steward passed me in his silver Cadillac. He slowed to get a good look and I caught his surprised frown.

Yes, I was hanging with the Wydells again. I hoped he couldn't tell that I'd spent the night.

Nothing to do about it now. I dialed my sister before pulling out.

"You're up early," she said as Frankie and I rumbled onto the main road.

"How was your run?" She liked to get in a few miles before

breakfast. Some days, I swear Melody had more energy in her little finger than I had in my whole body. And not because she was five years younger. She'd always been that way.

"That's not why you called me," she said.

Darned sisterly intuition. I adjusted my hands-free earpiece and fought with the wire because, well, it was an out-of-date, off-brand, garage-sale purchase that was probably going to electrocute me the next time it rained. "Don't flip out," I said by way of warning, "but I have a secret and you absolutely can't tell Mom."

She gasped. "You sold the house."

"What?" I jerked. The wire pulled and almost came up short. "No," I said, making sure the earpiece stayed in. I think Mom would find out about that. "The job I had to do last night…" My courage faltered and I glanced at Frankie lounging in my passenger seat. "I'm working for Ellis Wydell."

"The middle son of the devil?" she burst out, her voice going up an octave and a half.

I gripped the steering wheel. Hard.

Then I popped the piece out of my ear voluntarily as she listed the reasons why the Wydells were no-good dirty scum, Beau's brother included.

It's not like I hadn't heard them all before. But I was starting to learn that Ellis was different, and I didn't feel like lumping him in with the rest of his family.

Frankie leaned a little more toward the window as my car bounced over the back roads toward my house. My sister's tinny voice launched into a fire-and-brimstone monologue that would make any Southern preacher proud. "Is she going to take a breath?" Frankie asked.

I focused on the road. "This is going better than it looks," I told him. "Melody was especially hurt when things went bad." At least she'd avoided the public fallout.

My sister merely had to let off some steam.

Frankie gave me the 'iffy' motion with his hand. "She sounds like a gal I knew. Suds's old lady. He'd dial her up, tell her something simple, like hey, we got to drive to Cleveland and bust a few heads. You don't want to hear the racket that dame made."

My car's blinker made a heavy *clink, clink, clink* sound as I steered the land-yacht of a Cadillac left toward town. "Melody's cautious when it comes to the Wydell boys."

She had every reason to be.

I lifted the earpiece up. She was still going. I let it dangle over my shoulder.

Frankie braced an elbow on the door, the tips of his fingers trailing out to catch the breeze. Of course, he did this without needing to crack the window. "Tell her how it fits in with the twenty large."

"Not yet." My sister might have been a bit of a free spirit, but she'd certainly want to know what I was doing for that kind of money.

I sighed. Despite the fact that I'd trust her with my life, I wasn't quite ready to tell her about Frankie yet.

How could I tell her about Frankie when I couldn't quite explain it to myself?

I tended to charge in and trust my gut. I'd figure out the details later. Only Frankie was quite a detail.

We were driving right toward the sunrise. I squinted as I raised the hands-free headset to my ear again. Melody hadn't slowed down a bit. "Haven't the Wydells done enough to our family?" she pleaded. "Why would you open the door to more abuse? You can't trust him farther than you can take his left nostril and bend it over to his—"

"I'm talking now," I said, fishing my sunglasses from on top of the visor. "It's a lot of money. And it's something I can do. Well, with your help."

"I don't believe it," she mused, as if I hadn't heard a word she'd been saying.

Yes, well, just because she was right didn't mean she couldn't help.

"I need you to research the Wilson's Creek distillery property. All the buildings. I think there are at least nine. It was up for sale a few years ago and Ellis bought it. But I want to know who owned it before, as far back as you can go. I also need to know if anything out of the ordinary happened there. Ever."

"Is that all?" she asked, with more than a touch of sisterly sarcasm.

"For starters," I said, refusing to take the bait. This wasn't my first rodeo. "I also want to know about any ghost stories or burials there. I have it on good authority there's a family cemetery on the land." Speaking of such, "Have you ever heard of Colonel Maker? He rode with the Rough Riders."

She absorbed that for a long moment. "One evening with Ellis and you've gone catawampus."

I'd tell her later I spent the night.

She took a breath, then hesitated, which was very unlike her. "What's going on with you?" she asked, her voice quite level. Sane, even. A little too calm if you asked me. "I need to know."

When she spoke that way, I wanted to tell her more. But of course I knew better. "I'm helping Ellis renovate the property."

That was the truth, right?

Mostly.

"You're a graphic designer. You don't renovate. You can barely change a shower curtain."

I passed my old second-grade teacher driving the other way and we waved. "It's more big-picture work. Look, you have to trust me on this one. If I can pull this off, I can save Grandma's house."

"Okay," she said, drawing the word out in a way that suggested I'd most definitely be hearing more later. Like I'd expected any different. "I'll head in to work early and research for you."

Good. "Don't tell Mom," I reminded her.

"Her heart couldn't take it."

What about my ears? "I don't want to hear any more lectures from you, either."

"Now, I can't promise you that."

At least she was honest.

I hung up and shot a triumphant grin at Frankie, who leaned

back against the headrest. "Now we're getting somewhere," I told him. He let his entire arm trail out the window. If it were anybody else doing that, I'd tell him it could get cut off or something. Instead, I dug around in my console for a mint. I was getting hungry. "Aren't you psyched?"

He lolled his head my way. "Sure, babe." He turned his attention back to the riot of colorful trees out the window. "You don't know how exhausting it is to hang out with the living. Everything is drama."

"And you're always a model of tranquility," I muttered. I finished off a roll of half-petrified wintergreen lifesavers while Frankie sought peace and quiet in nature for the rest of the ride. Poor ghost. I kept the radio off for his benefit, but I appreciated the quiet too. It gave me time to think, and to recognize the exhaustion creeping up on me.

It wouldn't be long before I had answers to a few of my questions. Melody was a heck of a researcher. Two of her almost-degrees were in history and Shakespearean literature. I'd let her access the information I needed while I took the morning to clean up and take a quick nap. Five hours of hard sleep on a kitchen floor did not do a body good. And I swore I'd had one eye open the entire time.

Frankie promptly disappeared the minute I started up the long drive to the house. At least I knew he couldn't go far.

I parked in the front and enjoyed the sight of my home in the early morning light. The porch columns gleamed white against the pots of pink geraniums. My freshly washed dollhouse windows sparkled. Hydrangea bushes lined the front walk, shining wet with the dew. I ran my fingers along the leaves and blooms, enjoying the cool moisture along with the hot sun on my face. Yes, my head felt fuzzy and I could probably curl up and go to sleep on my front lawn, but despite the terror of the night, I found myself strangely energized.

It felt good to actually do something about my situation.

For the first time since I left Beau, I was in the driver's seat. My decisions, my wits could make the difference in whether or not I

could keep my home. Yes, I still had to figure out what the heck
I could do about real-life vandals and that horrifying poltergeist.
I shuddered to think what would happen if I ran into either one
of them again.

But knowing it came down to me… It was a heady feeling.

I opened the front door and Lucy toddled down the front hall
toward me, grunting and carrying on.

"Hey, sweetie pie," I said, lifting her up into my arms. Her
fur felt warmer on one side, most likely from sleep. She wore
a brand-new pink bandana, compliments of Melody no doubt.
"Did I wake you up?"

She shoved a warm, hard nose right into the crook of my
elbow, which was skunk for *You're worth it, babe.*

We walked through the front room and back to the parlor,
where she'd tossed the red blanket from my futon and rolled
it into a nest of sorts. It was her prerogative since I hadn't been
around to protest. Although I would throw it in the wash.

I scooped it up and took both skunk and blanket into the laundry room off the kitchen.

It felt good to settle into my own home this morning instead
of packing to leave.

Sure, the house could have used a few things to spruce it up,
but when you came down to it—I gave Lucy a kiss on her furry
head—"I have all I need right here."

She struggled to get down and I let her go.

I started the wash, grabbed a granola bar, and let Lucy out
the back door. She scampered out onto the porch and into the
sunshine.

Frankie sat out back, under the apple tree again.

I supposed everyone needed a spot to call their own. I set his
urn in a place of honor on the mantel. He deserved some respect
for what he'd done for me last night.

Ready to relax, I grabbed a towel and headed upstairs to
the black and white tile bathroom for a nice, hot soak. My
great-grandmother had won her large, claw-foot tub in an auc-
tion back in the 1930s, if you can believe that. Seems they were

a luxury item back then. Four generations of our family had treasured it, and I was looking forward to spending some quality time with it now.

The hot water steamed and swirled. I even added a touch of honeysuckle bubble bath, the good kind. It wasn't as if I could have sold a half-bottle of Olivina. I stirred the water with my hand, watching the bubbles break against my skin.

Last night had been a success, of sorts. Sure, I'd been attacked by a poltergeist and Ellis's kitchen hadn't exactly come out unscathed. Then there was the issue of my mysterious nighttime intruder. But I'd learned where to look next. And I'd gained some trust from Ellis.

Not that I cared, my mind said automatically.

I undressed and slipped into the deliciously hot bath.

Only, surprisingly enough, as the steaming water and sweet-smelling bubbles embraced me, I realized Ellis's opinion did matter to me. No telling how that started or why.

I leaned back, thinking.

I liked how he'd given Harry a job, how he'd been willing to hire me despite my past differences with his family. He hadn't been the one to start anything. It was always his mother or my ex.

I swirled my arms in the suds, releasing the scent of honeysuckle into the damp air. I appreciated how Ellis saw something special in that old distillery complex, and how he was working to make Sugarland a better place. It would make a difference for a lot of people around here.

Maybe he truly was the black sheep in that family. He saw things differently. He cared about people.

It seemed we had that in common.

"It'll be all right," I told myself.

I'd work hard to make it so.

When the water cooled, I treated myself to my only remaining fluffy towel before heading downstairs to grab my last clean sundress, the one with blue hydrangeas and a lovely white trim. It leaned toward the more formal end, especially considering I had to make up for some of the sleep I'd missed last night, but it felt comfy as I lay down on my futon and closed my eyes.

Home. What a wonderful feeling.

I woke to Frankie hovering over me, frowning. "You sleep like the dead."

"Aren't you busy recovering?" I asked, rolling to my side, hoping he'd go away.

"I'm too keyed up to go into the ether right now. Anyway, your phone keeps making strange giggling noises."

"That's just my text alerts," I said, reaching for my phone. "Those are minions laughing, from *Despicable Me*."

"I don't know what you're talking about," the gangster said, rubbing a hand down his face.

Sure enough, Melody had sent several texts. I leaned up on an elbow and scrolled through them. "She's found lots of good information. She wants to get together after her lunch meeting." I sat up. "What time is it?"

Frankie adjusted his Panama hat. "Does it matter?"

I stood, my legs stiff and my back a little achy. Moments like this, I missed my real bed. "To the flesh and blood among us, yes."

My cell phone read 1:14 p.m. At least I'd gotten a good nap in. I was supposed to meet Ellis at five. That left me a nice amount of time to see Melody.

"So are we leaving now?" Frankie asked. He was still missing his lower half. "I don't know how much longer I can keep this up."

I smoothed my dress. "Let me grab something quick to eat and we'll go." I headed into the kitchen.

He rubbed at his neck. "You don't get it. I've never been stuck before. It's freaking me out."

I opened the cabinet, grateful that I didn't have to root around for another granola bar. The Quaker Chewy Variety Pack was the only thing on all three shelves. While I unwrapped one, I reminded myself to give the ghost a break. He was going through a big change too. "We'll fix it," I said. I hoped.

Lucy scratched at the door and I let her in. She gave Frankie a wide berth as she ran to cuddle up on my still-warm blankets.

"What did you do to her?" I asked. Lucy was usually very friendly.

Frankie shrugged. "She won't come near me."

I poured myself a glass of water from the sink and made sure Lucy had food and water too. She was the best-kept skunk in Sugarland.

The nap had done me a world of good. My head felt clearer, my reflexes sharper.

"Okay, let's motor," I said, grabbing my keys.

Then I did something I'd never done before, on a quick trip into town, at least. I locked the back door. And after I'd given sleepy Lucy a pat on the head, I locked the front door behind me.

I probably should have done that before taking the morning to sleep. But, well, I wasn't used to it. It had always been a point of pride that we didn't need to bar our doors around here. I'm not sure Grandma had even known where the key was.

Still, I didn't like the way that car's headlights had lingered on me last night. I didn't know who had come to the property, but I had a hunch he'd seen me. And if he was from Sugarland, he knew exactly where I lived.

C

The city library stood in the middle of the town square, as it had for the past one hundred and seventy-three years. On the way we passed the Candy Bar, which was set up like a buffet for chocolate lovers, as well as the B Sweet Boutique, which specialized in locally harvested honey, preserves, and other delicacies.

"I designed that logo," I said, pointing out the stylized honeybee swirling around the s in sweet.

Frankie merely grunted.

"And look, I did the one for the New For You as well," I said, pointing to the whimsical antique-looking sign out front. "Think of the best estate sale you've ever been to and that's it."

If he was impressed, he didn't show it. "So you basically draw stuff?" Frankie asked.

"I make things look good." I'd done logos for a lot of the businesses in town. "I also design restaurant menus. And when the Broadway Diner redecorated, they hired me to pick out new colors and do the new brand look."

Frankie's brow furrowed. "Store owners pay you for this?"

"Yep. It's pretty good money," I insisted.

At least it had been, when I was the fiancée of the youngest prince of the community. Now, no one would hire me for anything. Some people had even reverted back to their old logos. Those things weren't nearly as bad as the silence.

He sighed, returning his attention to the parade of stores out the window. "And people said I was guilty of highway robbery."

I kept an eye out for a parking spot. "I'm going to pretend you didn't just insult my job," I said, locating an empty spot up ahead in the town square, right across from the mayor's office.

The buildings in this part of town had been constructed at a time when every door and window was considered a work of art. While they'd used brick and wood for Main Street, the town square was done in white limestone. After a lifetime of seeing it on an almost daily basis, it still impressed me.

They'd spared no expense on the town hall, with its red limestone accents, arched windows, and even a small clock tower at the center top.

After feeding the meter, I rushed across the square, past the large statue of our founder on a horse. Colonel Ramsey Larimore had fought in the Indian Wars, planted the first sugarcane in Tennessee, and served as the first official mayor of the city.

It wasn't long before everyone realized sugar didn't grow as well here as it did farther south. His son served as the second mayor, built his father a statue, and founded the Sugarland Candy Company. Even at the present day, that factory employed a lot of people around here. He's the one who should have gotten a monument.

I took the steps of the library two at a time. Red limestone columns flanked the entrance and the door resembled something out of a medieval castle. I pushed it open and was rewarded with the heady scent of old books.

"Huh," Frankie muttered, craning his neck at the tall ceiling of the lobby, taking in the painted scenes from Sugarland's history.

"Don't tell me you've never been in here before," I murmured, heading into the main room, past the displays of fall craft books and seasonal mysteries.

"Yeah." Frankie took his hat off and absently pressed it to his chest as he eyed the place. "The entire South Town gang used to have a Saturday night book club here."

"Don't let Melody hear you making fun," I said, spotting my sister at the desk. She wore her blonde hair up in the kind of loose, twisty French braid that I'd only seen in magazines, and on her. She'd tucked a pink flower pen behind her ear and managed to look both studious and charming at the same time.

She ducked around the desk and met me halfway, treating me to a sisterly embrace while giving a short tug on my hair, same as she did when we were growing up.

"You took long enough," she said, pulling back. Her blue eyes clouded with suspicion. "You didn't do anything crazy, like meet Ellis for lunch?"

"Of course not," I scoffed. I was seeing him tonight.

"In here," she said, motioning me toward one of the research rooms lining the back wall. The library had four total, all with thick wooden doors and old-fashioned windows that looked out over the courtyard below.

On a heavy dining-room-sized table at the center, she'd laid out several old newspaper articles and other print offs. I gave a low whistle. "You've been busy."

"I had fun," she corrected, tucking a wisp of hair behind her ear as I closed the door behind us. She noticed, but didn't comment.

Instead, she slid an article across the table at me. "What I learned isn't exactly surprising. It seems Ellis and his uncle, Vernon Hale, came about the Wilson's Creek property with the usual Wydell charm. That is to say underhanded, sneaky, and downright vicious."

"Can we do this without the editorial?" I asked. I could judge the facts on my own.

Melody pointed to a historical feature article from the 2010 issue of the *Sugarland Gazette*. "These are the best pictures of the original property that I could find." They showed the Victorian as it was being constructed. I even saw the start of the foundation for the carriage house. No tunnels, though. Yet. "Caruthers Wilson bought the property in 1874 as a family farm. Later, when motor cars replaced horse-drawn carriages, the family converted the carriage house into a whiskey distillery."

She showed me pictures of the red brick distillery in its heyday, with old-fashioned delivery trucks loaded with barrels.

"Evidently, the Southern Spirits brand was pretty popular," Melody said. "I was talking to Jeanie at the front desk and she said the library even had some of the original bottles as part of a display on Sugarland history a few years ago for the two-hundredth anniversary celebration."

I returned my attention to the article as Melody continued. "Prohibition hit. They turned the distillery back into a carriage house. Officially. But then they got busted for illegal operations."

"No kidding," I said, glancing over my shoulder, toward Frankie by the door.

Eyes wide, he shrugged. "Don't blame me."

Melody pulled out another article from her stack. "It says in this one that there was a famous jewel heist right about that time. There was speculation that mobsters from Chicago took the jewels down here and hid them when they were on a whiskey run."

"I thought gangsters didn't bury their money like pirates," I said, this time looking directly at Frankie.

"They don't," he insisted.

"What are you talking about?" Melody asked, trying to see where I'd focused my attention.

"It's nothing," I told her. Nothing she'd believe anyway.

The newest article showed trays and trays of cut gemstone jewelry, all of it in black and white, of course. It looked expensive as heck.

"Police at the time knew these gangsters were operating in the area, but they didn't know exactly where to look for the stolen gems. So they started checking out the places where the mob could have been running alcohol. That's how they learned about the illegal distillery at Southern Spirits."

"Actually, it was because Skinny Pete sold us out," Frankie grumbled. He leaned against the wall, his arms crossed over his chest, glaring.

"If anyone has facts they're not telling me…" I mouthed, looking at Frankie.

"Running booze there don't make a guy no expert on the poltergeist," he muttered. "My people don't like it any better than you do. My own brother barely had enough energy to cuss me out last night."

Poor guy. I couldn't imagine what caused that kind of a rift. And I doubted he wanted me asking.

Melody handed me another article. "Treasure hunters dug around the distillery after the feds shut it down, but nobody reported finding the stolen jewelry."

"Doesn't mean they didn't," I remarked. "Maybe someone found it and didn't tell anybody. Or maybe it's still there." Could our vandals be treasure hunters? It seemed plausible.

"If the stolen goods even came through town in the first place," Melody pointed out. "Anyway," she said, "Jonathan Wilson went to jail for mob-related activities and the family slowly went bankrupt. Even after Prohibition ended, they never could get the business to run at the same level as before." Melody turned to her stack. "And here's where it gets interesting." She laid another paper in front of me. "The family sold in 1968 to none other than Thaddeus Bolivar Steward, age twenty-two."

"The mayor?" I asked, trying to picture our white-haired mayor as a young man.

"His fiancée lent him the money to buy it," she explained. "Of course, instead of paying her back, he just married her. Thad had big plans for the property. He was going to start brewing again, revive the old brand. Whiskey was starting to grow more popular. But I suppose he was more of a politician than a businessman because once he got elected to city government, he focused on that. Word has it he always loved that property, though. It tore him up when Wydell and his uncle stole it out from under him. Supposedly, it was more the uncle than Ellis Wydell, but still…"

"Might as well despise them both?" I asked.

She gave me an all-too-innocent look. "Something like that."

"Why did the mayor sell?" I asked, walking over to the window, careful not to catch my skirt on any of the papers covering the table. "He has money. Certainly, he could afford to keep the property, especially if he enjoyed having it."

"Thad Steward married a Wydell," my sister said, as if that were a crime in itself. "Beau's cousin twice removed."

"Ooh." I stopped and spun a bit, causing the papers to flutter. "I forgot crazy Genevieve was part of the clan." They didn't exactly invite her to family Christmas.

Melody quirked a brow at me. "She took the property in the divorce. She's the one who sold it to Hale and Ellis."

"Ouch." I winced. "A woman scorned."

Melody rested her hands on her hips. "Are you listening to yourself?"

"Don't start," I warned her, "or I'm going to stop telling you about all of this."

She didn't appear to believe me. "Why did Ellis contact you?"

"I'm good," I told her.

Her eyes narrowed. "At what?"

Oh my word. My ears grew hot. "Not *that*."

She began gathering up the papers we'd scattered. "Last I heard he was dating some model."

I didn't like how my stomach twisted at the thought. "I don't know any models around here. Unless you count Suzie Conners, who walks in the Fourth of July parade every year, wearing outfits from her mom's prom dress shop."

Melody rapped a stack of papers on the table. "She's from New York. He met her while he was doing that FBI thing in Virginia. Word is she likes men in uniform. Probably out of uniform as well."

Fine. She could have him. "Look, I'm only helping him get his restaurant open," I said, trying to convince both her and myself. "I'm good at branding and graphic design," I added, really stretching it. Come to think of it, I really should try to sell Ellis graphic design services if he ever got this entertainment area off the ground.

"Mom's going to find out," Melody warned. "She has a sixth sense whenever one of us is about to screw up."

I wasn't messing up. Besides, "We're not telling anyone," I reminded her.

She handed me a red folder full of papers. "You'd think that would be enough to keep a secret around here, but it's not."

Didn't I know it?

"This has copies of everything I've shown you so far," she said. "I'll keep digging here. I didn't have a chance to look into those burials you talked about."

"See if you can learn about any unusual architecture. Specifically," I cringed, "if there are any hidden passages or secret hiding spots."

She looked at me as if she could dissect me with her stare. "You are not just doing branding for that man."

"I love you," I said, in the most sincere way possible.

She closed her eyes for a moment. "I know I'm the worst one to be giving this kind of advice, but for the love of all that is holy, you need to think about what you're doing."

"I will," I promised her. "Starting now."

Like right now, I was thinking it would be a good idea to drop in on our mayor and learn his side of the story. And ask if he'd seen anything unusual at the former Southern Spirits distillery.

CHAPTER 14

I MADE MY WAY ACROSS THE square, toward city hall.

"Now that is one anatomically correct horse," Frankie said, chuckling as we passed the statue of Colonel Ramsey Larimore and his stud.

"Truly?" I asked. I couldn't stop myself from hazarding a look. I hated to admit it, but the gangster had a point.

Frankie had gone invisible somewhere to my left. It was disconcerting to say the least. "You doing okay?"

"I think those books relaxed me enough to take a little snooze."

"You didn't even read any of them."

He sighed, ignoring me. "If you need me, I'll be in the ether."

"Okay." I'd let him rest. Until tonight, at least.

The air inside the city hall building felt unseasonably cool, as if someone had cranked up the air-conditioning at the worst possible time. I rubbed at my arms, wishing for a sweater, as I checked a directory on the wall. The mayor's office was on the second floor.

My sandals clacked against the marble stairs, the mishmash in my bag rattling along with it. Heaven above. Where was my sense of Southern decorum? If I didn't know better, I'd think I sold it with my grandmother's antique fainting couch.

I slowed, smoothing my hair, trying to exhibit an air of professional calm as I approached the door with hand-painted gold letters that read Mayor Thaddeus Bolivar Steward III. I hoped he had the decency not to assume too much based on where he'd seen me this morning.

Nancy Tarkington sat at the outer desk, as she had for the past three decades. She wore her auburn hair short, paired with diamond-chip earrings and a fall sweater.

She braced a black office phone against her shoulder while she wrote out an incident report. "Yes, Mr. Lemon. I agree. Those teenagers should not have positioned your garden gnomes like that. Yes. I do believe I've heard that is in the *Kama Sutra*. No, I don't know what page."

She wheeled her chair over to one of the massive file cabinets and pulled out a yellow folder packed with paperwork. "Just tell Mrs. Lemon the gnomes were wrestling," she said, stuffing the report inside. "I'm sure there is a nonviolent solution, but I don't see how the mayor can help. Nevertheless, I'll put it on file immediately." She held the phone away from her ear. "Oh my. I'm losing the connection. Have you tried calling the police? They filed a report as well? I'm so glad," she said, before she swung around in her chair and dipped a finger down onto the hang-up button. "Whoops."

The smile on her face faded when she saw me standing there. I tried not to fidget. People saw me differently now, even those who should know better.

It would pass.

It had to.

"Hi, Mrs. Tarkington," I said, with a bit more cheer than necessary.

At least one thing hadn't changed. I found it impossible to call the woman by her first name. Growing up, my mom would have boxed my ears for addressing adults by their given names. Mrs. Tarkington attended our church and used to play bridge with my mom every Tuesday afternoon. I'd climbed trees with her daughter, Callie, and tried not to lose my shoes in the creek every time I'd visited.

Mrs. Tarkington frowned slightly, as if she were trying to figure out exactly what to do with me. I pretended not to notice.

"How's Callie doing?" I asked. We'd lost touch when I went to college and she moved to Atlanta.

Mrs. Tarkington played with the overlarge, Home Shopping Network-style ring on her right hand. "I'm sure she thinks about you, Verity. We all do. Bless your heart."

It seemed that was the best I was going to get, at least for now. Rather than make her more uncomfortable, I stated my business. "I'm here to see the mayor."

"He's not here," she said, dismissing me.

She busied herself gathering papers on her desk, rearranging them, no doubt wishing her phone would ring again, even if Mr. Lemon decided to call back.

I'd heard most of what people said about me after the Incident. That I was out of control, a manipulative gold-digging fool. That I didn't appreciate what the good Lord had given me. That I'd used my womanly wiles to sway the prince of Sugarland.

As if boobs in a push-up bra wielded some kind of magic powers.

Maybe I could have handled things better. In fact, I know I could have. But I was no PR expert, and I'd been heartbroken at the time. Nobody's perfect, and if you wanted to get right down to it, I was probably a lot less perfect than most people. But I did my best.

I couldn't spend all day trying to change Mrs. Tarkington's opinion of me. I still had a job to do, so I pressed on. "Do you know when Mayor Steward will be back? I'd like to talk to him about a property he used to own."

Mrs. Tarkington tensed, as if she feared I'd park myself in the outer office and wait. "He'll most likely be gone all day," she said, searching through her immaculate pen drawer for something that evidently was not a pen—or she would have found it lined up with the half dozen already there.

The door behind her clicked open and out stepped the snowy-haired man that, in my youth, I had sworn was the real Santa Claus. He'd grown even more round over the years, as if he were auditioning for the part. He kept his white beard clipped short and wore a gray suit with a white shirt, a tie with pumpkins on it, and gold cuff links.

"Hello there." He moved slowly, leaning heavily on the walking stick he'd been using for a few years now, ever since his old Vietnam War injury started acting up again.

Mrs. Tarkington flushed with embarrassment.

I was just grateful I wouldn't have to come back.

Our encounter this morning had embarrassed me. Before that, the last time I'd seen the mayor, I'd thanked him for his service and my coffee had gone cold while he told me stories about the men he fought with. He'd been kind to me in the middle of a diner where many might not have even passed me the salt shaker, and I was grateful.

I met him halfway around Mrs. Tarkington's desk. "I'm so glad to catch you here, sir," I said, shaking his hand.

He smiled and adjusted his glasses. "Has anyone ever told you how much you resemble your sister?"

Even if I'd had black hair and twelve tattoos, I would have agreed. "All the time."

He pressed against his cane and reached with his other hand to steady himself on the wall. "I was expecting your sister. Melody drops by with the minutes from the Sugarland Heritage Society meetings. I keep them all. They're planning an antique quilt display at the senior center. You could join, you know."

"I've been a little busy lately," I told him.

"So I've seen," he commented.

I let it go. I didn't owe him an explanation for this morning. Although if it meant he'd answer a few questions, I'd offer to stitch him a king-size Irish Swag Bohemian Bell quilt. With my toes.

"Can I talk to you?" I asked. "I only need five minutes of your time. This does have to do with town heritage," I added, sweetening the pot.

"Of course," he said, leading me back into his office. "I need to sit down anyway. How's your mother?"

"She's great," I told him, checking out his office. It was smaller than I would have expected for an eleven-term mayor. He'd certainly had the time to build himself some fancy digs if he'd wanted them.

Framed photographs jammed the walls, many of them black-and-white prints that showed Sugarland's early development. Other, more recent pictures showed Mayor Steward posing with prominent citizens, church groups, and school kids. I probably knew everyone in those pictures—if they'd been born in the last fifty years, at least.

He had two more canes leaning up against the wall. One had been done up in red, white, and blue stripes with a brass eagle-head handle. The other was metallic toned, stylized to look like a sword, with a woven metal handle on top. He placed the walking stick he'd been using, a carved wooden cane with a brass handle in the shape of a trout, against the wall with the others.

"Is your mother coming back soon?" he asked, struggling a bit as he situated himself in a red leather tufted chair. "It's a real shame she felt she had to leave in the first place."

I took a less fancy, but quite comfortable chair across from him. "She's enjoying the new RV," I said, as if she were the child. I felt a twinge of guilt at that. She had every right to live her life the way she wanted. She'd certainly been supportive of me. "I think Mom's down along the Gulf Coast this week. Pensacola." In fact, I was one hundred percent certain. She'd been there since June.

Chances were the mayor knew as well, if he'd talked to Melody. He didn't need the conversation. He was trying to make me feel at home. I used to take that kind of gesture for granted until some of the people I thought I knew began doing the opposite.

He leaned back in his chair, the leather crackling. "Your mamma was never one for politics," he said fondly, folding his hands over his ample stomach, "but your father went door to door for me on my first campaign. He was a good friend."

"I remember him telling me about that," I said, almost wishing we hadn't begun a whole new line of small talk. Normally I enjoyed sharing stories, even ones I knew quite well. It was what living and working in a town like this was all about—being seen as a person, someone to be remembered and cared about. I liked that he wanted to honor my father, who had died when I was in fifth grade. Only right now, I needed to talk about passageways and ghosts. About who might be sneaking around the old distillery.

So I launched right into it. "I'm so glad my dad helped you. And I'd love to chat more, but I actually came to you because I need your help."

The request lingered between us.

Perhaps it was the abrupt switch in topic or the fact that I'd barreled right over Sugarland etiquette, either way, I'd gotten his attention.

His focus sharpened. "What is it, my dear?"

I leaned forward. "I know you used to own the Wilson's Creek property." If my knowledge surprised him, he didn't show it. Then again, look where I was living. I pressed on, trying to figure out how to start the conversation without being so crass as to discuss Ellis Wydell or what had happened with the mayor's divorce. That would shut him down for sure.

I really should have thought about this before I brought it up.

It felt awkward, but I gave the gentlest summation I could. "I was hired as a…consultant on the new renovation there—"

It didn't work.

His breath came in even puffs, like an idling freight train. "You went to work for Ellis Wydell," he said, as if I'd set fire to the square.

"Yes," I admitted. "I ran into trouble last night. Bad."

His expression changed as a realization dawned over him. "Did he hurt you?" the mayor asked, horrified.

"Wait. No. That's not what I meant—"

His face flushed and he appeared flustered. "My dear child, if this is something you're afraid to go to the police about, we can go directly to the chief." He reached across the desk, as if to take my hand. "I'm so very honored you felt you could come to me. Your daddy would be proud, too."

Why did he keep bringing my dad into this? "It's not like that," I said quickly. "Ellis has treated me fine. Better than fine." My ears heated and I pushed past the skepticism I saw. "I know it's crazy to work for him after what happened with Beau, but he's paying me well and heaven knows I need the money if I want to keep my grandmother's house."

"Oh dear." The mayor ran his hands along the arms of his chair.

"What I wanted to talk to you about," I said, hoping I still had his attention, "are some strange goings-on at the old carriage house. We had an intruder last night. I think he wanted to tear up the place. It was really scary."

He rubbed his fingers along the chair arms, his chin tucked back. "That Wydell boy is with the police. He should be able to handle it."

When he put it that way, I almost felt silly for stopping by. Damn. This conversation wasn't going the way I wanted and I had no clue how to turn it around. In a minute, the mayor would remember he was terribly busy and I'd get left out in the cold.

"The place is also haunted," I said, before I could change my mind.

"What?" he sputtered. "Are you daft?"

In for a penny, in for a pound. "You never saw any ghosts in the carriage house?" I pressed.

He looked at me like I was crazy. "Absolutely not."

"So the people who owned the property before you never said anything about a tragic event occurring there? Something that might cause a haunting?"

He opened his mouth. Closed it. "My dear, I don't have time for such nonsense. I think you'd better leave. I have a lot of work to do."

"I'm sorry. Forget about ghosts for a minute. I came to you because I want to learn more about who might be vandalizing the site. My sister is helping me research," I said, throwing him a bone. "She said something about treasure hunters looking for an old stash of jewelry on the property, and I thought that might be related to the damage we've found."

"Melody is involved?" he asked. "Don't you get her in trouble." He ran a hand over his chin.

"What kind of trouble?" I asked him. "Did treasure hunters disturb the property when you owned it, too? Were they dangerous?"

"Sakes alive. I don't know what I should tell you."

"The truth," I urged. "Please don't hold back. I'm going to be at the property tonight, and I'd feel better if I knew everything you do."

"I don't like being put in that position," he said, crossing his hands over his ample stomach. He leaned back. I felt about six inches tall as he studied me. "All the same, I won't let you go in blind." He rocked slightly, the springs on his chair squeaking, as if he were buying time to decide how much he should tell me. He cleared his throat. "You realize the Wydells have a lot of power in this town. So I'd appreciate it if you didn't tell anyone we discussed this."

"Believe me, I understand." He probably did as well. I'd heard his divorce was messy, although he'd never made his dissatisfaction known in public.

He'd left the sideshow to yours truly.

The mayor pressed his lips together. "Here's the rub: there have been problems on that property from the get-go. Mind you, I'm not talking about anything as outlandish as ghosts." He shifted uncomfortably. "Have you found the tunnel in the cellar?"

"Yes," I said, surprised. "I suppose it's been dug out for years."

He let out a huff. "The thing nearly came down on me in '72. Yes," he said, when he saw my shock. "I thought it might be a fun diversion for the tourists and the locals, a little bit of Sugarland underground history. According to some old plans, it goes all the way to the main house. But the entire structure is unstable." He frowned. "It's certainly not worth getting killed over."

"There must be more to it than that," I told him. "Someone's been excavating down there."

He seemed surprised. "If your vandals are in there, Mr. Wydell might be liable for a lot more than damage. No. Lock that place up and throw away the key. Anyhow, your real concern with the treasure hunters is the spot overlooking the river."

"No kidding. I haven't been back there."

"It's probably as hazardous as that tunnel. There are cliffs back there and unstable rock. That's shale. It breaks off in layers. You don't know how solid the rock under your feet is going to be. Do you understand me? That's very important. It's dangerous."

"I got it." And it made me distinctly uncomfortable. "What makes you think anything's back there?"

He was slow to answer. "I found a brooch once," he said non-committally. "This delicate thing with a bright red ruby in the middle. It was in a leather bag stuffed into an alcove in the cave on Wilson's Point."

I hadn't even been aware of a cave. "Is that where you saw most of the digging?"

He nodded, rueful. "Figured I'd try my luck, too," he admitted. "But it was treacherous and dumb and I'm wiser now."

"Believe me," I said, "I'm not one to take unnecessary chances, either."

He drummed his fingers on the table. His sunken eyes sparkled. "I have to admit, that brooch was fun to find. I gave it to Genevieve for a birthday present. She didn't appreciate the fact that I basically 'found it in the woods,' as she said. Then again, we were always very different." He stilled, growing serious. "But now you're going to go back there and I might have just made things worse."

"You've allowed me to make an educated decision. I appreciate that." I was a big girl. I could handle it.

He obviously didn't share my confidence, but he didn't press it further. He settled back in his chair. "Yes, the Wilson's Point Cave. That's where I saw most of the digging and where I found that brooch." He reached up, as if he could see it and pluck it out of the air. "The bag was brown, caked with dirt. I almost didn't even see it."

"And that was it? You left the trespassers to the rest?"

He chuckled. "No, I dug. I spent quite a few Saturdays out there. I goofed around when I should have been fixing the property up. But I didn't find anything else. Other than a busted ankle when I nearly fell off the cliff." He smiled, remembering. "Then my career set sail, my bum leg got worse, and I didn't go back there at all. Just didn't have the time."

"Where is the cave? Melody could look it up," I reminded him, "but it would be easier to hear it from you."

He gave me a long look. Yes, I was strong-arming him again, and he knew it.

"Perhaps you're the one who belongs in politics," he said. The accusation sounded friendly, but I could feel the ice underneath.

He drew his fingers in circles over the desktop. It was clear the man could not be rushed. "Thing is," he said, glancing up at me, "if there's a stash of jewelry—and there might not even be, but if there is—it's not in a good spot or someone would have found it by now." He waited until I acknowledged the warning. Then he surprised me. "If you go down, it's safer to walk along the left side of the overhang. Also avoid the shale ledge near the leaning juniper bush, if that's still there. It's unstable. It might have fallen down the cliff already."

"I'm going to write this down," I said, reaching for my bag.

"I'll draw it out for you," he said, pulling a sheet of paper from his top drawer. "I'll block out the dangerous parts as I've experienced them." He grabbed the gold desk pen from its holder and pointed it at me. "That doesn't mean they're the only spots to avoid, and it doesn't mean I approve of what you're doing." He put pen to paper. "I'll also show you where most of the digging's been and where I found the brooch." He made bold lines across the page, filling them in with a fairly detailed sketch. "The only thing I ask is that you don't share this with Ellis. If anybody's going to find another bit of treasure, I want it to be for you and your grandma's house, not some damned Wydell."

"Thanks," I said, meaning it.

"I hope I'm doing the right thing." He drew a cliff face and the trail down to it. He made the cave and drew a circle near the upper left and wrote something next to it. "See that? That's my chicken scratch. It says brooch." Then he made a series of x's all around. "These are where I found evidence of digging and where I poked around, too." I noticed he marked the shale cliff overlooking the site.

"You didn't find anything else on the land? Not a belt buckle or a button?" Anything like that might offer a decent clue as to where the gangsters had gone.

"Nothing." He slid the paper across the desk at me. "If you see any strangers on the property, you avoid them. It's an isolated piece of land and you don't know what some of these people are willing to do."

"I understand," I said. Then I reached out on a limb. "I'm sorry you had to sell the place. It seems like a really neat property."

He gave a wry smile. "The truth is, I didn't spend as much time out there as I'd hoped. It was one of those good ideas that fell by the wayside."

"Ellis really does have some impressive plans for the place," I told him, hoping he could at least see value in the new ownership.

"I saw the permits," he said wistfully. "Don't feel bad. I had my chance." He straightened in his chair. "It was fun when I was young, when I first got married." He leaned his elbows on the desk. "I fought one too many zoning restrictions and ended up in politics. I'm glad Genevieve took the Wilson's Creek property instead of the house in Palm Springs. I led her to believe it would hurt me more." He sighed, gazed down at the desk, and suddenly found interest in his fingers. "I thought I didn't care, but talking to you now, I do find I regret the loss. Life takes funny turns."

"You've certainly done plenty of other things," I said in the understatement of the year.

We all had our choices to make.

He pounded a palm on the wood. "Ah. Well. It's good for the

town if someone is doing something with the property. Even if it's one of those bloodsuckers." He cringed and I followed his gaze to the slightly open door.

"I don't think anybody's out there," I told him.

The corners of his mouth tugged up. "You can never be too careful."

He folded the map in half and slid it over the table to me.

"I appreciate your time, and this," I said, slipping it into my bag.

"I'm glad to help you, sweetheart." He stood when I did, a little unsteady as he went for his cane with the trout handle. He situated it in his hand, fingers shaking. "If I was twenty years younger, I might go barreling down the hillside with you. These days, I'm glad just to wake up in the morning."

"You don't look a day over sixty," I told him.

He laughed at that. Yet all too soon, he grew serious again.

He pressed his lips together as he regarded me. "I don't want to preach, but I will. Watch out for that Wydell boy. In fact, keep guarded against that entire family. You already know they have it out for you. They are mean, and they stick together. Trust me. I know."

"I do, too," I said.

He pushed the door open all the way and lowered his voice. "Also, don't mind the Nancy Tarkingtons of the world."

Embarrassment trickled through me, for myself or for her I wasn't sure. "You heard?"

He didn't give an inch. "My leg might be shot. My eyes could be better. But my brain and my ears work fine. I've seen a lot over the years and I can tell you with certainty—this too shall pass."

He seemed utterly convinced, and for that, I was grateful. "You're a good man, Mayor Steward."

He passed his cane to his other hand and reached out to shake my hand. The old man's grip was firm, even if his skin felt soft and paper-thin.

"You're a good girl, Verity Long." He gave my hand an extra

squeeze. "Your grandma would be really proud of the way you're taking care of her house."

It touched me that he understood in that way. Of course, he loved this place as much as I did. "I'm glad I stayed in Sugar-land."

His eyes twinkled and his mouth curved into a smile. "Me too."

CHAPTER 15

AFTER MY TALK WITH THE mayor, I figured I'd better be on top of my game. And so I made a quick stop before continuing on to the Wilson's Creek property. Yes, I'd be a bit late to meet Ellis, but he'd forgive me when he saw what I had. I couldn't help but smile. I hoped he liked surprises.

This one fit neatly into the trunk. Well, as long as I smushed my assorted bags, catalogues, and coupon books to the side and tossed my jumper cables in the backseat.

I slid into the land yacht and stowed my hemp bag on the floor of the passenger side.

"You doing okay, Frankie?" I asked. He hadn't bugged me much when I talked to Melody, or at all when I spent time with the mayor. "Frankie?"

I half expected him to shimmer into focus, sitting on the seat next to me. He didn't.

I supposed I should be glad he was resting up in the ether. I hoped it was comfortable.

The urn in my bag rattled as we bounced over the older, rougher roads south of Main. Thick, mature trees lined the road. The neat, bungalow-style houses along Magnolia Street had stood since the early 1900s. I loved the wide variety of styles and personal touches as well as the inviting porches. No two were alike.

I fiddled with the radio as the town gave way to country roads and farms.

"Are you with me?" I asked Frankie as we turned right onto the drive.

Silence.

There were times when I didn't mind him quiet. Believe me. But this had me worried. I needed him tonight.

The old brick carriage house hunkered under gray skies as I pulled up. Perhaps it looked more ominous because I knew what resided there. My fingers tightened on the steering wheel. If I couldn't see the spirits lingering on the property, if I had no warning before a poltergeist attacked, it could get ugly.

Ellis sat on the front steps, taking a break, and oh my—he looked filthy. His gray T-shirt stuck to his chest and arms, and a layer of dust coated him from head to toe. A construction helmet lay at his feet and his hair spiked up like he'd been rubbing out a serious case of hat head. I did a double take when I saw his gun holstered at his side, but I supposed he couldn't be too careful.

I parked next to his black Jeep and put on a brave face as I slammed my car door shut.

"Tough day at the mine?" I asked, going for a little levity.

He grinned and poured lemonade from a round cooler. "I was excavating the tunnel."

My chest pinched at the thought. "I'm glad you're okay. Did you find anything?"

"Stale air, rocks," he said. "I got closer to the cave-in. It looks old."

"You shouldn't go down there," I said, trying to think of the best way to bring up Mayor Steward's warning. And his revelation about the cliffs.

So I went behind your back and talked to the previous owner of the property...

"Want some?" he asked, holding out an empty glass for me. When I hesitated, he went ahead and poured. "Homemade from the diner," he said, pressing the cool glass into my hand. It was a genteel kind of offer, a very Southern one, even if it came from a beat-up cooler leaning against the crumbling porch. "I also grabbed us some cold chicken," he added. "Since dinnertime's coming up."

My stomach growled at the thought. I hadn't eaten anything but granola bars and Life Savers all day. "You're spoiling me here," I told him, embarrassed that he'd done all of it, and that I liked it.

Of course, I couldn't get used to it. I was about to torpedo the goodwill we'd built.

I took a sip of lemonade. It tasted sweet and refreshing with the right amount of tart.

"Maybe I just don't want you to quit," he said, glancing at me as he tightened up the cooler lid.

I tried not to read too much into that. Last night had been a disaster by all accounts. Of course Ellis wanted to stay and protect his property.

I needed to tell him about what could be buried out back. He deserved my honesty and he also needed a true picture of who could be poking around.

"Listen," I said, placing my glass down. "I did some investigating on my own. I stopped and talked to the mayor on the way over here."

"Thad Steward?" Ellis's shoulders tensed as he turned to face me. "I asked you to keep our arrangement private."

"He's not a gossip. And we need to know more about what's happening here."

He pressed his lips together. "And you think he's the one to tell you."

"He drew me a map of things to look at today," I said. "And he told me not to show it to you. I don't think he's made peace with your family yet," I added guiltily.

He flinched at that. "Who else did you tell?"

I drew back, offended. That was assuming a lot. Although I couldn't get too miffed because he was right.

"I told my sister, Melody," I said, trying to make it sound as innocent as possible. Who was I kidding? It was innocent. I didn't share his story around town for kicks and giggles. I was looking for answers, same as Ellis. "I thought someone in my family ought to know where I am, just in case something happens. Besides, she did some research at the library and learned that you may have goodies from a 1920s jewel heist buried out back by Wilson's Cave."

He stiffened. "I know where that is."

"The mayor confirmed it. He also told me about the tunnel you were in and said it's been in danger of collapsing for years."

He made a dismissive noise. "The old man hadn't been down there in decades, I guarantee. Thad can barely walk a flight of stairs."

"So you think it's grown more stable over time?" I'd rather be safe than sorry when it came to cave-ins. "There's a ghost down there asking for help. Another trying to block us from the place."

"And the poltergeist in the kitchen," he finished for me.

"That about sums it up," I said.

Ellis sighed. "We should stick to the kitchen tonight. I need you to solve my vandalism problem first."

"I agree," I told him. "But your ghost always comes after dark." And Frankie hadn't even lent me his power yet. I hadn't specifically asked the gangster, but from what I'd experienced, it appeared he had more power at night as well. "In the meantime, we need to explore every lead we have. It'll give us the best chance to figure out what's going on around here."

He shook his head. "You're not going to let this go, are you?"

Of course not. "Maybe there's another underground tunnel from the kitchen to the cliffs out back. It can't hurt to check it out while we still have some daylight left. Come on," I said, standing. "I have a surprise for you."

A grin flashed across his features. "Lady, you're a walking, talking surprise."

He had me there. "You find it charming. I know you do." I drew the keys from my pocket. "You're going to like this even better."

He followed me to the car. "I can't wait," he said with a touch of irony as I popped open the trunk.

Maybe this would wipe the smile off his face. I presented my find with the panache of a *Price is Right* model. "This is the Garrett ATX ultimate multifrequency detector. It has a military-grade design, advanced pulse-induction technology, and the new DD coil design for enhanced sensitivity."

"It's a metal detector," he said, a little underwhelmed considering what he had in front of him.

"It's the George Clooney of metal detectors," I corrected. "I borrowed it from Lauralee."

Her husband made a hobby of hunting for civil war memorabilia, things like belt buckles and lead bullets and even the occasional pocket watch.

Of course he'd needed the Garrett ATX metal detector. Well, Lauralee hadn't been so happy about that. She'd thought the military-grade design and the "deep seeker" package with a super-steady handgrip was overkill.

For my purposes, it was ideal.

"This can search up to twenty feet deep," I told Ellis. He needed to get how impressive this was. "We can also submerge it in up to ten feet of water."

"I sure hope we don't need to do that," he said.

"I hope we don't either, but it's nice to know we can," I said. "If we don't get any pings, then we'll know the cliffs are a bust. We can focus on hunkering down in the carriage house and we'll just cross our fingers that the poltergeist attacks us tonight."

Ellis gave me the once-over. "That's very practical of you." He held the metal detector for me as I closed up my car and slung my bag over my shoulder. "I can't believe I'm doing this."

"You'll see," I said.

⌀

We headed for the woods at the back of the carriage house. The trees and shrubs grew tall there, wild with tangled blackberry vines and undergrowth. I could hear the river churning far below. The drop-off had to be steep. And close.

"I'm going to have to fence this off before I open," Ellis said, carrying the metal detector easily as we navigated the uneven ground. "The trails down to the river are downright dangerous."

"I'll stick close," I promised.

Movement rattled the woods to the left and I jumped as a man emerged from the brush. He wore a brown jacket and jeans, and seemed to be as startled by us as I was by him.

"Harry," Ellis said, his voice warming.

The handyman appeared even grungier up close.

Harry tilted his head up, frowning. "Hey," he said, his voice rusty, as if he never used it.

He could have been handsome if his face weren't gaunt and unshaven. He wrapped his jacket around his body and brought his shoulders up.

"My name is Verity. I'm working here too," I said, smiling even though he had a wildness to his eyes that made me distinctly uncomfortable.

He gave a curt nod.

"We're heading down to the cliffs," Ellis said, as if he were having a conversation with a normal person and not some guy who looked like a wild mountain man. "If you've got a minute, I'd like if you could show us the best way down to Wilson's Cave."

Harry angled his head away. "I got glue drying. Got to put the tiles up now."

"We need five minutes," Ellis said.

The strange man's breath came harder. His eyes darted from side to side. "It'll dry. I'll have to scrape it." Panic tinged his voice.

"Hey," Ellis said. "No worries. Go take care of your gluing. We'll take the curved path, the one that washes out at the bottom."

Harry nodded in agreement and brushed past us.

I watched him go. That man was odd on top of strange. Truth be told, I found myself glad he didn't come along. Besides, if he had taken this job to dig up treasure on the side, he'd be hindering us instead of helping.

"Come on." Ellis led me to the break in the woods. "Don't let Harry get to you," he added under his breath. "He's a good guy."

We'd see.

I glanced back and saw him standing at the back of the carriage house, watching us. He frowned as I pushed through the opening in the brush.

Insects buzzed all around me. I batted back tree limbs and thorny bushes and scratchy parts of Lord knew what kinds of plants.

Maybe this wasn't such a good idea.

Think of it as a nature walk.

In the South's version of a jungle, on the edge of a cliff.

The hill sloped downward fast and I had to brace myself as the path curved sharply to the left. Railroad ties supported it along the sides, but some of those had fallen down the hill. The rest sagged under the tumbling weight of the trail.

"You okay?" Ellis asked as he waited for me to catch up.

"Yes," I said. "Of course." Bits of rock and earth dislodged under my feet as I moved slowly, carefully. A natural spring bubbled from the rock face next to me, spilling a steady trickle of water over the trail. What a lovely way to make it even more slippery and unstable. Go, nature.

I never could have dragged the metal detector down here by myself. "Wait," I said as Ellis pulled ahead. I stopped and pulled the mayor's map from my bag. His hastily drawn curve didn't at all accurately portray the steepness or danger of this trail. I hoped he hadn't underestimated the rest.

"Sorry," Ellis said, steadying himself against an ash tree. "It's harder to go slow."

"I'm going to forget you said that." I wiped the sweat from my forehead and shoved back the hair tangled in it. Leaves rustled in the trees and I felt the steady, low presence of *something*. "Do you feel that?" I could have sworn I sensed movement behind me, a chill in the air. But when I turned, I saw nothing. Only leaves, trees, and shadows.

And here I'd believed the mayor had been trying to scare me.

"We're almost there," Ellis said, encouraging me as we continued down.

The hillside grew steeper and I heard the bubbling of another stream farther down. It emptied out into a pool near a rock face below. I could see the glistening water through the thinning leaves on the trees.

A leaning juniper bush caught my eye. I used it to brace myself and peered over the slippery shale overhang. Below, I saw a larger overhang on the edge of a steep cliff. Great.

"You can do it," Ellis said, reading the fear in my eyes, the stiffness in my movements as I picked my way down the rest of the trail. I wasn't cut out to be a mountain goat.

I leapt the last few feet to get it over with.

"Wilson's Cave," Ellis said, nudging the nose of the metal detector toward the small opening burrowed into the hillside we'd tackled. I realized with a sinking in my gut that the opening stretched about five feet across and three feet high. There couldn't be a lot of hiding places in a space that small. I found the flashlight on my keychain and shone it inside. The dull gray rock arched back about eight feet, narrowing as it went, until it ended in a cluster of leaves and debris.

"It looks like something may have built a nest back there," I said, panning the light over the sticks and twigs.

"Bobcat," Ellis said with certainty.

The light in my hand jumped as I whirled to glare at him.

"Kidding." He grinned.

Yes, well, as a police officer, he might be good at joking around in serious situations, but I found my nerves to be a bit prickly at the moment. "I need the metal detector," I said.

It felt weird to be five feet from the edge of a thirty-foot drop-off. But we'd made it down here and I'd gotten us the equipment we needed to see if there was still any truth to the rumor of treasure. I had to think it would have been picked clean by now.

Metal detectors had been around for decades.

Of course, I had the monster of them all.

Ellis wiped the sweat from his forehead as I powered it up. His lips quirked. "And here I thought you weren't a Ghostbuster. That looks about as complicated as a proton pack." He moved closer. "You need help?"

"Lauralee showed me how to work it," I said, adjusting the sensors, calibrating like an expert, "plus it's light enough for me." At about thirty pounds it would wear on me eventually, but he didn't need to know that. "Let's start here," I said, hovering over a spot of dirt and rock at the entrance. It didn't look at all special.

We'd see soon enough.

"You're enjoying this," he said, giving me a lopsided look as I pulled out a pair of deluxe submersible headphones.

"You're right," I said. No harm being honest about it. I'd done too much worrying lately—about the house, about my finances, about a ghost trapped on my property. It felt good to have a problem that I could actually do something about.

Either there was treasure here or there wasn't. I liked the certainty. And the idea of buried loot.

I swept the round sensor coil over the entrance to the cave. Nothing. I marked the searched area with a swipe of my foot in the dirt. I backed up a step to make sure I had the whole entrance covered before we moved inside. With uniform precision, I made another pass.

Ping.

"Ha!" I said, admittedly loud because, after all, I was wearing headphones. I swept the scope of the detector over the rocky soil. *Ping.* It grew louder. I moved the scope toward Ellis's work boots. *Ping.* And then up and then all the way to his pocket.

"Oh," he said, pulling out a pair of keys. "Wait," he added when he saw my disappointment. "I found this in the tunnel."

In his hand, he held a rusted decorative button shaped like a daisy.

I braced the detector against my leg and took the button from him, turning it over. "What is that? From the '60s or something?" I didn't think Victorian women wore trendy buttons.

"Exactly. Here," he said, retreating. "I'll get rid of this and anything else I still have in my pockets."

I watched him stash his things on the rock face behind us. "You can put it in my bag," I called to him.

Dang. He'd see Frankie's urn. I didn't feel like explaining why I carried it with me. While I was borrowing trouble, I also didn't like that my bag was only a few feet from the edge. But we couldn't have our stuff on us with the metal detector going. The narrow rock face made it impossible to do anything else.

I nudged the earphones back up and resumed my scan of the cave. I didn't imagine myself as any sort of expert, but I was thorough and that counted for a lot.

About six feet back, I was on my hands and knees, sweating, the heavy metal detector braced out in front of me when—*ping.*

I nearly jumped out of my skin.

Ping.

There was no mistaking it.

Ping.

I held still over the spot, just to hear it again.

Ping.

The depth gauge estimated its depth at less than a foot. "I've got something!" I set the metal detector aside and began digging with my hands.

"Let me help." Ellis drew the detector out of the cave and settled in next to me. He passed me a stick and started in with one of his own.

"Too bad we didn't think of shovels." I grinned, working hard, but not caring. Then my stick hit hard metal.

I gave a small shriek. We were both breathing hard as I reached into the hole and pulled out a round, flat object. Ellis shone the light on it and we both held our breath and saw...a penny.

"Oh my," I said, turning it over in my hand. The date read 1982, so it wasn't even a particularly old or interesting penny.

We dug at the hole some more and found nothing. I swept the

metal detector over it again. Nothing.

Ellis saw my disappointment. "Want me to take over?"

"Yes," I said, scrambling out of the cave, needing some air. I'd never thought of myself as claustrophobic, but these tight spaces were wearing on me.

Perhaps the penny was a marker for an old and valuable jewelry stash. Or maybe it was only a penny.

I looked out over the woods, listening to the river churning below. I didn't dare walk close enough to the cliff edge to see it. The back of my neck prickled. Quickly, I glanced behind, to the path leading up the hill. It stood empty.

"Nothing else in the hole," Ellis called out. "I'll check out the rest of the cave."

"Good," I called to him, folding my arms over my chest. I couldn't escape the notion we were being watched.

I took a step toward the path, then another. My throat felt tight. "Anybody there?" I called.

Trees rustled above, but not a soul—living or dead—revealed itself.

If there was ever a time I could stand to have my gangster friend around, it was now.

"Frankie?" I asked as I caught sight of a gray image among the trees. My heart sped up. It could be nothing. Still, I didn't dare leave Ellis with his back exposed.

A hollow voice floated down, chilling as it settled over me. "Come."

I glanced back at the cave. "What do you want?" I called.

A sharp breeze rustled the woods, sending up a chorus of squawking black birds.

Ellis emerged from the cave, eight kinds of dirty. He saw me and his eyes narrowed. "What's wrong?"

"I think I see a ghost, up the path," I told him.

He froze, unsure of what to say.

Join the club.

"I don't know who it is," I said quietly. It had to be Frankie. He hadn't restored my ability to see other ghosts. Although I supposed a ghost with enough energy could manifest whenever it wanted to. I searched for it among the trees, but didn't see it anymore. Heaven knew I wasn't about to go up there and look for it.

I glanced back at Ellis. "What did you find in the cave?"

"Nothing," he said, carefully placing the Garrett ATX on the ground. "If there was a treasure, it's long gone."

Then the trees rustled and I saw our visitor clearly—Colonel Maker of Teddy Roosevelt's Rough Riders. My heart thundered in shock.

He beckoned me furiously.

It took a lot of energy to manifest. Whatever the colonel had to tell me, it must be important. I blew out a breath. "I've met this ghost," I said to Ellis. "Give me a second to go see him." I didn't know if he'd talk to me with Ellis around. Besides, now that Ellis was out of the cave, he could watch out for both of us.

I scrambled up the muddy trail. The colonel spoke to me now, frantically, but I couldn't hear what he said. His image faded at the edges and he appeared weaker than I'd seen him last.

"Hold on," I called to him. "I'm coming."

He grew more agitated, holding his hands out, screaming at me, his voice silent, his body turning to smoke before my eyes. Something bad was happening to him.

Cripes. He was fading. "Hey." I grabbed the leaning juniper bush as I pulled myself up onto the cliff face. "Calm down." I tried to spot the flicker of him in the trees. "Don't try to manifest. Just talk. I'll listen." Sweat trickled down my forehead. My body flushed. "Colonel?"

I felt a hard shove at my back. My legs went out from under me, and I screamed as I fell face-first off the path.

CHAPTER 16

I'D NEVER BEEN SO TERRIFIED as I hurtled down. I saw the stark horror on Ellis's face as he tried to catch me. I hit him with a bone-rattling crunch, taking him down with me onto the hard shale.

My muscles shook as I braced my arms and lifted myself to my knees, straddling him. I should have been crushed on impact.

He swore. "You okay?" He lay with his head in the dirt, staring up at the sky.

A startled, panicked laugh escaped me, as if his asking that were the funniest thing in the world. I knelt over him and took his cheeks in my hands. "I'm more worried about you." Carefully, slowly, I inspected his head for injuries, and when I found none, I contented myself to hold him a little longer, gently slicking the hair out of his face.

He leaned into my hands, wincing. "You're heavier than you look."

I refused to take offense at his snark at a time like this. He'd broken my fall. He'd most likely saved my life.

"Somebody pushed me," I told him. I looked up at the cliff face above and saw no one, not even the colonel. It was a long way up from here. And then it hit me. "Somebody just tried to kill me."

"That's it. Let's get out of here." He groaned, attempting to shove himself to his feet.

"Wait. You could have a back injury," I said, trying to hold him down.

There was a blossoming spot of red on his cheek where he'd hit and his hands were bloody as he warded me off. "See?" he said, brushing past me, struggling to his feet. "I'm fine."

"That's debatable." He bled from scrapes on his cheek and chin, and I could see more blood seeping from his shoulder, staining his gray T-shirt that had gone from dirty to downright disreputable.

"I like how you handled that fall," he said, patting his hands over himself to check for injuries, completely ignoring me. "No crying, no hysterics."

"That comes later," I told him in all honesty.

He chanced a glance up at the path. "Stay put. I'm going to see who's up there."

"It's too dangerous," I said, following. "We should call the police."

He moved fast for someone who should be flat on his back, recovering. "I am the police."

There was that. "Then I'm coming with you." I went back to recover the metal detector, my bag, and Frankie's urn, and somehow managed to haul them up the cliff face, where I joined Ellis in his search. I slowed as I approached the spot where I'd been shoved, feeling distinctly uncomfortable even being there. I felt no more ghostly presence, no malice, just a lingering sense of unease that was wholly mine. This was no accident. Someone wanted me dead. A fall like that could have easily killed me. But since it hadn't, and whoever pushed me probably knew that... What if he'd gone back to get a weapon?

"I don't see anyone," Ellis said. His hair stood on end and he swayed where he stood. He shot me a look that challenged me to say a word about it. "They didn't leave anything behind, either."

"Let's get you back to the carriage house." From there, I'd wrestle him into my car if I had to. The man needed to be checked out at a hospital.

Besides, I didn't like being in these woods. We were too

exposed.

Ellis kept his gun out as we picked our way up the path. He made short forays into the wooded spots, looking for God knew what. The entire time, he didn't move his shoulder. And he kept bleeding.

"Stay with me," I said, looping both my arms around his good one. "This way I won't fall down the hill." He might have been too bullheaded to admit he needed help, but I knew he wasn't above being gallant.

I was right. He didn't argue. And as I held him tight, I felt him leaning into me for the first time. It was clear he hurt everywhere.

He gritted his teeth. "I've had worse."

"I'm sure you have." He swayed as we hit a particularly rough spot. "I'll let you stand on your own and be a badass if we see anyone you'd like to arrest. Or shoot."

"Thanks," he said.

I felt pretty good about that until I looked up at the rest of the hill. Sweet heaven. We were insane to try climbing that in our condition.

He worked to steady himself. "Maybe get Harry to help."

"No," I said, urging us both forward. For all we knew, Harry was the one who shoved me from behind. "We're going to take it one step at a time."

"So you saw a ghost," he said, forcing himself forward, probably trying to take his mind off the pain.

My shoulders and back ached. My thighs burned as we struggled up the path.

"The colonel," I explained. "You'd like him."

"Why?" he asked, his breath coming harsh. "Because I was in the military?"

"I didn't know you served." At least I didn't remember hearing. I felt vaguely guilty about that.

"Marines," he said automatically. "Back when you and Beau were in college. Mamma didn't brag about it because she didn't like her son going enlisted. Or serving at all."

I'd never stopped to think what it must be like to be raised by a woman like Virginia Wydell. I didn't think he'd want my sympathy, so I didn't say anything. I kept my focus on the hill as we trudged forward.

"The ghost," Ellis prodded. He'd obviously said more, but I hadn't heard the question. A cut on his hairline bled down over his ear. He either didn't notice or didn't care. He was too focused on me. His hazel eyes bored into me as he repeated his question. "What was the soldier ghost trying to protect you from?"

I thought back on the colonel's grim features, his soundless warning. "My attacker, maybe. I don't know." I wasn't sure of the colonel's motives, or who he was prepared to stand behind. At least I knew he'd been too weak to shove me.

But what I couldn't figure out is how I'd seen him in the first place. Frankie hadn't helped me; I didn't feel his energy. If the gangster had nothing to do with it, then the colonel must have gathered the energy to manifest by himself. I hadn't realized he was capable of that.

Ellis and I struggled forward until we reached the area behind the carriage house. We didn't see anyone, but I didn't want to chance a confrontation if Harry was our attacker. Ellis was in no shape for it, and I didn't know if I would be on my best day. We kept going, straight to my lifeboat of a Cadillac.

"This is old," Ellis mumbled, practically falling into the passenger seat. My limbs tingled, grateful to be relieved of Ellis's weight. But my heart pounded. We weren't out of the woods yet.

"Here." I adjusted him so he leaned against the headrest. "I'm taking us to the hospital."

"Ow," he muttered, closing his eyes.

"How bad does it hurt?" I asked, checking out his injuries.

He winced. "It's getting better."

I didn't see how. I gave him a shake. "No sleeping."

His eyes cracked open. "But you don't know how good it feels to sit down."

"Nope." I tossed my bag into the backseat and hurried around to the driver's side. I wouldn't feel better until we were safe and moving. "You have to stay awake."

He began shaking. I knew how he felt—punch-drunk on adrenaline.

I slid my key into the ignition. "I didn't drag you up a hill so you could crash on me now."

He swallowed, nodded, and closed his eyes again.

Dammit.

I didn't feel Frankie's energy leave me as I drove past the gates. He'd had nothing to do with this. The colonel was even stronger than I'd thought.

Wow. I pushed the radio button and hit the gas.

First things first. I had to see to Ellis.

I turned the volume up high and jabbed the button for 105.9 The Slam.

Rap music blared through the car.

Ellis jerked up in his seat, eyes wide. "What the hell?"

"Oh, good," I hollered sweetly. "You're awake."

"And I thought it hurt to catch you," he said as I turned down the volume and steered the car onto the main road.

"Nope," I said blithely, even though his bold-faced assessment unnerved me. "Saving me is the least of your problems tonight. Now you have to deal with me taking care of you."

He reached for the radio off button, but I swatted him away. "No. This will keep us going." We couldn't afford to relax until we got him to the hospital.

He shoved past me and switched it off. "My head can't take any more."

"Have it your way," I said, trying to sound as nonchalant as possible while I gripped the steering wheel. "Just don't bleed on my seat."

He huffed at that. "It's purple velvet," he said, as if that in itself was bizarre.

"Really?" I asked, acting surprised. "That's what you see? Because it's really tan vinyl."

For just a second, his shocked expression was priceless. Then he saw me chuckle. "Gotcha."

"You don't know who you're messing with," he said, the corners of his mouth tugging into a grin. I considered that a victory.

I laid on the gas, hoping to get pulled over. We could use a police escort. I didn't like the way his hands lay limp on his legs or how his head lolled against the seat.

What would have happened to me without Ellis there—it was too horrible to comprehend. Now he was paying for saving my skin.

I could almost see the wheels turning as he tried to phrase his next comment in his head. Good. That meant he was thinking, trying to stay alert.

From his expression, I could tell he hadn't lost his sense of amusement. Lord help us.

"Excuse me," he drawled, "but why are you driving this piece of shit?"

I barked out a laugh. Random and honest. I liked that. "Because it's *my* piece of shit," I said proudly. Believe me, there was something to be said for that.

He let out a huff. "God, I'm sorry. Did I offend you?" He leaned back in the seat. "I'm always offending people…Mamma can't stand it when I open my mouth in public. I just say what I think and usually it's the wrong thing."

I'd been in that boat a time or two. "Lucky for you, I'm not sensitive about my ride." As long as it got me from point A to point B. Besides, he was in immense pain and slaphappy. And, I had him talking. We needed to keep it up. I tossed him a playful glance. "While we're asking uncomfortable questions, tell me about your girlfriend in New York."

He winced, but this time I wasn't sure it had anything to do with his wounds. "I don't have a girlfriend. My mom keeps trying to set me up with this model." He cradled his left arm in his lap. "I can't stand her. She's plastic."

"Hmm," I mused. I wasn't letting him get off that easy. "Isn't there a movie about that? Some guy and his blow-up doll?"

"She's fake," he said on an exhale. "I like girls who are real," he said, glancing at me, "ones who know what they want."

"Good," I told him. "I want you to stay awake."

He gave a slight grin. "I am. I will," he said, readjusting his injured left shoulder, grimacing. "There's no telling what you'd do to me otherwise."

We sang Christmas songs for the rest of the way, to keep his energy up. He had a better voice than mine, which wasn't saying much. But, hey. We were in this together. We'd survive.

At the Tri-County Regional Hospital, he got to listen to a doctor tell us both how lucky we'd been. Evidently several people had died on those cliffs over the years. It didn't surprise me in the least.

Ellis was in worse shape than me. He'd taken the brunt of my fall. I had bruises and scrapes. He had scrapes on top of his bruises on top of his scrapes. He also had a sprained shoulder, a badly bruised tailbone, and possibly a mild head injury, one he claimed not to notice.

"You want me to call anyone?" I'd asked. I'd even deal with his mother if it meant he'd be more comfortable.

His answer had been a definitive no.

His reward for that was to be sent home with me. Well, to his home, not mine. I promised to take him there and to keep an eye on him. I owed him that much and more.

The ride to his place was quiet, which was fine with me. We both needed time to settle down. And when we arrived, he didn't complain as I opened the door and let him lean on me as he got out.

Ellis lived in a tidy bungalow on Magnolia Street, about a block away from Lauralee's house. I took his arm as I helped him up the stairs.

"Where are your keys?" I asked when we made it to the porch.

"In my pocket," he said, attempting to reach into his jeans.

"Let me," I said quickly, sliding my hand down into his left front pocket…and pretty much down his thigh. Maybe I should have thought this through.

He grew still. "Um, wrong pocket," he managed to choke out.

"Gotcha," I said with forced cheer. He was right-handed.

I steadied him and moved to the other side.

"I got it," he said, shoving his hand into his pocket, most likely enduring shattering pain so I didn't feel him up again. Great.

He inserted the key in the lock and pushed the door open. "You don't need to stay," he said, glancing back at me as I followed him inside. "It isn't part of your job."

This had stopped being about the job the minute I'd fallen down that cliff. "You helped me, now I'm helping you," I said simply.

"You're going to be the death of me," he muttered.

"That's the spirit," I told him.

Sure, if you'd asked me a week ago, I'd have sworn there was no way I'd voluntarily spend a red-hot minute in the company of Ellis Wydell, much less a whole night. But now? I'd learned a lot about him since then.

And, oh my goodness! Shock hit me as he flipped on the overhead light and I learned one more thing about Ellis. The man could *not* decorate.

His man cave looked as if a blind bear had outfitted it.

A black leather sofa rested against a white-painted wall. He had a black leather coffee table that doubled as storage. Either that or it was in the process of giving birth to a bunch of video game controllers hanging from their wires.

An immense TV hung on the opposite wall and that was it. Finito. As if the Y chromosome demanded absolutely nothing decorative or appealing be allowed in the room.

"Let's get you into bed," I told him, leading him past the empty dining area on the right. A card table and chairs stood in the small kitchen and the back bedroom contained only a basic black platform bed and nightstand.

"I'm sensing a theme," I said.

"What?" he asked. His voice stayed even, but the lines of his shoulders betrayed him. He was unsettled. He shifted away from me and toward the bed.

"Nothing." I was running off at the mouth. It didn't matter

what I thought of his hastily put together home. Or the fact that I'd be spending the night here.

The truth was, there was something incredibly intimate about being in his private space, where he slept, and I'd rather focus on anything but that.

His brother, my ex, had surrounded himself with the best—expensive furnishings, professionally decorated rooms. He had a large home and plenty of objects to fill it.

One of the last things Beau ever said to me was that he believed everything and every*one* could be bought for a price. Objects, people, women—you name it, they were all commodities to Beau. I was glad I'd slammed that door and never looked back.

I hadn't wanted to be owned. And I refused to be yet another thing for him to collect.

But Ellis was different.

I hadn't thought so at first, when he'd come to me with his offer. But now I understood. Ellis wasn't entitled. He was practical. And if anything, he didn't treat himself with the care he deserved.

He sat on the edge of the bed, his legs wide, his left arm in a sling and his right braced on his thigh, as if he'd run out of energy right there. "I'm fine now."

"Let me look at that cut on your forehead," I said. They'd cleaned it at the hospital, but it had opened up again.

"No," he said automatically.

"Wasn't asking," I said as I gently lifted the bandage away.

He shifted in his seat, but didn't argue anymore. I located a first aid kit in his bathroom and used it to clean and redress the wound.

"You finished?" he asked as I stepped away from him.

"I am for now, but don't worry. I'll find new ways to torture you," I teased.

Most likely without even trying.

His shirt clung to his chest, stiff and beyond dirty. It wouldn't be a picnic to sleep in those jeans, either. I swallowed down the flutter in my stomach. "Do you need me to help you undress?"

I tried to consider the logistics of sliding his gray T-shirt over his broad shoulders without disturbing his sling and not on the fact that I'd just asked if I could help him take his clothes off.

For a split second, it appeared as if he'd agree. He drew in a sharp breath. Then he let it out as if I'd punched him in the gut. "No," he said, his voice deepening, as if he were imagining what it would feel like to have my hands on him.

I felt myself flush.

"I'm not asking so I can ogle," I clarified. I wouldn't mind seeing his body under other circumstances, but in this case I was asking because I cared. It's not like anything could happen between us. He was my ex-fiancé's brother. I wasn't supposed to like him, much less touch him.

All the same, I was a little relieved when he scooted back to lie down on the bed.

Maybe I'd been out of line to ask. I wasn't always the smoothest around men. With our history, I probably should have been more cautious. But it bothered me, deeply, that he felt uncomfortable letting anyone truly help him.

Yes, I hated asking for help, too, but even I knew when to buck up. If I acted as stubborn as Ellis, sweet little Lucy and I would be in an apartment by the railroad tracks by now.

"Call me if you need me," I said. "I'll be out on the couch." His eyes were closed, his breathing even, as if he'd already dismissed me.

I turned to go.

"Verity," he said.

I paused in the doorway. "Yes?"

The light from the dresser lamp spilled over the bruises forming on his jaw and cheek. "You can fall on me anytime."

I hoped he didn't mean that literally. "Thanks," I said, before slipping out into the hall.

☾

That night, I checked on him every hour or so. I was too keyed up, too achy to get much rest.

He slept soundly, on top of the covers. He didn't even take off his shoes. It puzzled me until I saw the empty pill envelope from the hospital. He hadn't even asked for a glass of water.

I tried to locate a quilt for him, but found his linen closet empty. The top of his closet held a few shoe boxes. Dust bunnies lived under the bed. Where did he keep his things?

Did he even have much of anything?

It also bothered me that he hadn't called any of his buddies. As far as I knew, he hadn't even reported the assault to the police. He'd simply let me bring him home and collapsed in a very sparse house.

I found a few Tylenol in his bathroom and washed them back with a glass of water. I'd never met anyone so powerful, so in control of himself, who was also so alone. I wanted to do something about that. It was hard to figure out what, but I wanted to at least try.

I didn't sleep well for thinking, and besides, his couch felt harder than the ground. I slipped out shortly before sunrise and went home to go gather a few things. I wanted to take a shower at my place anyway.

When that was done, I changed into my purple dress, the one I'd worn on that first night. Good thing I'd had the sense to run laundry the other day.

By 7:00 a.m., I'd returned with three bags full of supplies and Lucy. She'd been so excited to see me, I didn't have the heart to leave her again. I'd been so busy, she'd hardly gotten any attention in the last few days. And when she gave me those wide, hopeful skunk-eyes, I just had to scoop her up and bring her along.

Ellis was still asleep, but that didn't matter. Little Lucy crawled right up next to him and snuggled in tight. Sometimes, animals just *know* when you need a little extra TLC.

I paused, admiring the scene in front of me. Ellis had barely moved from where I'd left him last night. I laid my grandma's quilt over him and Lucy, and went to start the bacon on the stove. Thank goodness the Circle K was open twenty-four-seven.

We hadn't quite gotten around to that chicken last night.

I was cracking eggs into a frying pan when I heard him stir. Then he let out a yell.

The man moved quick because by the time I turned around, he was standing in the doorway behind me, clutching the frame. "There's a skunk in my bed!"

I smiled. "That's just Lucy." She toddled out after him and I flipped her a tiny sliver of bacon. She gobbled it right up.

Ellis ran a hand over his face. He looked cute all morning rumpled.

"I know I hit my head, but this is ridiculous," he said, eyeing the skunk as she sniffed at a chair leg. "And what are you doing in my kitchen?"

I ignored the ire in his voice. Some folks just weren't morning people. His hair was mussed, his shirt even more wrinkled than before, but he looked good. He had his color back, and that sparkle of interest lit his eyes.

"Lucy likes to cuddle, and I'm making breakfast," I said, turning back to the stove. "How do you like your eggs?"

"Scrambled," he said, easing into the room, as if he couldn't quite believe what he was seeing. I didn't see what the big deal was. It was only breakfast. He paused, searching for the right words. "I didn't think you'd still be here."

I stirred the eggs and added some milk. "You needed me."

He came up behind me, his interest turning to the crisp bacon on a plate lined with paper towels. "I could have made my own breakfast."

"Color me impressed," I said, pretending not to notice when he stole a slice. "Considering all you had in your refrigerator was a bottle of ketchup and a pack of triple-A batteries."

"What's this on my table?" He touched the edge of the green tablecloth like he'd never seen one before.

"A touch of home." He was actually cute when he was confused.

He watched me as I plated the bacon. "I don't want you to give me your tablecloth."

"I'm not giving it to you. It's on loan. Besides, I don't have a table anymore." I placed the plates in front of two chairs and went back to finish the eggs. If I was going to have a real breakfast for the first time in two months, we could least pretend we weren't eating it off a card table.

"Fine." He sat and reached for a pair of salt and pepper shakers that looked like watermelon slices.

"Those you can keep," I told him, placing a paper napkin on my lap. "I got them on summer clearance at the dollar store."

They'd ridden around in my trunk for the past month because it turns out you don't need to salt crappy dollar-store ramen noodles.

I poured the coffee and as soon as I picked up my fork, he dug in.

"This is good," he said, treating the meal as if I'd gone gourmet on him.

"I've always enjoyed making breakfast," I said, taking a slow sip of my coffee, feeling quite domestic.

"But I don't need it," he added, reaching for his mug.

"Of course you don't." I took a broken piece of bacon from the plate in the center and fed it to Lucy under the table. "Tell me. How are you going to run a restaurant if you can't stock your own kitchen?"

He took two slices. "I hadn't gotten that far."

"Now you sound like me."

He laughed at that and I found I enjoyed the sound of it. "I'm glad you stayed, Verity."

I could feel my skin heating up. "You scared me. But I'm pleased to see you're doing better. You look good."

"Sore," he admitted. "But alive, and that's what counts."

It was something to be thankful for.

I leaned my elbows on the table, ignoring my manners. I didn't think Ellis would mind. This was important. "I don't know why anyone would push me. I mean, say they're after the gangster treasure. Wouldn't they just wait until we left? We didn't even find anything."

He frowned. "Unless they were after something else."

"What?" I couldn't imagine.

"Last week, I was installing a dishwasher in the kitchen. Easy stuff. Only somehow the electric got switched back on. It sparked and I was okay, but as far as I knew, I was alone."

The weight of it settled over me. "Somebody tried to hurt you." It could have killed him. "Where was Harry?"

Ellis shook his head. "He'd gone home for the day. I was trying to do one last thing."

Someone wanted to hurt Ellis, and now me. And his uncle had been shot in the chest on a routine call. I felt Lucy's little nails on my leg and I reached down to pick her up. "Do you ever wonder," I asked, folding her into my arms, "what really happened to Vernon?"

Ellis didn't even flinch. "Not until last night. My close call could have been written off as an accident, but yours? No." He pushed his empty plate away. "My uncle had been first on the scene of an arson call. No one had reason to suspect he'd been targeted specifically."

"They never found out who shot him, though, did they?"

He scooted his chair back. "No. We believed it was a random, senseless act of violence. But how random was the electricity being turned back on? Or your fall off that ledge?"

My sister was right. Perhaps I shouldn't have involved myself in this. Of course, I didn't see any way to back out now. In fact, I wasn't sure I wanted to be alone until we figured this out. And we would.

We had to.

I deposited the plates in the sink, then turned and leaned against the counter. "Where was your uncle killed?"

"At an abandoned house off Rosewood, south of Main," he said, thinking. "Neighbors spotted smoke billowing from one of the windows. He got there before the trucks."

I held my skunk closer. "Do you think this has something to do with the Wilson's Creek property?" Maybe someone found a significant fortune and wanted both Ellis and his uncle out of the way. Of course, that didn't explain why I had to die.

Maybe the attacks were connected to the vandalism in the kitchen somehow. We knew about the ghost, but maybe a person was riling up the ghosts on purpose. "Does Harry know about the hidden jewelry?"

He could easily sabotage Ellis's plans from the inside. And he'd watched us head down to the cliffs.

Ellis shut down when he saw where I was going. "Harry's a good guy," he insisted.

"We both know supposedly good people can surprise you." At one time, I'd thought Beau was a good person. He had to look at the facts here. "Your uncle was murdered. You were almost killed. Now me. We can't afford to overlook any possibilities."

Ellis stood, thinking. "The night he died, my uncle discovered something. He was really excited." He scrubbed a hand over his chin. "I don't think it was about money, though. He wanted to talk in private, but we didn't get the chance before he went on duty that night." He turned to me, as if he had an idea.

"Oh no," I knew where this was going.

"Find my uncle," he said, approaching me. "Talk to him."

He had this all wrong. "I can't just call people up." Frankie wasn't running a ghostly AT&T. Besides, I hadn't seen him since he'd gone into the ether yesterday.

"You're tuned into the spirit world," he said, as if talking to ghosts was something I did all the time, like a trip to the gas station or the store.

"I'll try my best," I told him. It really depended on Frankie, or anyone else I might get to help me.

Ellis stood over me, determined, looking stronger injured than most men did fully well. "Verity, it could be a matter of life and death."

It disturbed me deeply to realize he was right.

"I'll do it," I told him. "I'll start now. Only, I need a little privacy." And Frankie's urn.

CHAPTER 17

"COME ON, FRANKIE," I SAID, holding the urn as I slid into the backseat of the police cruiser.

Luckily, Ellis had taken his Jeep to the old carriage house last night and left his official vehicle in the driveway. He braced a hand on the open doorframe. "Do you need any help in there?"

I had a hard time meeting his eyes. "No. You can close the door now." I felt dumb enough sitting out front of his house and holding an urn in my lap.

I didn't need anybody staring.

Yes, this was the best approach to get the answers we needed. It just wasn't the way to appear sane, normal, or date-able.

I wasn't sure where that last part came from. Of course I could never go out with Ellis.

The seat felt hard, uncomfortable. I squirmed a bit and sighed.

Truth was, I sort of liked Ellis. Which made it even more awkward when he backed off a few feet and stood watching me through the window, as if Hale would manifest in the seat next to me, in full view of him and the entire neighborhood.

It would certainly make my job easier if he did.

Now I had to hope my favorite ghost hadn't checked out on me. "Frankie," I said, rubbing the urn. "I hope you've rested up because it's go time. I need to see."

Morning sunlight streamed into the car. Birds chirped outside.

And not one ghost appeared—not even Frankie.

My stomach twisted.

I hoped the gangster was okay. What if the poltergeist had attacked him at the same time I was shoved? Lord almighty. I hadn't even stopped to consider if yesterday's assault hadn't stopped with me.

"Are you hurt?" I asked, hearing the edge in my voice. "In trouble?" I adjusted the bronze lid and ran my fingers over the blue, square-shaped tiles on the outside. "Can you try to bang on the side? Even if you can't appear right now, I need to know you're all right."

A low groan echoed throughout the car and the hair on my arms stood on end. "You realize I don't live *in* the urn."

Oh, thank goodness. I could have kissed him. "Frankie! It's so good to hear your voice."

"You could say I have more of an attachment *to* the urn," he yammered on, as if I hadn't spoken.

"Where have you been?" I searched for any sign of him in the car. "Where are you now?"

"I've told you how hard it is to manifest," he grumbled from somewhere to my left. "I've used a lot of energy on you. It takes a while to build back up."

A thin wisp of a white shadow caught the sunlight. "Is that you?" I leaned toward it. I couldn't tell.

He groaned, as if he was having trouble coming back to the living. "You still think I'm your personal, portable ghost."

I waved a hand over the empty seat next to me.

"Stop it," he snipped.

"Can I at least take a look at you?" He sounded like his normal cranky self. Tired. Probably not hurt. But I'd feel better if I could see for myself.

The ghost chuckled. "Well, ain't that a gas? You usually get all bug eyed when I manifest."

Oh, please. "That's because you like to pop up and scare the bejesus out of me."

"Yeah," he said, the grin evident in his voice. "I'm starting to get the whole appeal of haunting."

Lovely.

At least I had him back. "Listen," I said. "I don't know if you realize, but I was attacked last night."

A chill wound through the air. "Damn. I was out of it."

"The colonel tried to warn me. Without your help, how did I see him?"

"I told you he was powerful. He show up right after sunset?"

"Late afternoon."

"Boy howdy," he muttered, "that takes even more juice."

"I think he was warning me. Someone tried to hurt me. Bad." I couldn't quite bring myself to say kill. "Ellis had an accident in the kitchen that may have been no freak thing at all. It makes us suspect his uncle might have been murdered. You met Vernon Hale. He was the one who needed a light for his cigarette."

"The fuzz," Frankie said, with a hint of contempt. "I never mixed with Hale before the other night, though. He don't hang with my crowd."

That didn't surprise me. "You think you can help me locate him?"

He huffed. "I can't go much past the urn, but if you take me to him, I'll make it so you two can have a conversation."

The vase tipped in my lap and I hastily straightened it. "I can't drive all over town, hoping we run into Hale. I wouldn't know where to start."

"Try heading to the place where he died. This is going to sound strange, and trust me, it's not as depressing as it seems, but when you get killed by surprise, sometimes it helps to hang out where it happened."

"All right. Thanks," I said, appreciating both his guidance and his honesty.

Although… I sank back into my seat. Poor Ellis would have to show me where his uncle died. I hated to put him through that.

I had to think if we could contact Hale, it would be worth it.

I chewed at my bottom lip. I didn't care what Frankie said. I couldn't help but feel sorry for Hale lingering at the site of his tragic murder. I usually tried to avoid places with bad memories.

Maybe it was a ghost thing. "Frankie," I said, knowing I might be out of line, but I wanted to understand. "Did you? Hang around?" He'd never told me where he'd been murdered. I assumed it had been a surprise.

It hadn't even occurred to me that he'd want to go back.

For a long moment, he didn't answer. I suspected he'd gone. Then he let out a sigh. "Yeah," he said simply. "I hung around."

My heart broke a little for him. It couldn't have been easy. "I'll take you back there if you want." I wasn't sure what ghosts did at the scene of death, but I'd certainly give him his time and his privacy.

"No," he said sharply. "I'm tired. Leave me alone."

The wisp of light in the seat next to me flickered and disappeared.

Fair enough. I tamped down the urge to apologize. An apology would only make matters worse. Maybe after he thought about it, Frankie would let me help. I sincerely hoped so.

I slid Frankie's urn back into my bag and opened the car door.

Ellis waited expectantly, which only made me more nervous about what I had to tell him.

"Hey," I said, attempting to exit gracefully. It wasn't always easy while wearing a dress.

But Ellis only had eyes for the backseat of his car. "I saw you talking. What did he say?"

"Your uncle isn't in there." I clasped my hands in front of me. "I was talking to a, er, friend of mine, a ghost I know and trust. He thinks we have a good chance to find your uncle at the place where he died."

Ellis visibly paled. "All right," he said simply.

"I can go by myself if you want," I offered.

He paused for a moment. "No, of course not." He seemed distracted, on edge. "Let me lock my front door."

I resisted the urge to tell him that I'd started doing that too.

☾

"I'll drive," I said, ushering us to my caddy. He shouldn't be behind the wheel of his cruiser with that sprained shoulder. "We'll drop Lucy off at Lauralee's."

To Ellis's credit, he didn't protest, but I could sure tell he wanted to.

He handled Lauralee's stare well enough. In fairness, it only took a minute for me to hand her the skunk and ask for a few hours of pet sitting. The kids always enjoyed Lucy anyhow. They were well on their way to teaching her how to sit and shake.

"I won't tell Melody," she called after us as I started up the car.

To Ellis's horror, I leaned my head out the window and shouted back to my friend, "She already knows."

Ellis set his jaw in what could have been a grimace (I preferred to think of it as focused dedication) as he directed me west onto Sherman Avenue. We took that for several miles and then wound over a few blocks toward the railroad tracks. The roads grew bumpier and weeds cropped up between the cracks in the sidewalks. Most of the houses in this neighborhood were shotgun-style, small. Many hadn't been kept up like they should.

Rusty chain-link fences gave way to scraggly lawns. Children played in patches of dirt where the grass had given up altogether. Paint peeled from some of the eaves; window shutters hung at odd angles or were simply missing. Old couches and other junk crowded front porches.

We also passed abandoned houses, many with their windows broken out, some with soot marks streaking above the casements.

Sirens wailed in the distance.

I hated to think of Hale spending the rest of his afterlife here.

"Maybe there are other places your uncle liked to go," I suggested to Ellis. "We can try those next." It could be that Hale was having an enjoyable afterlife with his friends. I wanted that for him. "Is there any place that he loved?"

"There was Curly's Bar," Ellis said, "but it closed down. It's a maternity store now."

"Oh," I said, disappointed.

"Let's hope he's not hanging out there," Ellis added, far more lightly than I would have imagined.

Perhaps he was more used to seeing this side of Sugarland.

I slowed for an older man crossing the road. "Was your uncle here a lot?"

"Whenever he needed to be," he said, scanning the neighborhood as we drove. "Same with any of us." Ellis leaned forward. "On the night he died, my uncle responded to an arson call." He pointed to a squat, pea green shotgun-style house coming up on our left. "There."

It hunkered between an empty lot on the left side and what appeared to be a vacant one-story on the right. Tiles peeled from the roof. The house numbers ran with a rusty sludge, next to windows shrouded with what appeared to be flowered bed sheets.

At least we had no trouble parking.

Cigarette butts littered the front walk.

"How long has this place stood empty?" I asked, noticing fast-food cups on the porch. They appeared to be filled with chewing tobacco spit.

"Officially," Ellis said, "nobody's lived here for three years. In reality, with the economy being what it is, people have to make do."

"Wow." Golden boy Beau would never have understood. He'd never be here in the first place. "You're nothing like your brother," I said, stumbling up the last step.

He caught my arm and steadied me. "I know."

We approached quietly. He had me hold the storm door as he scanned the rough wood of the main one. Satisfied, he leaned in and twisted the handle. "Stay behind me," he said, before announcing, "Coming in." He shoved hard and the door burst open.

Ellis stayed in front, blocking me as we entered.

The house smelled like stale smoke and wood rot.

"I don't see anybody," he said softly as we entered a small front room.

The flowered bed sheets tacked up over the windows let in a weak light, making the dank room appear even less inviting. In the corner, a metal folding chair stood vigil over a pair of dirty mattresses. Cans of food clustered nearby.

"There are homeless people living here," I said, adjusting my bag on my shoulder.

I don't know why it surprised me. Ellis had said as much. At that moment, it hit me. I might be sleeping on a futon in my parlor, but I was one of the lucky ones. Despite my problems recently, I'd led a very sheltered life.

Ellis glanced at me, as if he wondered whether or not I could take it. "This is how I met Harry," he said, moving into the hallway. "There's a bedroom on the right and a kitchen in the back." His footsteps echoed off the scarred wood floors. "Anybody home?" he called.

I followed, noticing a small bathroom to the right of the empty bedroom. It was dirty, but serviceable. The bedroom hadn't been used at all. "Why don't they sleep in here?" It didn't have a bed, but it had to be more private than the front living room.

Ellis shrugged, checking out the backyard through dirty windows. "I didn't ask."

My boots crunched over the dirt on the floors. My nose twitched at the reek of mold. "Harry lived here," I said, trying to get it through my head. He'd had no running water, no heat.

"Next door. I got him into the Good Samaritan House," Ellis said, giving up on the backyard. "It looks like we're alone."

A large burn hole charred the linoleum floor near an open space where a refrigerator had once stood. The floor had melted at the edges.

"We're on a slab, so the floor is stable," Ellis said simply.

"This is where your uncle died."

He was silent for a long moment. "He was first on the scene. He put out the fire with a handheld extinguisher. Then somebody shot him in the chest."

"I'm so sorry," I told him.

He stood motionless. "Me too."

I slipped my bag off my shoulder and placed it on the counter, careful to step around the charred mark, as if it were somehow sacred.

Ellis watched me. "Are you getting anything?"

"Not yet." This wasn't an exact science.

Ellis crossed his arms over his chest. "At first I thought someone living here did it. That they mistook my uncle for an intruder or an arsonist," he said. "But at the time, I didn't find any evidence of recent occupation. And Harry insisted there was no one staying here."

That was all well and good, but, "Why do you trust Harry?"

Ellis stiffened, as if maybe he'd wrestled with that very thing. "He didn't have a reason to lie," he said. "He was camping out next door. He was the one who called in the fire."

I didn't like it. "Harry was working with you right before the electricity got turned back on and nearly zapped you. Harry was in the woods yesterday right before I got shoved off a cliff." Ellis didn't react, so I pressed harder. "Come on. You're a police officer. You know how this works. I know it's not fun to suspect people you know, but I'm thinking Harry also has a key to the carriage house."

"I assume he's over there right now," Ellis said.

"Doing what?" I asked. "Digging up your cellar?" Someone had been down there before Ellis and me. I'd seen the freshly turned dirt. I had no clue what might be down there, but someone was certainly anxious to find it.

Ellis stopped in front of me. "You don't know him like I do. I get that he's not the most socially adept guy. It's easy to suspect someone like that."

"I'm only looking out for you." Someone had to. "Harry has been near or present for every potentially deadly incident so far. Now you're telling me he called in the fire that resulted in your uncle's death." It was too much of a coincidence to ignore.

Ellis frowned. "There is absolutely no evidence to suggest that Harry is behind any of this."

"That doesn't mean I'm wrong."

He clenched his jaw. "Let's talk about a little thing called motive. What does Harry get out of it if he kills us off?"

I stood my ground. "Whatever's in that tunnel."

He shook his head. "You want everyone to like you. Just because Harry didn't smile and shake your hand doesn't mean he's up to no good. Some people have a tougher time being friendly."

"Or they're criminals," I shot back.

"He's had a tough life. He works hard," Ellis said, staring me down as if he could convince me by sheer force of will. "If forgetting my manners was a crime, I'd be in jail for life."

I couldn't help but grin a little.

Ellis softened too. "Look, Harry didn't attack either of us. We're helping each other." He watched me carefully. "I'm not an idiot. I've dealt with lots of lowlifes and I've met plenty of people who deserve to be locked up. But trust me when I tell you Harry is one of the good ones. I've got a solid instinct for that kind of thing."

I cocked my head, refusing to back down. "Are those the same instincts you used on me?"

He jerked away as if I'd slapped him. "I don't know what you're talking about."

"Oh, please," I said, following him. "You misjudged me on sight."

"Can you blame me?" he huffed. "After what I saw you do with that cake?"

I glared at him. "I got emotional."

He cracked a smile. "Yes, you did."

I couldn't help but join him. "And you're always so smooth."

He huffed. "Damn. I know. I didn't mean for it to come out like that." I thought for a moment he was going to reach out to me with his good hand, but he hesitated and seemed to think better of it.

Smart boy.

"It's okay," I told him, simply because I was used to saying it. Not because it was true.

"Did he hurt you?" Ellis asked softly.

"Yes, but not in the way you think."

Beau hadn't gotten physical. The wounds he left went much deeper than that.

"I'm sorry," he said.

I glanced up at him and saw that he truly meant it. "Thanks." This time, I meant it, too.

I felt a prickling of energy down my spine and I knew in an instant that Frankie had tuned me in to the other side.

"What's going on in here?" a raspy voice asked.

I turned and, sure enough, the old police officer stood next to the charred hole in the floor. He held a fire extinguisher in one hand and his hat in the other.

"We were hoping to find you here," I told him.

Ellis moved up behind me.

The ghost shimmered at the edges, the morning light streaming through him.

I didn't think I'd ever get used to seeing the departed, even when I expected them. But I screwed up my courage. I found my voice. This was a gift, an opportunity, and I'd take it as such.

"Officer Hale," I began, "I hate to tell you this, but we're here because we think you might have been murdered."

CHAPTER 18

H E WASN'T NEARLY SURPRISED ENOUGH. "Who did it?" he challenged.

That broke my heart. "You knew you'd been targeted," I said softly.

He cleared his throat. "I suspected." It was an emotional topic for all of us. He glanced at his nephew. "Every time Ellis came here, it damned near killed me that I couldn't tell him what happened."

"Your uncle's glad you came," I said out loud. Ellis gave a short nod and moved woodenly to stand next to me. I had a feeling he was still stuck on the idea of murder. It was one thing to suspect, an entirely different matter to have it confirmed by the victim.

Hale took a second look at his nephew. "What'd he do to himself?"

"We were attacked yesterday," I said. "We don't know who did that, either."

Hale cursed under his breath.

"We need you to tell us more about what happened on the night you died," I told him.

"Everything you can think of," Ellis added, addressing his uncle. "I've been over and over the reports, but we're missing something."

"Why's he staring over my shoulder?" Hale asked.

Hey, I had to give Ellis credit for remaining calm and upright.

I hadn't been this smooth when I'd first run into a ghost.

"He can't see or hear you," I reminded Hale. "Only me."

"Right," he said, his brow furrowing. "Sometimes I forget. It can get muddy on this side of the fence."

I hoped I didn't have to find out, not for a long time.

Meanwhile, Ellis jumped right in. "I could understand arson in this neighborhood," he said, addressing his uncle, "but if that was the case, why was someone inside when you got here? Arsonists will watch the fires they set, but they usually do it from a distance. It couldn't have been a burglary. There was nothing to steal in this house."

Hale stared down at the charred hole between us. "I'd barely finished putting out the fire. It was hell on the eyes." His watered, remembering. He held a hand up as if to block the smoke. "I could see a foot in front of me at most when this flashlight cut through the haze. I thought it was the firefighters, so I yelled to 'em, told them where I was. Said I thought I had it." He dropped his hand. "Fucking bastard shot me in the chest."

I couldn't imagine how horrible it would feel, knowing you'd given yourself away to the person who would use that information to kill you. "Did you see who it was?" I asked. When he didn't respond right away, I prodded. "Height, weight, build, clothes…" I'd take anything at this point.

"Nothing," he said, seemingly unaware as a red stain erupted on his shirt. I watched in horror as it bloomed across his chest.

Ellis touched my arm. "What?" he asked.

I shook my head at him. "Hale didn't see."

Hale grew pale as the blood drained from him. "It was me," he said, staring forward, lost in his thoughts, as if he'd forgotten we were even there. "The bastard wanted me." He stood in an ever-widening pool of his own blood.

It made me sick to imagine what kind of person could do such a thing. I quickly filled Ellis in as Hale's clothes and hair began to smoke. Oh my God. He'd burned.

At that moment, I was very glad Ellis couldn't see his uncle.

"What did you want to tell me the night you were killed?"

Ellis asked.

The older officer grunted. "It was the damnedest thing. I'd been pulling out that dead tree by the front of the carriage house, that old oak, and I found a purse inside. It had an ID for a girl listed as missing since the 1960s, one of the cold cases. I went straight to the station and called up her file."

"And?" I pressed.

"By the time records got it to me, it was time for me to go on duty," Hale said glumly. "Then I was killed. When I got enough of my wits about me to go back to the station and look for the purse, it was gone from my desk drawer. They'd cleaned everything out. The only other person who knew what I had was Merle in Records and he let it drop."

"Merle in Records didn't do anything?" I asked. Surely procedure would have dictated that he pass the information along. "Maybe he took the purse."

Ellis watched me carefully. "Merle died the same night as my uncle. Heart attack."

Maybe not. I tried to remain focused as I quickly relayed the facts to Ellis. We needed to gather all of the information we could while his uncle was here and had the energy to speak with us. It's not like we could call Hale on the phone.

To Ellis's credit, he took it all in stride. "What was the girl's name?" he asked his uncle.

"Joy Sullivan," Hale said, "she disappeared after a high school football game. She also lived on this block. I was here in this kitchen a week ago and I saw her, right out the back window. It was the first time I actually knew she was dead. She's still listed as a missing person."

My throat tightened and it hit me for the first time what was possible when we opened up communications between the living and the dead. "Joy Sullivan. Did you talk to her when you saw her outside?"

I noticed how Ellis's expression had lit at the mention of her name. "I tried," Hale said to both of us. "She seemed like she was in her own world. I followed her out to the Wilson's Creek property."

That couldn't be a coincidence. "What was she doing there?"

"Not sure," he said. "I thought she might look for her purse where the old oak had been. Instead, she walked right up to the side yard of the carriage house and sank straight into the ground."

Dread inched down my spine. "Where?"

He furrowed his brows, thinking. "To the left, as you're facing it."

Into the tunnel. I'd be willing to bet my life.

Hale paused as he went over it in his mind. "I don't even know if she could see me or hear me."

"I think she may have been trying to tell you something," I said to him. "And she had ties to this neighborhood and to your property." I was familiar with only one other person like that. "I wonder if she knew your handyman, Harry."

Hale drew his brows together. "Why would you ask that?"

Ellis glanced at me. "Harry used to live next door," he said, his tone letting me know he didn't appreciate where this line of conversation was going. "He was on the property yesterday when we were attacked."

Hale's nostrils flared. "He might have been in the report. I didn't get far." I could see his mind turning. "It's worth asking her. I only wish I could have gotten close. Maybe it was the property that made her squirrely. Every ghost that goes near the place gets jumpy. I don't know what it is." He looked from me to Ellis. "The night I followed her, I was attacked inside the carriage house."

"Wow," I said. I glanced at Ellis "The poltergeist went after your uncle, too."

"You've run into it?" The ghost frowned.

"Unfortunately," I told him. "Do you know which spirit it is?"

Hale's expression tightened. "It came at me too fast. I tried to ask around about Joy, but the ghosts there avoid me. They see me as an outsider," he said, taking one step toward me, then another. He crossed the blackened hole, his shoes squeaking on the bloody floor. "Watch yourselves. Stick together at all times. It's hard to explain, but in spirit form, you develop ties to places you love. I can feel the building and the land even now. There's some strong emotion tied to that place and it doesn't feel good. It's strong, aggressive."

He pulled aside his uniform collar. His neck bloomed purple with bruises. They darkened by the second.

Oh my God. "Did it try to hang you?"

Hale drew close. I could feel his cold energy brush against my skin. "It tried to bury me."

"In the ground?" I gasped.

"I fought it off and escaped," he said, his eyes wide with fury. "But it's back there. It's waiting and it's angry."

I swallowed hard. "How do we get rid of it?"

"You don't," he said, backing me against the counter. "If I couldn't, you certainly can't handle it."

"No," I said, my mind churning. I refused to believe that. Sure, Ellis and I had gotten beat up a little, but we were figuring this out. We couldn't give up now.

"You run," Hale insisted. "You stay away."

"We can't," I said. Not now. "We need to stop it."

He leaned so close I could see the sweat beading on the skin of his cheeks. "Then I might be seeing you sooner than you think."

And with that, he disappeared.

⸿

I didn't tell Ellis about the bruises or the blood. I was shaking bad enough as it was. I didn't want to relive those things. And it would only upset him.

"We have to go back to the property," he told me. "Now."

I got that. It was our only option if we wanted to question Harry. But I had a feeling he had something else in mind. I stopped, studying him. "Why do you want to go?"

"I want to see if we can dig up more on the poltergeist," he said, as if it were that simple.

We made our way to the front door. "You think it could be

the murdered girl," I said.

"I don't know," he answered. "I also want to take another look at where you were pushed yesterday. I didn't call it in, but it is a crime scene."

We'd been so focused on investigating for ourselves. "We should have told the police."

He gave a short laugh. "I told you, I am the police."

We stopped by the grocery store for sandwiches on our way down to Wilson's Creek and ate in the car while Ellis peppered me with questions about his uncle's warning, about the attack in the kitchen, and exactly what his uncle had said about the purse he'd found.

He also called the station and put in a request for the case file on Joy Sullivan.

"Records room is pulling it," he said, hanging up. "I can sign it out tomorrow."

"Good," I said. "In the meantime, I have my own source of information."

"Please don't." He groaned.

"I'm going to tell her anyway," I said. We were too close for it to be any different. Besides, she could help with this.

Melody answered on the first ring. "Where were you last night? I stopped by with a chicken."

Damn. I'd be willing to bet Q never made Bond feel guilty for where he'd been the night before.

"Well...?" she prodded. "Lucy was tickled pink to see me. It's like she'd been left alone for hours."

I winced as I said it. "I spent the night—" Ellis's eyes grew wide. He waved me off, but I ignored him. "—at Ellis's house."

"Urgh!" I heard from both Ellis and my sister.

How sweet.

"You," I said, pointing at Ellis, "should be glad I helped you." He opened his mouth, but I shut him down. "And Melody will not tell a soul."

Not that I would clue her in on what happened yesterday. She'd never let me out of the house again.

"You," I said over the racket Melody was making, "you owe me for the time you superglued my ponytail to my headboard."

"This is way worse than that," she insisted.

I didn't see how. "Listen. I need you. We think there is a distinct possibility Ellis's uncle was murdered."

"What?" she sputtered. Okay, maybe I could have been a tad less blunt. "You're hanging out with your ex's brother and getting yourself involved with a murder?"

She really didn't have to screech.

"Nobody saw who shot Officer Hale," I said, pushing past her objections. We needed to keep our focus. "At the time, he was resurrecting a cold case involving a girl named Joy Sullivan."

"I remember that story. She's still missing."

"She's dead."

"You don't know that."

Unfortunately, I did. "Let's just say someone received some new information about the case. Ellis is going to dig into the files as soon as he can, but for now, can you look in the newspapers and get the facts of the case for us? That'll put us one step ahead of where we are."

"What is this?" she protested. "Do you think you're some kind of detective now?"

"I'm some kind of...something," I told her. Although I wouldn't be half as useful without the ghosts. "Just help me. Please," I added.

"You know I will," she groused. "That's why you called. But promise me one thing," she added. I could feel her worry over the phone. "Be careful."

"I'll do my best." It was all I could promise.

"And don't kiss him."

I wouldn't promise her that.

CHAPTER 19

I BLEW OUT A BREATH AS we pulled up in front of the carriage house. We simply needed to locate the body of a missing girl, who could be holed up in a collapsing tunnel, with a poltergeist on the loose.

And possibly avoid a murderous handyman.

I must admit I'd had better days.

I knew I was pushing it but, "I could use your help again, Frankie," I said as I slid out of the car. Clouds hung low over gray skies. I didn't see any sign of Harry the handyman or Joy Sullivan. Yet.

Ellis shot me a curious glance.

I slammed my door shut, a bit edgy. "Frankie's my friendly ghost, the one who tunes me in to the other side," I said, going out on a limb. The words hung between us, making me uncomfortable.

"That's good to know," Ellis said, pausing while I adjusted my bag over my shoulder and tried to regain my sense of calm. "Thanks for helping us out, Frankie," he said into thin air.

"That's it?" I asked, a bit taken aback that he'd accepted my ability with such calm.

"I'm with the police department. I've seen weirder things on an average Tuesday."

Point taken.

We began walking to the carriage house. "I met Frankie when

I dumped his urn out on my rosebushes," I said, for shock value, and perhaps to learn how much Ellis could accept about this. About me.

He stopped. "That would only happen to you."

"He's your great-great-uncle."

I smiled when I saw the shock register on his face.

"That would only happen to me," he said, his lips twisting into a wry grin.

"True." I shook my head. "I can't believe how well you're taking this." Maybe I'd misjudged him.

"Maybe I'm just glad to be alive after you landed on me." He became serious again. "Take a look at this," he said, running his boot over a slight dip in the earth. "The oak tree was about here. We filled it in." We continued to the side of the carriage house to the place where we'd marked the tunnel location with a few loose bricks. Ellis stood over it. "My uncle said this is where he saw her," he mused, as if the place itself would give us answers.

"Near as I can tell." I kept an eye out for both Hale and Frankie, although I didn't truly expect to see either of them. "It takes a lot of energy to manifest. I don't think Hale's going to be able to come out and help." And poor Frankie had been dead on his feet even before he'd helped us talk to Hale this afternoon.

As for the rest? I waited for a moment. "I don't see evidence of any spirits right now," I said. Not a wisp, not a glimmer. Only rocks, scattered trees, grass, and the decrepit main house in the distance. No doubt that held a few ghosts too, but we had enough problems right here.

Ellis drew his keys out of his pocket and unlocked the door. "Let's go inside." He motioned for me to enter ahead of him. Always the gentleman. Even when I didn't want him to be. And I didn't miss how he locked the door behind us.

Shadows cloaked the inside of the building. It felt stark in here, empty. Ellis's work boots echoed off the century-old hardwood.

Harry should have been there. A quick search of the place showed us he was not.

"Do you think he's hiding?" I asked.

Ellis frowned. "No." He appeared uneasy. "I don't know where he is. Come on," he said, continuing to my least favorite spot on the planet. "Let's check out the tunnel."

That was the last place I felt like searching, especially since Frankie's power hadn't kicked in. It must have shown clear on my face.

"Don't worry," Ellis said. "We'll go down together."

"Great."

I had to get a grip if we were going to see this through. The ghost of Joy Sullivan had sunk into the ground, down into the tunnel. Hale had seen it with his own two eyes. It would be irresponsible of us not to investigate. I just wished it didn't scare me so much.

"Come on, Frankie," I muttered. "Frankie the German," I added, resorting to his nickname, not sure if I was begging or trying to butter him up. I knew this was tough, but I just needed him one more time.

But I felt nothing.

I saw no silvery light, only the deceptive emptiness of the carriage house.

"Hey," Ellis said, his voice echoing in the open space as he tried to lighten the mood. "At least we're not going to the cliffs."

How sad was it when investigating a collapsing tunnel was the safer thing to do?

I caught a spark of light near the entrance to the kitchen, merely a flicker, before it disappeared.

We weren't alone.

"You okay?" he asked as he reached the cellar door.

"Sure," I lied. "Never better."

With a hard grunt, he cracked the door open. It tried to slam back down, as if an unseen force wanted the cellar closed tight. Ellis fought it, the muscles in his back and arms straining, until the wood door gave way with a resounding *boom*.

He glanced over his shoulder, slightly out of breath "Gets harder every time."

I didn't want to know why.

"Let's see what we've got," I said. He'd brought a Maglite and I still had my keychain flashlight. We shone them both down the hole.

An eerie silver light poured from the space.

Thank God.

"Looks the same to me," he murmured, casting the beam of his light down into the old cellar.

"I'm tuned in," I murmured.

He shot me a hard glance. "Good," he said, trying to sound casual.

The air felt a least ten degrees colder. Tendrils of smoke crept out of the opening, tickling my ankles.

Dread wound through me. I wondered if Harry experienced the same sense of unease, if it had kept him from sneaking around—or if he'd fought past it like we would.

I gave an involuntary shudder.

Ellis caught it. "I'll go first."

"Thanks," I said, meaning it.

I watched as Ellis began his descent, and when he was down, I followed. Ghostly cobwebs tickled my arms and legs. My fingers gripped the ladder a little tighter. One rung. Two. The air grew more frigid with each step down. Three. Four. I held my breath as the cobwebs wound against my cheeks and into my hair.

Keep moving.

Five rungs. Six. I froze when I heard the same faint, hollow sobbing echoing from the back of the cellar.

I jumped the last two feet. "There's a girl down here," I said softly. "I heard her once before when I was down here."

Ellis stood, grim in the silver light of the haunted cellar. "All right. We can do this."

Goose bumps prickled up my arms. "Right." I hitched my bag over my shoulder and took a moment to get my bearings. The cellar had changed. It was now completely empty, save for cobwebs glittering in the corners.

"There's a different ghost in charge down here," I said.

Ellis turned his flashlight around toward me. "What?"

I didn't need any lights. I could see the cellar perfectly in the gray ghostly glow. "How I see things depends on which ghost is in charge, whoever is dominant," I said. "Whoever has the most energy at the time." It must have been the colonel before, with his horse liniments and baskets of apples.

And now? I didn't know.

The air tasted stale, dead.

Ghostly sobs echoed all around us and strangely enough, I could hear the faint, tinny sound of an old rock song: "That'll Be the Day" by Buddy Holly & the Crickets.

"The ghost down here, the girl... she sounds upset," I said, pressing forward.

The sobbing grew louder as we passed through the arched doorway and into the back room.

Ellis's shoulders stiffened. "Can we get to her?" he asked, glancing at me.

"We may not want to," I said, remembering the bruises on Hale's neck. While I didn't see Hale getting beat up by a woman on the mortal plane, the rules down here seemed to be centered around emotional strength and aggression. I wasn't about to put anything past a suffering spirit.

The beam from his flashlight scrambled up the stone walls. I hated to break it to him, but we didn't need light to find the missing girl.

I worried we'd lose her if she stopped crying, but was also a little afraid of what we might find. I never knew what to expect when encountering a spirit, especially one who had been killed violently.

"Where are you, Joy?" I whispered as her sobs faded.

I aimed my light to the left, where shelves of ghostly mason jars had once lined the wall, to where the plywood board should have been wedged against the tunnel. My light shone into the narrow passageway instead. "She might be in there."

Ellis drew a sharp breath. "I put the board back."

My light bobbed over the freshly turned dirt at the entrance. "I have no doubt."

We traded glances as he shone his light on several piles of rock outside the arched entry. "This wasn't here, either. I removed the rock I found. Someone else has been excavating."

Dread settled in my stomach. "I hope they don't come back while we're down here."

Ellis lifted the back of his shirt, displaying the handle of a gun. "I wouldn't mind if they did."

The hair on my arms pricked as a small sob escaped the tunnel. "Help me."

"She's in there," I whispered, ducking past Ellis, bracing myself as I entered the tunnel.

I breathed in dust and decay. The temperature dropped with each step I took and this time, the silver light from the cellar didn't fade. The ghost was still influencing this space. I pressed forward, guided as much by the glimmering light as the solid brick tunnel looming over me. I flinched as the hair on top of my ponytail skimmed the ceiling.

Ellis's footsteps scraped in the tunnel behind me. At least I hoped it was him.

I turned, just to make sure.

Shadows shrouded his features. "I'm here," he said, as if that would make this all right.

As if anything could be right about creeping through a claustrophobic old tunnel underground, searching for a murdered girl.

"Take it slow," he added as the beam of his light found a spot on the wall directly to my right. A white chalk mark slashed over the brick. "This is as far as I got." He paused, his voice lowering. "The rest is someone else's excavation."

I eased past Ellis's line and stumbled over a large rock, then stepped directly onto another. The floor was rough with debris. I glanced up as the back of my head brushed a jagged piece of brick. "This is where they had the cave-in." Packed dirt and plant roots clustered above my head. Broken bricks clung haphazardly to the ceiling. It appeared as if it could collapse at any second.

This was insane. "We should turn back."

Then I heard the voice again. "Help me."

I swore under my breath. "Only a little farther." First I'd find Joy Sullivan. Then I'd escape. I'd run out of here so fast they'd never catch me.

I stumbled over another rock. Whoever had cleared this section hadn't been neat or thorough. They'd been in a hurry.

Jagged stones littered the ground, forcing me to walk over them, to crouch as I avoided the ceiling. I pressed forward until a waist-high pile of broken brick and rock blocked the way. My breath came in hard puffs. It felt like a refrigerator down here.

A slight breeze tickled my cheeks.

"I think we're close," I said, my voice sounding loud in the narrow space. "Talk to me, Joy." I pulled a large rock off the pile and tossed it to the side. There was either something buried here or we were about to break through to…what? "We're here to help," I said, digging away another rock. Then another. They clanked against each other and on the cement floor of the tunnel. For the first time, I saw cement instead of dirt covering it.

Ellis shone his light on the rocks in front of me. "Tell me what you see."

"Nothing yet." It was unsettlingly dark beyond the rock pile. Which meant we were likely in the right spot. "But why did they stop digging here?"

"Maybe they were interrupted," Ellis said as he started clearing the rocks from around our feet.

I knocked the top of the pile into the darkness, sending down a cascade of stones. I needed to see what our intruder had been digging for. What about this tunnel, this place, this jumble of stones was so important?

When I'd been so scared the first night, when the intruder had me cornered—that person had been headed down here. When the colonel warned me about uneasy spirits and tried to block me from the cellar—he feared for what was down here. And now Joy had shown Hale this exact spot.

I flinched as rock sliced at the soft skin of my palms, but I didn't care. It didn't stop me. Nothing could as I grabbed a large stone in front of me with both hands and yanked.

The pile collapsed.

"Careful," Ellis warned, drawing me back as rocks and broken bricks crashed down onto my legs, falling away from a gleaming white skull.

I shrieked. "It's…"

"Human," he finished for me.

It stared up at me with empty eye sockets. The beam from Ellis's light caught it at the jaw, where a rough scraping of skin still clung to the bone. The skull had been shattered on the right side. Large holes gaped where teeth should have been and if I wasn't mistaken, I saw an arm bone peeking out of the rock next to it.

"Help me," the voice whispered. It came from all around us.

Sweet Lord in heaven. We'd found Joy.

Ellis let out a sharp grunt. I turned as he jerked forward and collapsed right on top of me. "Ellis!" His body hit me hard, driving me backward onto the skull and the rock and the bones.

I felt the sharp sting of impact as his light spun away. Debris rained down. Lord in heaven. The tunnel was collapsing. I rolled to the right and encountered hard metal. A hot electric shock pierced my leg and then nothing more.

CHAPTER 20

M Y HEAD BUZZED. IT RESTED against a cold rock. Cripes. It could be a bone. I stiffened and brought my hand up to check, or I tried to. A sharp tug and the clink of chain at my wrist stopped me.

I froze, my heart pounding, every nerve on high alert.

I forced my eyes open. In the dim light, Ellis lay facing me. His head rested at an unnatural angle against a small mound of stones near the floor, the remains of the pile I'd found.

"Ellis." I reached for him, dislodging some of the rocks nearby. He groaned. Thank God. An iron manacle circled his right wrist. A thick chain hung from it, ending in a loop sealed into the concrete floor.

My left hand wore the matching manacle.

I sat up with a shock and realized I didn't have Frankie's urn anymore. My bag was gone. The only light filtered in from the way we'd come. Only now, there was a chest-high wall blocking the way.

I heard the rhythmic scraping of metal on brick.

I jerked upright as far as I could and saw Mayor Thad Steward on the other side. "Help me," I said automatically, unthinking, as he added another brick.

He pursed his lips, his head bent as he focused on the job. "You're awake," he said, diligently scraping the mortar on his side, neatening it up. "I should have set my Taser higher."

Oh my God. He was walling us in here.

He was burying us alive.

I searched for a weapon, a forgotten key, a way out of here. I slid against the debris, unearthing an arm bone, a scrap of a blue dress, the ring worn by the last girl he'd trapped down here and left to die.

Help me.

"If you're looking for your bag, I've got it. And his gun," Steward added.

My breath came in pants. My mind swam as I tried to reason my way out of this, how to escape my chains as the mayor added another brick.

Tendrils of hair had fallen into my eyes. I tried to brush them away and failed. I couldn't reach. "You don't have to do this," I pleaded. Whatever had driven him to bury us alive, there had to be a way to change his mind.

He shook his head like a stern parent as he added another brick. "I'm sorry, Verity. I tried to keep you out of it."

"I don't understand. Why are you doing this?" How could this be happening? It didn't make sense.

He added another brick. "I tried to dig up her body. Bury it again on some property I own that I'll never lose." He made a face. "Disgusting, even if she is only bones now." He exhaled loudly, reaching for another brick. "I only needed one more night. She would have been resting somewhere else by morning if you two hadn't started digging around." He scraped the mortar on the brick. "I'm getting too old for this sort of thing."

"You can barely walk," I said, trying to work out how kind, helpful Mayor Steward had managed to trap us in an underground prison. How did he even make it down the ladder? He had that war injury.

He snorted. "Right. The old bum leg. Guess I'll have to keep it up, but hell, it's a small price to pay. And the voters love a war hero."

I still couldn't believe it. Yes, Thad Steward had probably never been one of the most honest guys in the world. He'd made his living in politics. But a murderer? "You killed Joy Sullivan and buried her down here."

He gave a low grunt. "I didn't kill her. I walled her up. Chained her to the floor."

As if that were any different. He'd left her to die.

He frowned as he added another brick. The man moved fast, quicker than I ever imagined possible. Oh my God, we only had about a foot and a half left before…

"Joy didn't have the good sense to leave things alone, either," he said, slightly out of breath as he scraped his trowel over the mortar. "I loved her. I did. But she didn't understand why I had to marry Genevieve Wydell. The Wydells have the money and the power in this town." He pointed the trowel at me. "You of all people should know that."

I did. All too well. But still, "If you loved Joy, why did you kill her?" Maybe it was self-defense. Maybe he didn't need to kill me in order to cover this up.

"She thought she could keep me by getting pregnant. Big mistake," he added.

Oh my God. I struggled against the shackles until the metal tore my wrists. I fought them as if my life depended on it. Because it did.

"Don't," Steward said, as if I were the crazy one. "I installed them myself. They'll hold." Once again, the mayor's trowel scraped over brick.

And Ellis? I touched his hand. It was warm. I hoped he was okay. Yes, he needed to be okay so that he could be buried alive with me.

"This doesn't have to happen. Please. We can work this out," I reasoned, pleaded. "You were young. You didn't know what you were doing," I said, trying to find a way to justify what he'd done so he wouldn't have to kill me. We didn't have much time. And I couldn't afford to upset him. He probably couldn't tase me from over there, but if he did, I'd wake up chained behind a brick wall. I'd have no chance then.

He shook his head. "I'm just sorry you had to get caught up

in this." He added another brick. I could barely see him on the other side now. "I like you, Verity. I do. That's why I shoved you off the cliff. Figured it was a more humane way to let you go."

The truth of it hit me. He'd lied. "There was no treasure in Wilson's Cave."

"No. But there was a cliff above it." Bricks scraped on the other side of the wall. "That treasure story's as old as dirt. Nothing's ever come of it. But the cliffs, they're real. One fall. Snap your neck. You don't feel anything after that." He leaned his head into the hole, his fingers curling over the edge. "In fact, I should have tased you again when you woke up. Then you might not suffer so much. Sorry about that."

A shiver sliced through me. There was no getting through to him. I was going to die.

I gasped for breath as the panic welled up. I opened my mouth as my lungs seized hard, trying to suck in enough air.

"Screaming won't help," he said, getting back to work. "I imagine Joy screamed a lot. She was the dramatic type. Didn't have the lovely Southern gentility you possess. Most of the time. Still, these walls are thick. I didn't hear a thing."

I swallowed hard, trying to piece it together. Maybe I could find a way out. Supposedly this tunnel led to the old house. Of course the mayor was the one who'd told me that. He could have been lying. "You followed me after I talked to you," I said. It all made sense now.

"I did. I even had to miss the Sugarland Holiday Glee Committee meeting. Without me there, they approved yellow and white lights for this year's city hall holiday display. Yellow and white. Not red and green. See what I gave up for you?"

He was insane, a complete psychopath.

He tsked. "My knee still hurts from shoving you."

"Good," I muttered.

He chuckled, adding another brick. "Truth is," he said, slightly out of breath, "I'd have rather killed Ellis. He's the one who took my property. He started digging it up."

"And now you have us both," Ellis muttered.

His head still lay against the rocks, his eyes were still closed.

"Well, look who's awake," Steward crooned. "I have to get me a new Taser. This one doesn't work as well as it used to. Anyhow, don't start on me. Won't do you any good. Joy begged the entire time." He added another brick and we lost more light. "That was tough. This is cleanup."

The wall was almost to the top of the tunnel now. Shadows drenched our side of the wall.

Ellis tried to sit and failed. Rocks skittered down the pile where he'd rested his head. "People will notice we're missing," Ellis said to me, his voice low. "This will be one of the first places they look."

"Oh, I'll lead the search for you." Steward chuckled. I could hear him grunt as he leaned down to grab another brick. "It's the least I can do, seeing as I know the property so well."

I glanced at Ellis as cold fear settled over me. Ellis's gaze raked over the tunnel, desperately searching for a way to escape.

"I think you might be down by the river," Steward continued, "or in the old house." He chuckled. "We'll certainly have to question that scary-looking handyman you hired."

"What did you do to Harry?" Ellis demanded.

"I blessed him with a bottle of his favorite whiskey. He's in the alley behind my office, sleeping it off, with no alibi. We'll waste a lot of time blaming him."

"They'll look," I insisted. Melody wouldn't let this go, my mother either.

"We'll be worried sick," the mayor agreed. "Although I doubt they'll search too hard down here. I'm using original brick. It looks perfect from this side, undisturbed for decades, if I do say so myself." He wheezed loudly, adding another brick. "I'll also get my property back."

"Over my dead body," Ellis muttered.

"That's the idea, son. I have the money to buy it. Genevieve will throw a fit, but your mother never liked her anyway." I could hear the smile in his voice. "She'll sell it to me to spite your great-aunt."

Ellis struggled against the manacle. "My will states that this property will go to charity."

"You don't have a will," Steward said. "I asked your mamma. Seeing as you're a police officer and all. Dangerous profession." The trowel scraped the other side of the wall. "Your mother always felt I deserved this place, said it was a crime when I lost it," he mused. "No. This is error proof. Soundproof. All in all, there are worse ways to go." He slid the second-to-last brick onto the wall. "Now what has to happen to poor Melody...that part *has* kept me awake at night. She was a special one."

Was? I straightened, struck by a new energy. Blood pounded through my veins. "What did you do to Melody?"

"Nothing yet," he said simply. "But I have to kill her when I'm done with you. You told her too much."

"I didn't," I protested, all the while racking my brain. *How did he know?*

Steward tsked. "She searched for Joy this afternoon. Used my library to do it. I have an alert system in place, you see." He chuckled. "Old Mayor Steward doesn't know technology. Old Mayor Steward can't walk too well. Unless it suits him."

I stiffened. "What are you going to do to her?"

He sighed. "I was going to use the shotgun. It worked on Hale. But that's so loud. And messy." He let out a low grunt as he reached for the last brick. "I have a pistol with a silencer. Rest assured, I'll try my best to get her with one clean shot to the head."

The blood turned to ice in my veins. "You can't just kill an innocent person."

"I've done it before," he said, in that sweet, cloying, perfect gentleman's voice, before he slid the last brick into the wall.

CHAPTER 21

WE HUDDLED IN DARKNESS. WE were out of time and so was my sister.

"We have to save Melody." If he hurt her, if he *killed* her, it would be my fault.

Ellis's chains clinked. He grunted as he struggled. "I'm sure Steward's heading over there right now."

Yes, that was Ellis. He didn't sugarcoat the truth.

We could catch up to Steward. Maybe. If we could get out of here. A few minutes more and it would be too late. I searched through the rocks for any kind of tool, a weapon. I felt my skin tear, my fingers bleed.

"Frankie!" I called, keeping up my frantic struggle. *Come on.* If I ever needed a ghost, it was right now. "Frankie!"

He could already be too far away. If Steward took his urn, he might be lost for good.

The stark reality of that cut deep. I'd grown to like Frankie. *Stop.* I couldn't think about that right now. It wouldn't do us any good. I could only get his urn if I got out of here. In the meantime, I prayed I still had the ability to call on the ghosts. "Colonel!" I screamed. "Joy! Anybody!"

A glimmer of light flickered near the ceiling. Sobbing echoed in the chamber.

The air grew electric and I felt the same razor-sharp tingling edge that had cut through the kitchen moments before the poltergeist attacked.

That was the last thing we needed. "Joy?" Please. "Is that you?"

A woman's scream pierced the tunnel as a wall of energy barreled down, searing my skin, turning me inside out. It knocked the wind out of me. The blast shook the tunnel, dislodging brick and mortar.

She was out of control. Insane. "Joy, sweetie?" I gasped. She was the poltergeist. She had to be.

Frankie said poltergeists manifested due to an excess of negative energy, and if anybody had a reason to be ticked, it was that poor girl.

This was like Jilted Josephine, only ten times worse. But she wasn't evil. At least, I hoped she wasn't.

"Can I see you?" I asked, trying to get my breathing under control. "Can we talk?"

A frigid wind slammed through the tunnel.

A voice echoed behind it. "I'm cold."

I drew a shaky gulp of air, not at all surprised to see my breath puffing in front of me. This was a cold, dark place—for her especially.

I sat up as far as I could. "I know it's rough. I don't want to be here either. But Thad Steward chained me here." Just like her. I swallowed hard.

"I tried so hard to get away," she said, her voice echoing all around me. "Now I'm dead. I know I'm dead."

"You are," I told her. "I'm so sorry for what happened to you." I searched the tunnel, wishing I could only see her. "Thad is a monster. I'll make him pay for what he's done to us," I vowed.

"I…" She shimmered into view above me, a scared girl dressed for a date in a sweater and a skirt.

"Do you need me to help find your parents?" I asked, thinking of those she'd left behind.

She began to weep. "They're gone. They went to the light. I just…can't. I'm so angry."

She screwed up her face and hid it in her hands. "He said he loved me."

And he'd left her here to die. He'd come back only to dig up her bones.

"You deserved so much better," I told her.

She cried harder and I regretted my words. Sometimes listening is all a person needs. Her shoulders shook as she raised her head from her hands. "He killed me." Tears streaked down her face. "I was going to have his baby. And he killed me."

"Oh, sweet heavens." I felt tears prick my own eyes.

"When he started coming back, I was so happy," she said, remembering. "He never stayed. He'd just dig and cuss. Then he wouldn't come at all when your man would build."

So she destroyed Ellis's work and hoped he wouldn't come back.

"Your man even covered up my tunnel." She gave a shudder. "I had to get those bricks off me."

She'd torn up the patio. It had made her feel buried.

"I'm so angry all the time." She clenched her jaw. "It will never be right."

"You can get justice," I told her. "But you certainly don't have to give up the goodness inside of you in order to do it."

"It's so easy to hate," she whispered.

I wouldn't argue there. "I'm on this plane still," I told her. "Your Thad has a key in his pocket that can set me free. I'm sure he's gone from this property, though. You can leave, can't you?"

"Yes," she said, breathless.

"Get the key. Get me out of here and I'll make sure he knows you helped me. I'll make sure everyone knows what he did to you."

She watched me, her nose flaring and her chest heaving. "All right." Her hair erupted into unearthly flames. Holy smokes. I could feel the anger radiating from her.

"Don't let the hurt control you," I urged. "You're stronger than that."

She snarled, a low unearthly sound, before plunging head-first into the brick wall after Steward.

Full darkness enveloped us. I knelt, drenched in sweat, my

wrist slick with blood, although when I'd come to my knees, I couldn't tell you.

Ellis's own chains clanked. "What did you do?" he asked, his voice low.

"I think I created a monster," I said quietly.

I'd meant to give her love and support. I wanted to give her courage, not rage. I didn't know if she'd be able to maintain her focus. Or if she'd return.

Steward could be in his car, halfway to my sister by now. I'd sent a killer after her. And now I'd sent a mad ghost after him.

My head pounded as I sat down on my heels. I'd never wanted it to turn out this way. "I'm so sorry," I whispered.

"Don't," Ellis said softly.

"About everything," I told him. I'd failed on all accounts. "I took on this job when I didn't know what I was doing." I sniffed. "I wore out Frankie until parts of him were plain disappearing. I told you I could get rid of a poltergeist, but then I led Mayor Steward here to shove me off a cliff and then I led you down here to get buried alive with a dead body."

"The job was my idea. So was coming down here." The chain on his wrist clinked as he reached for me. He took both of my hands in his. They were warm, comforting. "Nobody's getting buried alive."

My eyes felt wet, my throat clogged. "We are right now. You're a police officer. You should know that."

I wished I could see him. It was so dark.

His free hand gently eased the hair away from my eyes and tucked it behind my ear. "We can tackle this."

I wondered if Joy had thought so too.

"Stranger things have happened," he said, daring me to contradict him. "Especially to you."

"My life is never dull," I told him, resting a hand on his leg. "You should have run when you could." Although truth be told, I was glad he'd stuck around. Ellis was the nicest guy I'd ever yelled at, fallen on, or hit in the head with a ring.

To my surprise I could hear a slight smile in his voice.

"I haven't been the same since you offered to undress me in my room."

I snorted. "You were injured. It was a mercy disrobing."

"Too bad," he said pragmatically. I could hear the amusement in his voice, even down here, facing what we were. He leaned close. "I was really hoping to do this."

"What?" I asked as his lips touched mine. He kissed me sweetly, gently, the way every girl deserves to be kissed at least once in her life.

I couldn't believe it. I shouldn't have done it. But I found myself kissing him back, if just for a little while.

A cold wind blasted the tunnel, forcing us apart. "I did it!" Joy announced, dropping a key into my lap.

CHAPTER 22

"THANK YOU," I WHISPERED AS I grasped the key.

"What happened?" Ellis asked.

"This." It took a few tries in the dark, but I inserted the key into the lock on Ellis's manacle and twisted. It clicked open.

"I'll ask you later how you did that." He whooshed out a breath.

"You didn't think we'd get out of here," I said, quite smug for someone who had thought it was impossible until about thirty seconds ago.

I passed him the key and he unlocked me. "Now we move," he said, catching hold of me as we regained our feet. Both of us stumbled on the rocks on the floor. "Stand back," he said, launching himself against the wet brick wall.

He hit with a dull thud. I couldn't see a thing. Another thud and faint silver light streamed through. It must have been the glow I could see in the cellar, the spiritual haze that was invisible to Ellis.

"You've got it," I said, realizing he had to be killing his injured shoulder, even if he wasn't using that one as his battering ram. He'd knocked two bricks out. He just didn't see it.

"Wait." I took Ellis's hand and placed it on the wet wall to show him the hole. "Here."

He began yanking bricks out and so did I. We attacked the wet wall, pulling it apart until we could squeeze through. I grasped his hand in mine, forging the way as we faced the darkness.

His shoulder hung awkwardly. No doubt he'd injured it worse. We stumbled out of the trap and raced through the underground passage.

"Where's your sister?" he demanded.

"At the library." Mayor Steward would know that too. We had to get to her before he did, only he had a head start.

Joy dropped down in front of us, her eyes wild, and her hair streaming out behind her. "He's getting away!"

I couldn't stop. I ran straight through her, shivering at the wetness that soaked into my very bones. "Sorry," I called over my shoulder. "Can you delay him?"

Her mouth twisted into a grin. "I'll throw rocks into the road!"

Not what I had in mind, but I didn't have time to brainstorm with a ghost.

Ellis and I dashed out into the cellar, through the underground rooms, and straight for the ladder.

"Call the police," I told him. We should be able to get a signal outside.

"Steward took my cell phone," Ellis said, scrambling up the ladder after me.

Of course. I knew that. Horror crashed over me. "He has my keys." Both our keys. He had Frankie's urn.

Ellis rushed for the kitchen. "I've got a spare set."

We made it to his Jeep in under a minute flat. Thank God we'd left it here last night. I just hoped it would be fast enough. He shoved a police-issue rooftop flasher onto the roof and peeled out.

Ellis drove like a madman.

"Get the gun out of the glove box," he said, eyes on the road as he passed cars at an unholy speed.

"You have *another* gun?" I protested, fumbling with the push-button latch.

"I always have a gun," he muttered.

I pulled out a Glock.

"Now, load it," he said. "Ammunition's in the console. Grab

my extra cuffs too."

The man was a walking armory.

"You okay?" he asked, taking his eyes off the road for a split second.

They say you should never load a gun unless you intend to use it. With shaking fingers, I located the gun's magazine.

"Faster," he urged as we neared town.

I had us locked and loaded by the time he pulled into the back lot of the library. Good thing, too. I froze in horror as a smiling Mayor Steward escorted Melody out to his car.

His eyes widened as we blazed into the lot, and he reached for something in his pocket.

Ellis barely stopped the car before he was outside. "Stop! Drop your weapon!"

But I still had the gun. Steward drew a revolver and pointed it at Ellis.

I fired two shots and watched the mayor fall.

He hit the ground and his weapon went flying. Melody screamed. Ellis was on Steward in a heartbeat. He cuffed his hands behind his back, ignoring the mayor's bleeding leg and his own injured shoulder.

I stumbled out of the car, shaking. I'd fired straight through Ellis's windshield. He didn't seem to mind. In fact, Ellis looked quite stoic as he secured the mayor. "You are under arrest for the murders of Vernon Hale and Joy Sullivan."

A group of library workers and patrons stood at the back door, gaping. Library Director Sheila Ward gasped, "I hope you have proof."

Ellis glanced at her and at the rest of the horrified crowd. "I've got a body."

CHAPTER 23

ROCKS PINGED DOWN ON THE mayor's car as I hugged Melody tight. "What the hey?" she kept asking, holding me and refusing to let go.

"Mayor Steward killed a girl, back in the sixties, and buried her out at Wilson's Creek."

She pulled back as the crowd behind her drew in a collective breath. "Are you sure?"

I swore there were no secrets in this town. We were about to make that true again. "Mayor Steward left her body there, thought nobody'd find her. But Vernon Hale came across her purse during the renovation. He started looking into the case, and the mayor shot him."

My sister's eyes widened. "Verity, I—"

"Ellis abandoned the property after that. He was upset. It was a place he and his uncle planned to renovate together. When he went back to it, Steward realized he had to get the body off the property."

"Yes, but can you *prove* it?" Sheila Ward called out.

"Ellis can," I told her. He did, too. They found my bag in Steward's car, along with our keys and the Taser he'd used on us. And Ellis's gun.

And that was the scandal that gave Sugarland something else to talk about.

❦

Turns out the mayor wasn't as crippled as he'd claimed. He played up that old war injury for votes. And when he lost his property, he played hurt all the more.

No one would suspect a frail man could dig up a body, start a house fire, or hunt down an officer of the law. No one would suspect he struggled down a hill in order to shove me to my death.

The colonel had tried to warn me, just like he'd tried to warn Joy on the night of her death. Only he couldn't manifest so well outside the carriage house, and he couldn't stop Steward in any sort of physical way. So I'd fallen, and Joy had died all those years ago.

Poor Harry had been passed out in the alley just as Steward said, a sacrificial lamb ready to take the blame for the mayor's sins.

And they were many.

Judge Parsons didn't even grant him bail—said with all his money, he was a flight risk. I'd heard he was playing injured again in jail, trying for leniency. He could rot there for all I cared.

That night, I curled up on my futon with Lucy in my lap. The house smelled of the meatloaf Melody had brought over. She'd gotten takeout from the diner, and it was spectacular.

"You sure look happy," a voice echoed in my ear.

I jumped, startling Lucy. "Frankie!" I didn't even mind this time when he snuck up on me. "Where have you been?"

"On a ride with a killer," he said as he settled in next to me, a mere flicker of his usual self.

"Are you all right?" He didn't look so good.

"My legs will grow back, along with the rest of me," he mused. "I'm getting too old for this sort of thing."

"You're not even a hundred," I protested. "Well, maybe not a hundred and fifty."

"It's not the years, it's you," he said, tactful as ever. "You get my urn back?"

"No." It had been in Steward's car. Ellis hadn't been able to retrieve it before they locked down the scene. "The sergeant said he'd have it back to me soon."

"He'd better, or else I'm gonna haunt the fuzz."

I supposed he could. It was the only place for Frankie to lurk unless he wanted to hang out at my place.

"The good news is we saved the house."

Ellis had somehow found the time to deposit twenty thousand dollars into my account. As if the man hadn't already been shot at, buried alive, and jumped on by yours truly.

"We're safe for now," I told him.

"When we get my urn back, we gotta work on getting me ungrounded."

"Right," I told him, fighting the urge to chew at my lip.

Like Scarlett O'Hara, we'd worry about the rest tomorrow.

⸙

When things had settled down a bit and Frankie's urn was back on my mantelpiece, Ellis called me up and invited me back to the carriage house to check on everyone. He wanted to see what more we could do to alleviate their stress about the renovation.

"Is Joy here?" he asked as he closed the big doors behind me.

"She's not," the colonel said, from his favorite alcove. I went to join him as he fed a carrot to Annabelle the horse. Only this time, an elegant woman in an old-fashioned dress stood beside him. He smiled, drawing an arm around her. "Verity, please allow me to introduce you to my wife, Sally."

Her eyes sparkled as she gazed up at him. Then she inclined her head toward me. "Thank you."

She appeared happy and at peace. "It's so good to see you," I told her.

The colonel took her hand, weaving his fingers with hers. "Sally was here all along," he said, "but it seems she was too terrified to show herself. You must understand, Joy was a good person, but she could be quite frightening."

I'd experienced that myself. "She went to the light?"

The colonel chuckled. "After she ran out of rocks."

If putting dents in the mayor's car helped her feel better, then I was glad. "She saved us," I said. "I just wish I could have thanked her."

"She knows," the colonel assured me, his eyes sparkling. "She said to thank you as well. She wishes us all the best."

Then she was well and truly free.

Authorities had been by the day after Steward's arrest to remove the body. They'd positively identified it as Joy Sullivan. And they'd formally charged Thad Steward with her murder. It seemed he'd left DNA evidence behind.

I startled a bit as a trumpet blew in the kitchen. A few thump-thumps of a drum followed, and before I knew it, a jazz band had started up.

"Frankie?" I asked, nudging the urn in my bag. He had to see this.

My gangster friend's head popped out from the middle of one of the kitchen doors. "What?"

"Never mind," I said. He'd already made it to the party.

A bald-headed guy that I assumed was Frankie's brother stuck his head out as well. He caught my eye, winked, then grabbed Frankie in a playful headlock and dragged him back to the party.

"Gird your loins," I said to no one in particular. "The South Town gang is at it again."

The colonel wound an arm around his wife's shoulders. "They like to stick to the dance hall."

"And here I thought that was the kitchen," I said dryly.

"What you see must be very new," Sally reminded me.

Right.

"So no more damage?" Ellis asked, joining me.

The colonel gave a wry smile. "Perhaps a trick or two every once in a while, to remind you we're here."

"We should do something special for you and Annabelle," I said, nudging Ellis. "We know you were here first. Ellis could spare the table." We could display a picture of the Rough Rider with his war horse, maybe add a plate of carrots every now and again or encourage patrons to leave apples behind.

"We'd like that very much," the colonel said, nodding farewell as Ellis very gallantly slipped my arm into his and led me away.

"I'm going to tell my brother how you helped," he said, drawing me close, "that I know what you're really like."

"Please don't." I leaned into him. "Your good opinion is enough."

What we had was fragile, special. I didn't want to let others force their views on it.

Truth be told, I'd really like to kiss him again.

He stopped and I turned to face him.

"How's your sister?" he asked.

I had to smile at that. "Good. She's just hoping we don't go on a jewel hunt."

He grinned. "Maybe we'll find them. Harry and I still have a lot to do around here."

I felt bad at the mention of Harry. "I'm sorry I suspected him."

Ellis grew serious. "I'm not. You say what you think. It's refreshing. And you know, we never did get around to our dinner."

"I fell off a cliff instead," I told him. "I promise, I didn't do it so I could avoid you."

"No." He grinned. "You followed me home." He took my hands in his. His grip felt warm, safe. "You want to try again?"

The promise of a fresh scandal brewed. Of course, I jumped in with both feet. "I'd like that."

He relaxed, as if he'd been worried I'd say no. I probably should have. "I'll pick you up tonight at six."

"Good. That'll give me plenty of time with Lucy." I'd been neglecting that skunk lately.

Ellis smiled. "Just leave her at home this time. I'm not sure I can find a skunk-friendly restaurant in this town."

"Okay, but you'll owe her one," I teased.

"I'll see if I can find some skunk treats," Ellis promised. Little did he know, Lucy would hold him to it.

I couldn't help but smile. I had my health, my house, and a date with a most unusual man.

I couldn't ask for anything more.

Author's Note

OKAY, WARM FUZZY TIME. I have to say how much I appreciate you reading Southern Spirits. It's a dream come true to write for a living and Southern Spirits was a pure joy from start to finish. I'm excited to report that I'll be continuing the series for at least seven more books. The next book is called The Skeleton in the Closet and it is available now.

If you'd like an email when each new book releases, sign up for new release updates. You can find the sign-up link on the top right corner of my website home page: www.angiefox.com. The emails go out for new releases only and your information will be kept safe by Lucy and a pack of highly-trained guard skunks.

Thanks for reading!

Angie

Available now!

THE SKELETON IN THE CLOSET
Southern Ghost Hunter mysteries, Book #2
By Angie Fox

A haunted library is no place for a girl who can see ghosts, but when Verity Long stumbles on a dead body in the middle of the main reading room, she has to believe someone...even a dead someone...must have witnessed the crime.

Her ghostly sidekick Frankie warns her to stay out of it. The very alive, very handsome deputy sheriff, Ellis Wydell, inadvertently places her directly in the middle of it. And her ex-fiancé, Ellis's brother, is back with an agenda of his own.

Undaunted, Verity presses forward, uncovering scandalous secrets, long-forgotten ghosts, and a shocking trail of clues that places her directly in the path of a killer.

ENJOY THE FOLLOWING EXCERPT FROM

The Skeleton in the Closet!

Excerpt:

I CLOSED MY EYES, BREATHING THE clean fall air still tinged with the warmth of the fading summer. And I nearly ran smack-dab into the large Civil War reproduction cannon sponsored by the Sugarland Heritage Society. In my defense, it hadn't been there yesterday.

The lawn outside the library—heck, the entire town square—had been transformed.

With good reason.

Today was the first day of the annual Cannonball in the Wall Festival.

As far as parties went, Cannonball in the Wall Day was right up there with Christmas, Easter, and the biscuits-and-gravy breakfast at Lulabelle Mason's house.

This year would be even better. A History channel documentary crew had rolled into town to film the celebration, and it seemed every man, woman, and child from four counties had descended on us like bees to honey butter.

"Melody?" I called, spotting a blonde with a ponytail through the crowd. I strained to get a better look. "Melody!" I waved.

The woman turned and I realized it wasn't my sister. This perky blonde was an actress I'd seen on television. I didn't know whether to be impressed or frustrated.

I'd told Melody I'd meet her near the library, but that was before we realized what a spectacle this year's event was going to be. It might take some doing to pick her out of the larger-than-usual crowd.

I ran a hand along the gun barrel of the old cannon, over the layers of caked-on paint, warm from the sun. During the war, Tennessee was one of the most divided states in the nation, and our boys had gone off to fight on both sides. That left the town vulnerable when the Yankee army came through in 1863. The local militia fought to keep everyone safe, but our homes and businesses were on fire all around them. We thought it was over when the Yankees got their cannon up and shot straight into the town square. Wouldn't you know it, that ball did not explode. It lodged deep in the wall of the Sugarland Library for everyone to see. That small victory gave our ancestors the extra bit of spit and vinegar they needed to drive the invaders out and save our town.

The preacher at the time declared it a miracle. While I wasn't so sure faulty explosives qualified as the hand of God, the entire town had assembled to celebrate every year since. We'd come together—people of all different backgrounds and walks of life—and we'd saved the place we loved. The Cannonball in the Wall Festival reminded us to be grateful for that.

A smile tickled my lips and I couldn't help but gaze at the rusting iron cannonball still embedded in the white limestone near the foundation of the historic library.

Soon everyone would know our story.

"Five dollars for a picture with the cannonball," barked a scratchy voice to my right.

I turned to find Ovis Dupre's thin, bent frame nearly on top of me. The old man didn't understand the concept of personal space. Instead, he drew even closer with his vintage Polaroid.

"No, thank you," I said, doing my best to duck around him while taking care to be kind. He meant well. Besides, I couldn't afford to alienate any of my neighbors after a recent event had left my reputation a little questionable.

But Ovis was eighty if he was a day. And he did not get subtleties at all.

He lowered the camera to reveal the bushiest pair of silver eyebrows south of the Mason-Dixon Line. They stood out starkly against his mahogany skin. "Pretty girl like you deserves a picture," he said quickly. "Five dollars."

Ahem. Problem was, he'd trapped me between the cannon

and the crowd, and I didn't have five dollars to spare. Not after the incident involving my ex-fiancé. I'd managed to avoid selling my house—barely—after my ex-almost-mother-in-law had forced me to pay for the wedding she'd orchestrated, the one that didn't happen. But I'd had to empty my savings and sell most of my furniture. I scarcely had enough left for the things that really mattered, such as food.

Ovis cocked his head. "All proceeds go for historic preservation," he added, as if the cannonball needed my five dollars more than I did. "Did you know my great-great-granddaddy stood in almost this exact spot when he helped save Sugarland?"

He was good. If I'd had the five dollars, I would have produced it right then. But I didn't.

The entire town knew my predicament, but they didn't realize I was so strapped that I'd been forced to eat Royal beef ramen noodles for breakfast this morning. And for dinner last night. I'd kept those sorts of details to myself, along with the fact that I couldn't have preserved my own slice of Sugarland history, the historic home my grandmother had left to me, without the help of Frankie, the gangster ghost I'd grounded in my grandmother's heirloom rosebush, and Ellis Wydell, an unexpectedly sweet man who was tall, gorgeous, and very much alive.

To tell you the truth, I still didn't know what to do about either one of them.

"I've got it," said a familiar voice.

"Ellis?" I turned and saw my recent partner in all things spooky. He wore a Sugarland Deputy Sheriff's uniform and a smile that showed off the dimple in his chin.

I shot Ellis a bright smile as he slipped a five into a box marked "Historic Preservation."

Ovis captured my grin with a sharp *click*.

"Thanks for that," I said to the deputy sheriff.

He shrugged a broad shoulder. "I saw a damsel in distress."

Ovis watched us for a moment too long as he pulled the Polaroid photo from the camera. Ellis stiffened, and I fought the guilty flush that crept up my cheeks. We'd have to be careful how friendly we appeared together. Hardly anyone knew how close we'd grown after our recent adventure, and if any man in this town was off-limits, it was Ellis Wydell.

He was the brother of my ex-fiancé, the middle son of the woman who would give her eyeteeth to ruin my life. And even though I was highly intrigued by the black sheep son of the Wydell family, events like today had a way of reminding me of my place.

I turned to the elderly photographer. "I saw some people earlier with commemorative picture holders. If it's not too much of a bother…"

Ovis appeared pleased that I'd noticed. "I was just about to get you one." He weaved through the crowd toward a nearby table while I took a second to admire the scenery right in front of me. I'd almost forgotten how tall Ellis was, and how well his uniform fit over those work-sculpted muscles. He still had a slight scar under his eye from when he'd saved me from a killer. If anything, it made him even sexier.

"I see you're working today."

He gave a sharp nod. "Crowd control." He glanced over his shoulder at the reenactors lounging on the lawn. "Plus the Yankees have been drinking since ten o'clock this morning."

Oh my. "I suppose you can't blame them." Everyone who was anyone wanted to play a town hero in the reenactment. But the militia parts went to the older families in town, the ones with ancestors who fought. Anyone whose family had settled here less than one hundred and fifty years ago had to play the part of an invader. On television, no less.

"Poor Yankees," Ellis mused. "It must be tough to lose every year."

Yes, well, they should have thought about that before they shot at our library. "Your mother has to be loving this."

He shook his head. "She's convinced the family story is Hollywood material."

"More power to her," I said, meaning every word.

My ex-almost-mother-in-law might be slightly evil, but this

time she was using her power and sizable fortune for good. She'd formed a film production company dedicated to promoting the history of Sugarland, and her family's legacy, of course. So far, she'd managed to attract today's documentary crew and also finance an independent movie about the skirmish that forever entrenched the cannonball in the wall. Filming would start next week.

That kind of national recognition would do the town good. Plus, the more she focused on her family's fame and glory, the less time she had to meddle in my affairs.

Ovis handed me the picture, complete in its commemorative cardboard Cannonball in the Wall Day frame. I was stunned to see how happy I looked.

"For you," I said, handing the picture to Ellis. He *had* bought it. Plus, I sort of wanted him to have a picture of me.

He took it gallantly, but I saw how the tips of his ears reddened.

I was glad to see I wasn't the only one who might need to work on reining things in.

Bloodcurdling screams sounded from across the square, and from behind city hall, I heard shouts: "The Yankees are coming!"

Ellis checked his watch. "Twenty minutes early. Somebody needs to get them under control."

"Hop to it, lawman."

He shot me a wink and left to go check out the action while I wondered for the hundredth time whether I'd been blessed or cursed.

I also wondered if anyone besides Ovis had noticed me talking to the good-looking sheriff.

Melody made me jump when she drew up behind me and whispered in my ear, "Boo."

My hand went to my chest. "Can't you just say hello like everyone else?"

"So you're saying that scared you?" she asked, her blue eyes twinkling. "Impossible. Not after—"

"Never mind," I said quickly. "I'm just glad you found me." Melody and Ellis were two of the very limited number of people who knew about my ghost-hunting skills, and I intended to keep it that way. "Besides, I'm finished with that business." I wanted to forget about haunted houses, hidden passageways, and buried secrets. "The ghosts of Sugarland have caused me too much trouble."

Melody gazed down on me, thanks to her impossibly high platform sandals, and handed me a piping hot bag of kettle corn. "If you're serious about keeping out of hot water, you should stay away from Ellis."

"I know," I said, plucking a piece off the top. Nobody would understand the way Ellis and I had bonded over our adventure. They'd only see me chasing after the older brother of my ex-fiancé. "But he's like kettle corn. You can't have just one little taste."

Melody tsked. "You just like him because he saved your life."

"Yes, well, I saved his too," I pointed out. "Besides, you know it's more than that."

He was funny and brave. Kind. He was a darned good police officer, even though his family would never forgive him for joining the force instead of the high-powered Wydell legal empire. I admired a man who wasn't afraid to follow through with what he felt in his heart. I frowned. That kind of thinking could get me all tangled up if I let it.

Melody glanced out over the crowd. "We'd better get moving. The grandstand is filling up."

Portable metal benches took up the entire east side of the square. They were sponsored by the two leading families in these parts: the Wydells and the Jacksons. The Wydells ruled the roost in Sugarland. The Jacksons owned most of the land surrounding the town. Both families were careful to sit as far as possible from each other on account of a feud that had been going on since Lieutenant Colonel Lester Jackson may or may not have forgotten to salute Colonel Thaddeus Wydell during the War of 1812.

Melody took my hand and dragged me along. "Come on. My boss said he'd save us some seats."

"No kidding?" Montgomery Silas was not only our library historical expert, but he was also the man who literally wrote the book on the Battle of Sugarland, the one that was being made into the movie.

Melody waved to Montgomery as we made our way over.

"We are in high cotton," I said as he waved back. The eccentric scholar wore an ill-conceived pair of muttonchops and had a personal style that relied heavily on tweed and bow ties, but he was the closest thing to a celebrity we had around these parts. At least until filming started.

I couldn't wait.

We were just about to enter the grandstand when Darla Grace, Sugarland Heritage Society Volunteer of the Year—every year—closed a hand over my sister's arm. Darla stood five feet nothing, not counting her stacked auburn hair done up with daisies for the celebration. It looked nice, and I could tell she felt pretty.

She gave my sister a conspiratorial grin. "Thank you so much for all your help in the library this morning. I don't think I could have handled that fiasco without you."

Melody let out a small laugh. "It was nothing."

"I really appreciate it," she continued. "I mean, who in their right mind would think it's a good idea to add Myra Jackson's false eye into the jewelry display? Even if it is a family heirloom." Darla Grace shuddered.

My sister chuckled. "You just need to learn how to say no."

"No," I said under my breath as Virginia Wydell sat down in the front row, right next to Montgomery. "Those were supposed to be our seats. He just let her take them."

"Oh." Melody cringed. "Well, the Wydell Family Foundation is funding the movie. He probably didn't think he had a choice. Don't worry. We don't have to sit anywhere near them."

"We won't," I said. Not while I was still breathing. "But we'd better find a spot. And soon."

Melody and I started toward the stands with Darla in tow

when one of the young college volunteers rushed us. Panic widened her ice blue eyes and her bangs tangled in the sweat on her brow. "Disaster. Anarchy. I need you and Darla right now. The Jacksons are demanding we expand the exhibit."

"Don't you dare," I told them both. "I'm sure you've already done a wonderful job." They deserved more than political bickering in return. "Let's go, or we're going to miss the whole Yankee charge." I'd witnessed every reenactment since I was three years old, and I wasn't about to be left out this year.

"Expanding the exhibit is the only way to keep the peace," the student pleaded. She held up her phone. "I have a text from Montgomery. He says to work it out."

Darla groaned. "We don't want to offend the Jacksons or the Wydells, not at this hour."

Melody shot an apologetic glance to Darla. "I shouldn't have put out the Wydells' vintage corsets and lingerie. That might have tipped the scales."

"It did." Their panicked coworker looked ready to swoon. "The Jacksons retaliated with two muskets and a fainting couch." She drew a deep breath before rushing on. "Rumor has it Virginia Wydell just sent her eldest son to go dig into the family taxidermy collection."

"Perfect," I said. I had the solution. "This is a fine time to teach our fellow citizens the meaning of the word *no*."

Both Melody's and Darla Grace's heads whipped around to cast equally horrified stares at me. "No!" they sobbed in unison.

Hmm...perhaps this was why I tended to get into trouble, while they did not.

Melody touched her forehead, gathering her wits. "Don't worry. We'll sort everything out. As long as the heirlooms don't keep coming." She dropped her hand. "Verity, I have to handle this. You might as well go ahead and enjoy the reenactment."

"Not in a million years," I told her. I couldn't have fun while Melody and Darla were in such a spot. Besides, I didn't want to be anywhere near Virginia Wydell without my sister there for moral support. "If you simply cannot leave this undone, then you can count on me to help." Besides, it would be neat to see all the old relics and knickknacks.

Darla's brows pinched together. "We'd love that, but you can't. We had to sign papers. Approved personnel only."

Melody cast me a helpless look. "I'm afraid the rules are pretty strict."

"Okay, then." I felt for them, I truly did. "Just think," I said, trying to make it better, "after tomorrow's brunch it will be all over."

Both of them winced.

"Thanks for the deadline reminder," Darla groused.

Shoot. I hadn't quite thought of it that way.

"Go," Melody urged. "Find a seat."

That could be hard. The crowd had thinned around the grandstand, which meant most of them were in it. I watched as Melody and Darla made their way toward the library, trailed by the volunteer. I wished I could have done more.

Well, at least I could watch history being made. Again. I joined the last of the audience filing into the long benches and began working my way up, hoping to find a single seat...anywhere. I was craning my neck, distracted, when the last man on earth I wanted to see climbed up behind me and blocked my escape.

"You look gorgeous today, Verity." He had that slight, sweet, humble-if-you-didn't-know-him Southern drawl that made me want to punch him in the face.

I straightened and turned, already knowing what I'd find. "Beau."

Beau Wydell appeared quite harmless on the surface. Tall, with Matthew McConaughey good looks and a self-effacing charm that had bedazzled plenty of women over the years. He'd sure fooled me.

My ex-fiancé tilted his chin down and treated me to a shy smile, as if he didn't have a care in the world. And why should he? He was the one who'd cheated on me, lied to me, and then made me look the fool when he tried to force me to show up at our wedding. That was the day after he hit on my little sister, by the way. She'd gone to get another bottle of wine for our suite and he'd trapped her in a corner to paw at her. I didn't dare mention that here. No one knew. So far, Melody had stayed clean of this and I intended to keep it that way.

I'd told him the wedding was off. He'd waited at the altar anyhow, in front of the whole town. He'd made it appear as if I'd stood him up, and I became persona non grata to just about everyone who ever mattered to me.

"Please leave," I said, knowing I'd have to face him sooner or later, my heart racing all the same.

He shrugged. "The way I see it, you're standing in my family section."

I was? I almost dropped my popcorn. "Then I should leave," I said, trying to figure out a way to make it around him. We had folks on the seats above watching us, along with several packed rows underneath straining to hear.

Lord have mercy.

"It's all right if you sit by me, darlin'," he said, drawing closer.

"I'd rather set my teeth on fire." Before today, I hadn't seen or spoken to Beau since he'd invited me to join him at our reception. The whole town was there, he'd said, enjoying our five-course sit-down dinner. Dancing to the ten-piece band his mother had insisted we hire. Consoling him. Assuring him he was better off.

He'd sent me photos of the cake.

I'd snapped. That he would play the victim, that he would humiliate me like that after what he'd done... I'd like to plead temporary insanity, only I knew exactly what I was doing when I drove straight to the Hamilton Hotel, marched right into my almost-reception, and plastered Beau's face straight into our almost-wedding cake. Only I hadn't counted on everyone taking pictures. And videos. Not to mention the way I'd slipped on frosting and fallen on my rear.

I needed to escape. Now. Maybe I could shimmy under the seat and drop down to the ground below. Would I even fit? My luck, I'd get stuck. Then we'd have more embarrassing pictures of me for Beau's Facebook page.

His mouth tipped into a slow smile. "Are you going to make another scene?" he asked smugly, as if he'd read my mind. "Can't say that I don't enjoy your moxie."

His words hit me like a bucket of cold water. My outburst at the reception had consequences. Beau's mother had sued me for the entire cost of the production she'd orchestrated. I'd had to sell everything I owned. I'd darn near lost my family home. Half the town still thought I was crazy.

No. I would not let Beau Wydell humiliate me again.

A cry erupted from the crowd around us. "Sit down," the woman behind me hissed. "The Yankees are coming. For real this time!"

I sat, next to Beau Wydell, and tried not to cringe as our shoulders touched.

He took it as an invitation and leaned his lips toward my ear. "I'm kind of glad we got stuck like this, darlin'. We should talk."

"Don't call me darling," I said, keeping my voice down and my eyes on the town square. "We have nothing to say."

The camera crew from the History channel sprang into action. I focused on the drama of the advancing army, on our outnumbered, outgunned small-town militia as they were pushed back, on Miss Emily Proctor's dance classes, ages five through sixteen, as they danced in front of the limestone buildings of our town square, dressed as red and orange flames.

"I'm sorry about what my mother did to you."

He actually sounded sincere, and I felt my cheeks redden. I glanced up at him. "What about what you did?"

He huffed out a breath. "You know I didn't mean that, sugar." His fingers inched toward mine on the bench. "I'd had a couple of beers. Your sister looks a lot like you. I made a mistake." He shrugged. "It happens to a lot of guys."

"No, it doesn't." I folded my fingers in my lap. "And you didn't have to embarrass me later."

"Hey," he said. "Look at me. I was hurt." He appeared so sincere a girl would be tempted to believe him. If you didn't know him. "I didn't hear that my mom sent you the bill until after I got back from our honeymoon."

And then he'd done nothing to stop her when she unleashed her team of lawyers.

The Yankees were now overrunning the square. Our men were trapped, flanked, through no fault of their own. I knew exactly how they felt.

"Excuse me!" a woman protested on Beau's left side as someone knocked into her popcorn, scattering pieces.

"Sorry," a familiar voice called back. "Pardon me," Ellis said as he shoved past his brother. I hoped it wasn't an accident that he stepped on Beau's foot.

I scooted over as far as I could to make room.

"What the hell?" Beau protested as Ellis squeezed in between us.

I'd never been so glad to see him. "Shouldn't our sheriff be protecting the town?" I asked. It was too late to save me.

Then again, having him here did make me feel stronger.

"It's all going well," he said pragmatically. "The whole place is on fire. There's hand-to-hand fighting in the streets. They'll be talking about this for years." He angled for some space and elbowed his brother in the process.

Beau elbowed back. "You're an idiot, Ellis."

Everyone watched as the Yankees pointed a cannon and fired on the Sugarland Library. Well, most everyone. Virginia Wydell sat six rows down, her platinum hair pulled back into a girlish ponytail, her pearl earrings large, and her eyes hard as she glared back at us.

Fun day.

My ex leaned over his brother as if he weren't there. "I miss your back rubs," Beau murmured to me.

Ellis stiffened. "You realize she dumped you, right?"

"Oh, look," I said, "one of the Yankees just lost his uniform pants. He really should have worn a belt." Or laid off the hooch. "I wonder if that will make it into the documentary."

Both men ignored me. They were too busy glaring at each

other. Of course, Beau had no idea about Ellis and me. If I wanted to be perfectly honest, even I didn't even quite understand what was going on between us. It had begun innocently enough.

But now, seeing the two brothers together, I was starting to realize I might have started something I didn't quite know how to finish.

Ellis and I hadn't gotten to the back-rub stage. We were barely at the dating part. We'd fought for our lives together and had gotten close. Too close, maybe. Then we'd enjoyed one very nice, very quiet dinner a few miles out of town. He'd brought me daisies, and I'd baked cookies and pretended it was no big deal. He'd said they were delicious.

It had been wonderful.

Until now.

Beau groaned. "Can you move out of the way, Ellis?"

"No," Ellis said simply.

Oh, brother.

I'd never been so glad to see the Sugarland militia push the Yankees back and save our town.

We watched the two colonels, a Wydell and a Jackson, shake hands, as they did once a year. The patriarchs of the two families put aside their differences to lead the militia, a moment of cooperation before they went back to hating each other. Everyone in the grandstand stood and cheered. The cameras rolled.

Beau leaned past his brother to get to me. "I don't care if my family thinks you're bad for me. Let me take you out tonight."

"No," Ellis and I barked out.

Virginia Wydell looked ready to climb over six rows to get to us.

Suddenly shimmying underneath the grandstands wasn't looking like such a bad option.

Ellis cleared his throat. "I love you, brother, but sometimes you don't have the sense God gave an ant. What you had with Verity is over. You need to give up."

Beau shook his head, rueful. "You have no idea. You never

kissed a girl like her."

Maybe I could just whack my head on the metal bleachers and hope to forget I'd met either one of them.

"I've got to go," I said, sliding past the brothers, ignoring it when Beau ran a hand up my leg. Ew. I was done—with this, with him, with the whole blessed day. I had no more celebrating left in me. I was heading home. By myself, mind you.

And if I had a wish left in heaven, nobody would follow me. Then again, if wishes were fishes, I wouldn't be eating ramen for dinner tonight.

New York Times and USA Today bestselling author Angie Fox writes sweet, fun, action-packed mysteries. Her characters are clever and fearless, but in real life, Angie is afraid of basements, bees, and going up stairs when it is dark behind her. Let's face it. Angie wouldn't last five minutes in one of her books.

Angie earned a journalism degree from the University of Missouri. During that time, she also skipped class for an entire week so she could read Anne Rice's vampire series straight through. Angie has always loved books and is shocked, honored and tickled pink that she now gets to write books for a living. Although, she did skip writing for a week this past fall so she could read Victoria Laurie's Abby Cooper psychic eye mysteries straight through.

Angie makes her home in St. Louis, Missouri with a football-addicted husband, two kids, and Moxie the dog.

Sign up at *www.angiefox.com* to receive an email from Angie Fox each time she releases a new book

Made in the USA
Coppell, TX
24 August 2020

34674914R00152